# DIE FOR

# JESUS

## By Dave Earley

Cover design by Michael D'Attoma.

# <u>SUNDAY, DECEMBER 20</u>

## CHAPTER 1
## 6:33 PM

"CRACK!"

"CRACK!"

"CRACK!"

Pain exploded in Daniel's chest. He was falling. His chest was on fire. He couldn't breathe. Everything went black ... and silent.

*

"Pastor Daniel! Pastor Daniel! Can you hear me?" Someone was gently shaking him and calling in his ear. It sounded like Matthew.

"Pastor Daniel, keep breathing. Help is on the way. Hold on," Matthew urgently pleaded.

Then Daniel heard another voice, "Oh, dear God! Help him. Please, help him." It sounded familiar. It was Rebecca.

He wanted to reach out and hold her and tell it would be all right. But he did not have the strength to open his eyes. Plus, his chest was burning. Every breath was torture.

He just wanted to sleep.

*

*Stay strong*, Rebecca told herself. *Stay strong*. She felt light-headed and sick to her stomach. Just a few minutes earlier she had been in the back of the building, teaching a children's class when the shooting occurred. Rufus had burst into the room and told her "Come quick, Pastor has been shot."

Now she leaned over a pale man lying on a platform in front of hundreds of terrified people who had come to a Sunday evening worship service. The man, her husband Daniel, was stretched out on the platform like a rag doll, blood covering his upper body.

He looked dead.

*Oh dear God, help him.*

"Everyone be calm," a voice cut through the air. Pastor Carlos had a microphone and was standing by Rebecca and Pastor Matthew as they huddled over Daniel on the platform. "The shooter is gone. The doors are blocked and secured, so no one can get in."

He lifted his hand and continued, "An ambulance is on its way and the police will be here in just a moment. Pastor Daniel always says, 'God is big enough!' We need to believe that and trust God. Our job right now is to get into groups of three or four and pray for Pastor Daniel. Pray also for the man who shot him."

Then he gulped and his voice cracked a little. "Pray hard. Our prayers make a difference."

*

*Made it*, Zeke thought as he raced down the narrow driveway next to the ancient, dilapidated office park that housed Grace City Church in urban Las Vegas. Apart from the office/store fronts facing the street, nearly all of the rest of the crumbling office suites were empty. The back part of the property had only a few small lights that worked. The lights on the buildings were either burnt out or broken. It was dark, very dark. It was easy for Zeke to sprint through the shadows unnoticed.

He quickly replayed in his mind the events of the last few minutes.

He had slipped into the church service after the music had started. The lights were low and he found a seat in a section on the left near the exit door.

Making sure that he was unnoticed, he slipped on a glove. Patiently, he waited until the band stopped and the audience sat down. After the pastor walked out onto the platform, and had talked for a minute or two, Zeke had stood and shot him several times in the chest. Somebody bumped him hard from behind. Zeke stumbled to the door and was gone before anyone could stop him.

Now, he ducked into a dark shadow, glanced behind him, and quickly pulled the glove off and stuffed it in the back pocket of his jeans.

He turned into the alley moving more deliberately and limping slightly. Slowly he shuffled toward Tamarus Ave. As far as he could tell, no one had seen him. If they did, he would look like any one of hundreds of drunks or addicts that populated the neighborhood.

*No one out,* Zeke mumbled to himself as he looked up and down the street. There were some large, empty garbage cans off to his right, but he did not see anything unusual.

*No one saw me.*

Quickly and quietly he slid into a big, black SUV that was parked in the shadows. He took a deep breath and slowly let it out. Then he pushed the ignition and slowly pulled out into the street.

*Must be careful,* he thought. *No fender benders.*

He was surprisingly calm. The preacher was not the first man he had shot and was not even the first he had killed. He felt a rush. A job well done.

*The preacher got what he had coming,* he thought. That man reminded Zeke too much of his father. Plus, he was trying to ruin Zeke's family. Because of that preacher, Zeke's wife was talking about Jesus all the time.

*Life could go back to normal now that the preacher was gone.*

Zeke smiled. The voices that had been in his head for so many years would finally stop.

# CHAPTER 2

## 7:01 PM

"Nee-Naw, Nee-Naw, Nee-Naw!"

Rebecca's nightmare continued when the ambulance arrived. Thankfully, they turned off the ear-piercing siren when they drove into the office complex that housed the church. But the flashing light of the ambulance still spun around and reflected eerily off the walls of the buildings of the office park.

Suddenly Doris Garcia appeared beside Rebecca. "Don't worry about the boys."

Rebecca nodded.

Doris continued, "I'll take them home with me. We'll stop by the house, get their things for school tomorrow and take care of the dog." Doris smiled reassuringly. "They will be fine." Then Doris gave her a big hug.

"Thank you," Rebecca said weakly. She was still struggling to comprehend what had happened.

She turned and saw the paramedics lift Daniel up into the back of the ambulance. One of them jumped in the back with him. The other one reached out a hand to help Rebecca.

"Thanks," she said as she sat awkwardly on a bench beside where her husband lay on a stretcher.

Another paramedic jumped in beside her and closed the door. He began adjusting and monitoring Daniel's oxygen.

Rebecca was jarred almost out of her seat as the ambulance bumped off the curb and swung out onto the street. The ambulance had pulled out of the complex and turned left onto Flamingo Road. She did not have to look to know where they were. She felt the ambulance race west a few blocks to Maryland Avenue, and dash north to Paradise Hospital.

*This can't be happening,* she thought. *I was teaching the elementary kids a half hour ago, and now I am in the back of an ambulance watching my husband fight for every breath.*

Rebecca was nearly thrown from her seat as they pulled around the parking lot of the hospital and stopped in front of the ER entrance. The paramedics quickly had Daniel out of the ambulance, through the doors, and directly to the triage area.

A tall, thin, Asian doctor; a younger doctor; a petite, older nurse; and a huge, male nurse were waiting inside.

"Gunshot wounds. Three bullets wounds. One in the shoulder, two in the chest," the lead paramedic said. "Lost a lot of blood. Not sure how he is still breathing."

"Thank you." The tall, thin doctor nodded. Quickly he examined Daniel's wounds.

Then he spun and turned to the other doctor and nurse, "We need to operate right away if he is to have any chance. Prep him."

"You'll need to step out for a moment, ma'am," the male nurse told Rebecca.

"No, I want to stay with my husband," Rebecca said.

"We have to get him ready for surgery. There is no time to lose. You will just be in the way," the nurse said firmly. He pulled the curtain back so she could step by him into the cluttered hall of the ER.

In the hall were numerous people with various levels of medical emergencies. Rebecca had not even noticed them on the way through the ER. She leaned against the wall nervously.

"That your man come in with all the blood?" a ragged, old lady with thin strands of dirty, white hair, and very few teeth asked her.

Rebecca nodded.

"He don't look so good," the lady said, shaking her head. "He still alive? He don't look it."

\*

"Dear Jesus, please touch Pastor Daniel's body right now!"

"Heal him, Lord! Heal him!"

"Oh Father, carry your lamb close to your chest right now."

African American, Hispanic, Asian, Caucasian, young and old, rich and poor, educated, and uneducated, throughout the auditorium of Grace City Church voices cried out in a passionate symphony of intercession for their pastor. College students, homeless people, business men, ex-addicts, and housewives all linked by a common thread -- God had powerfully transformed their lives and Pastor Daniel had been a part of that process.

Quietly the keyboard and a guitar played in the background. Then, just as the chorus of prayer began to ebb, the young worship leader stepped to the mic and began to sing,

*God is able. He will never fail. He is Almighty God.*

*Greater than all we see. Greater than all we ask. He has done great things.*

She sang the song more slowly than usual, letting the words wash over the audience. One-by-one they joined her, declaring their faith and prayer for God to save their Pastor.

*God is with us. He is on our side. He will make a way.*

*Far above all we know. Far above all we hope. He has done great things.*

*

Darkness. Daniel felt darkness surrounding him. It was as if the darkness was living somehow. Well, not really living, dead, but alive. It seemed to be reaching out for him.

*Jesus! Jesus! Help me. Don't let it take me. Please don't let it take me,"* Daniel silently prayed like scared child.

Suddenly, the darkness stopped.

Off in the distance, a warm light was speeding toward him.

It was golden, beautiful and comforting.

As it neared, Daniel felt better. Almost good even. Well, not good, but the pain was bearable. He was captivated by that light – a silver, golden light. It was both familiar and other worldly.

Like smoke, it swirled until it slowly surrounded him. Then it hesitated.

*"Don't stop!'* he thought. He wanted to scream out, but he couldn't open his mouth.

*"I'm here, Jesus. Help me."*

After encircling him, the light stopped.

*"Please don't stop,"* he thought. Then his world went dark again.

## CHAPTER 3
### 7:18 PM

*Don't think he saw me,* Johnny Mulholland thought after the man in the dark coat shambled by him.

Johnny was slumped in the shadows behind several large trash bins. Earlier that night, he had heard music at the church and had stopped by hoping for some food. He knew that they had a meal and Bible studies on Wednesday nights. He had attended a few times.

But, tonight, he went by the church only to find that they did not serve food on Sunday nights. Disappointed he left and headed out the back of the office complex into the alley behind the office area. When he got to the place where the alley met Tamarus Street, he felt tired and decided to rest. So he slumped down in the shadows between a few big trash bins. No one should bother him there.

When the man in the dark coat shuffled down the alley, Johnny pulled deeper into the darkness, not sure if the man would try to rob him or not. The man wore a large overcoat, a hoodie, and a cap pulled down low.

Johnny watched the man in the dark coat walk out of the alley, walk north a little ways, look around, and slide into a big, black, Cadillac SUV. It had a small, silver skull on the bumper.

*Whew,* Tommy sighed. *Wonder what he is up to?*

*

"What is your name?"

"Matthew Meadows. I am an assistant pastor here at the church," answered a young man.

"I am Detective McCauley and this is Detective Marino. We need to ask you a few questions."

Matthew nodded his cooperation.

"So tell me in your own words what happened here tonight?"

"A man must have slipped in during the end of the worship time," Matthew said.

"When would that be?" McCauley asked.

"Sometime between 6:30 and 6:35 PM," Matthew said. "Soon after, when Pastor Daniel stood up and started to speak, I saw the man stand up right over there." He pointed. "He had a gun in his hand. Then he started firing at the pastor."

"Where were you?" McCauley asked.

"I was on the other side of the auditorium, over there in the back," Matthew pointed. "I was trying to count the attendance. When the man stood up, Big Tony started toward him. After the man fired the gun, Tony was close enough that he dove and knocked the man off balance. But the man righted himself and ran out that side door before anyone could get to him," he continued. "We tried to follow, but he disappeared. Everyone was kind of in shock... I guess we still are."

"Can you describe the man with the gun?" the detective asked.

"We keep the lights fairly low during the message, so as best I could tell, the man was not tall, but had broad shoulders." Matthew replied. "He had a ball cap pulled down low, a hoodie over his head, and was wearing a large, loose coat."

"What color was the coat?"

"Dark. Black, grey, or green I think. It might have been an army coat."

"Can you describe his face?" the detective asked.

"I didn't get a good look. Like I said, except for on the platform, the lights are turned down during the message," Matthew said. "I only saw him from behind."

"Where is this Big Tony?"

"He's over there," Matthew pointed to where a group of people were in a cluster praying. "Hey, Tony. Can you join us?" Matthew asked.

"What can I do for you, Officer?" Tony asked as he walked over.

"That's *Detective*," McCauley said. "What's your full name?"

"Tony. Tony Jones."

"Tony...Big Tony," Detective Marino said the name slowly. "You look familiar. Do I know you?"

"Sir, I used to gang bang in this neighborhood. I am not proud of it. I had my run-ins with the police a few times. But that was a few years ago. Jesus changed all of that."

"Good for you," Marino said with a bit of a smirk. "Glad you found something to help you." Then he added, "I think I remember you. I walked a beat here for a short time, then got transferred to North Metro, then promoted to detective.

"Congratulations," Tony said sincerely.

"Thanks, now what can you tell us about this shooter?"

"I shouldn't have let this happen," Tony shook his head slowly. "I was supposed to be on security duty tonight, but I got off work late and didn't get here until after the service started. I got here right before the message. I didn't see the guy come in."

"What happened?"

"When Pastor started preaching, the guy stood up and began shooting," Tony said. "When he stood up, I went for him. I dove over a few rows of chairs and hit him from behind as he was shooting. He stumbled but took off before I could get up and get to him. He ran out the door and disappeared," Tony continued. "I tried to follow, but I lost him in the dark. As you can tell, there isn't much light outside around this office complex. The few lights they have are burnt out, and the people we rent from won't fix them."

"Can you describe the man?" McCauley asked.

"Short, strong, dark. A dark hat pulled down low, a grey hoodie over his head and a loose dark gray or black coat with the collar turned up," Tony continued. "They pull the lights down for the service, so I didn't get a look at his face."

"When you say he was 'dark,' do you mean like a black man?" the detective asked.

"No," Tony shook his head. "More like Hispanic or Arab, something like that I think."

"Anything else?"

"Oh... yeah," Tony said. "When I hit him, he mumbled something. It was like he cursed under his breathe. It might have been Spanish, but I am not sure."

"Thanks, Tony. Anybody else see this guy?" the detective asked.

"Anybody see the shooter?" Tony yelled.

A couple of hands went up around the room.

"I saw him when he came in," said an old, black man with a snowy beard and white, fuzzy hair.

"Come here, old man," the detective said. "What's your name?"

"Rufus. Rufus Johnson."

"Ok. Rufus Johnson," McCauley said as Marino typed on his iPad. "Tell us what you know."

"They had turned the lights down and were starting the last song of worship. The little kids are sent out right before the last song in order to go to their classes," Rufus said. "The guy comes rushing in the door and heads for the auditorium. I tried to give him some sermon notes, but he just pushes me aside and goes in."

"Did you think it strange the way he rushed in?" the detective asked.

"Well sir, we have a lot of down-on-their-luck people in this neighborhood. Sometimes they are just mad, sometimes they are drunk, and sometimes they are high," Rufus said. "I was one of those people when Pastor Daniel came to town seven years ago. But I came in here one night and listened to that man preach about the love of God. By the end, I put all my anger down and let Jesus heal my wounds and fill my heart with love," Rufus grinned.

"So you just let him in?"

"Yes, sir," Rufus said proudly. "I invited Jesus into my heart."

"No, not *Jesus*," the detective said shaking his head. "I was asking about *the shooter*. You just let *the shooter* into the auditorium?"

"Oh, *him*," Rufus smiled. He was smarter than people often gave him credit for.

"Well, usually, Tony stands back here with me. He kind of screens the people. If they might be trouble, Tony has someone like Pastor Matthew or Pastor Carlos sit with them. Sometimes, Tony won't let them in and he sits out here with them until they calm down."

"I see," the detective said.

"I was going to get someone to sit with the guy, but Miss Maria needed me in the back to go with Billy and take the little boys to the bathroom because Marcus didn't show up."

"Did you see the shooter's face?"

"No, not really," Rufus said. "I'm sorry. It all happened so fast.… I am so very sorry." Rufus turned his face away.

"Anyone else see the shooter?" Detective Marino said.

A lady raised her hand and walked toward them. "I was sitting in the front row. When the shooting started I turned around. It was dark, but I caught a glimpse of his eyes… just his eyes," the young lady said.

"What is your name, miss?" Detective Marino asked.

"Amelia Ruiz," she said. "His eyes," she said shaking her head. "They looked like devil eyes."

"What do you mean by devil eyes?" The detective said.

"I just saw them for a second, but they were wild and evil."

*

Zeke turned left on Flamingo and a few blocks later, took a right on Maryland. He drove a few blocks north and turned left into the parking lot at Vons Grocery. He drove all the way across the front of the parking lot close to the front of the store on the far west edge of the nearly empty parking lot. Then he slid quietly into a parking space that butted up against Molaskey Family Park.

"*Family* Park," he said chuckling as he read the sign by the path leading into the park. "It's only a *family* park if your *family* is made up of homeless dudes, addicts, drunks, prostitutes, and gang bangers," he chuckled. He was feeling good about his success so far this evening.

It was dark, and he saw no one nearby. He quietly slid out his car. As he walked toward the park entrance, he passed a dumpster. Smoothly, in one fluid motion, he flipped a brown bag into the dumpster. The bag landed with a clunk,

With the hoodie and hat pulled down low over his face, and the collar of the coat turned up, he shuffled through the park toward a few trees in the distant corner. Asleep under a tree was the homeless man he had been watching the last few weeks. The man was passed out and snoring loudly.

Based on his observations, Zeke had noticed that the bum could not resist whiskey. Earlier in the afternoon, he had made sure the man had found the bottles of whiskey he had "hidden" by the man's make-shift camp site. Now, Zeke saw the empty bottles resting by the drunk's outstretched hand. The drunk had downed every last drop. Zeke chuckled and looked around to see if anyone was watching.

No one.

The unusually cold December night in Vegas had limited the number of people in the park tonight. Many of the homeless were elsewhere sleeping in shelters. The others seemed to have left the park and camped under a bridge and gathered around fire barrels. But not this guy. He was all by himself on this side of the park.

Zeke, looked around again and made sure no one was watching. Then he slipped off the large coat, the hat, and the hoodie. Quietly he dropped the hat and the hoodie beside the passed-out drunk and laid the coat over top of him. Then he pulled another hat out of his back pocket and pulled it down over his eyes. He had another sweatshirt on underneath the first and he pulled the hood of that sweatshirt up over his head. Then Zeke shuffled off back toward the grocery store and his car.

Obeying all the traffic laws and staying off the main streets, Zeke drove west toward Las Vegas Boulevard and the famous Strip. He turned north and drove past the massive newer casinos as he headed toward the older part of the Strip. As he drove north, he passed seedy pawn shops and tired wedding chapels. Just north of the Stratosphere Casino he turned right into the parking lot of Esquire Limousine Company; he drove around back and parked the car.

*

*The nightmare continues*, Rebecca thought as they wheeled Daniel to the Operation Room.

"Ma'am?"

Rebecca felt a hand on her arm. She turned and saw the huge, male nurse.

"Ma'am, you can wait in the OR Family Waiting room," he said pointing down the hallway. "They will give you updates as to when he gets out of the OR and when you can see him. Just follow the blue signs that say, 'Operating Room Family Waiting.' It's all the way over on the far side of the building."

"Thank you," Rebecca said numbly. Her adrenaline must have died down. She felt exhausted as she started walking down the hall.

# CHAPTER 4
## 8:03 PM

"Pastor," Detective McCauley called out while signaling for Matthew. "If you don't mind, I have just a few more questions for now."

Matthew sat down across from him.

"So, you are the assistant pastor, is that right?

"Yes, sir," Matthew said. "Pastor Carlos and I are the assistant pastors."

"So, you worked pretty closely with Pastor Browning?"

"Yes, sir," Matthew said. "We prayed together every morning and were in meetings together a few times a week. Plus, he ate lunch with me every other week. My wife and I had dinner with his family every couple of weeks."

"Did he have any enemies that you knew about?"

"Everyone loved Pastor Daniel. You can ask the officers that work in this precinct. They know him," Matthew continued. "Our pastor has helped so many people. Before he and Rebecca came to this neighborhood, it was nothing but darkness… drugs and prostitution, gangs and violence. Pastor Daniel and Rebecca brought light, healing and hope."

"What about the gangs? I imagine they lost some business."

"Yes. That's right," Matthew said slowly. He had a far-off look as he remembered. "I do remember our first few years here, he had some death threats from gangs. Also, a few pimps were really mad at him when he rescued a few of their girls and got them safe houses."

Then he smiled at the detective, "But we had a weeklong prayer marathon and it seemed to die down."

"Anything recent?" the detective asked.

"No. Nothing that I know about."

"Thanks," McCauley said to Matthew. "Here is my card. Let me know if you can think of anything else." Then he turned to his partner.

"Marino, tell these people they can leave now. I think we have got all we can get for tonight."

\*

"Oh no. Oh no. Lord, no!" Maria Cruz, gasped as she looked at her phone. It was filling up with texts.

"Maria, what is it?" her sister asked.

"Pastor Daniel got shot at the church!" Maria's face turned ashen and she began to cry.

"What?" her sister asked.

"Some man showed up at the church service tonight and shot Pastor Daniel. They are not sure if he is still alive."

"*The man* is still alive?" her sister asked.

"No!" Maria said. "If *Pastor Daniel* is still alive. The shooter got away." She paused and then added, "Poor Rebecca."

Then Maria dropped to her knees, "Dear Father, please be with Daniel and Rebecca right now. Our only hope is in you. Please don't fail us now. We need him."

Her eyes grew moist. "You used him to save my life and my son, and my kids."

She groaned. "God, Pastor Daniel cannot die. We need him to reach Ezekiel."

*

As Zeke drove quietly down the street, thoughts raced through his mind. The plan worked. He had just gunned down a pastor, in his own church, while he was preaching ... and *he* had got away with it!

Initially the adrenaline made him feel elated. But as it wore off, he felt empty and even a little sick. He had had beaten a lot of men, shot several, and had even killed a few. But this was different.

He felt nauseated.

The feeling was like the first time. He was sixteen when he was forced to slash a homeless guy as part of his gang initiation.

It had been colder than usual that night, and the old man was trying to sleep alone in the park.

Big mistake...for that guy.

He did not see Zeke coming. When the old man saw the knife and realized what was about to happen, he looked at Zeke with helpless, pleading, tired eyes. Zeke had felt a twinge of guilt, but gritted his teeth and pushed ahead.

His family needed the money he'd make being in the gang and selling the drugs. Plus, Zeke needed to prove that he was a man. A real man.

That was the night the voices started in his head. Ever since, no amount of power, money, alcohol or drugs could make them stop.


*

"No, Mom, we don't know why the man shot him." Rebecca said into the phone. "That does not matter right now. What matters is that you and Dad pray and get your church to pray."

"Thank you," Rebecca said. "Yes, the boys are with the Garcias. You met them. They will take good care of them."

"Yes, the Garcias are the couple with the older kids. They are a great family."

"I know that God does have this under control." Rebecca nodded, but then she began to cry again. "Oh Mom," she sniffed back the tears, "If you could have seen him lying there with all that blood…."

Rebecca was huddled in the corner of the waiting area with Pastor Carlos and his wife Freda when a few ladies burst in.

"Mom, I've got to go," Rebecca said. "Yes, I'll call you if there is anything to tell you."

"Oh Rebecca, Rebecca," Roberta said, swooping her up in her big arms and hugging her close. "Any word?" she asked eagerly.

"No, the doctor said it would be at least three or four hours," Rebecca said. "Then he'll have to wake up from the anesthesia… if all goes well." Her voice dropped and she turned her head so they could not see the moisture in her eyes.

"Ladies, we need to get to work," Roberta commanded. "We are going to pray that the doctor will operate better than he has ever done before."

*

"Oh my!" Maria said looking at her phone.

"What is it?" her sister asked.

"They brought Pastor Daniel to *this* hospital," Maria said. "They are operating on him now. Rebecca is in the OR Family Waiting area down on the first floor along with some of the ladies from the church. I've got to go be with her. You stay here with Mom," Then she gathered her stuff and headed out the door to find the OR Family Waiting room.

Maria was not good at directions. Put her in a mall and she could find anything, but in strange places like this hospital it was a different matter. Oh, she knew the ER of course. Ezekiel had been there several times when he was younger. But the rest of the hospital seemed to be laid out like a maze.

"Jesus, help me find them," she prayed as she got off the elevator on the first floor. She saw a sign and headed out. "But most of all, help Pastor Daniel."

"Maria!" Maria had just turned the corner from the west to the south wing and toward the OR Family Waiting area and was stunned and relieved to see the familiar faces of the ladies from her prayer group, the Prayer Force, rounding the corner from the opposite direction.

When they reached the OR waiting area, Roberta said in her big voice. "Well thank the Lord. Now the Prayer Force is complete."

"Come on Sisters. We got to pray that God will get Pastor Daniel and Rebecca through this operation," Roberta said. "We got to pray them through it."

"Join us," Roberta motioned for them to kneel by her. "Just on the other side of those doors and down the hall in an operating room, Pastor Daniel needs our prayers. We're praying for miracles."

*

Zeke unlocked the door to the office and slipped behind the dispatcher's desk. Sunday night was often one the quietest nights of the week, especially this time of year. The tourists poured into town on Thursday and Friday nights. The convention people, who came in for the week, usually got cabs their first night in town and did not venture out to the strip clubs until later in the week.

Zeke had given his usual Sunday evening dispatcher the night off.

He tinkered with the security footage and phone call records to make sure it looked as if he and the SUV had been there all evening and that he had left the desk for nothing more than an extended bathroom break. Then he sat down and lit a cigar.

*I have an alibi, if needed. I have proof that I was here at work tonight.*

# CHAPTER 5

## 10 PM

*"You did it! You killed him!"*

*"Serves him right."*

*"He won't be ruining your life anymore."*

The voices shouted in Zeke's head as he tried to sit calmly at the dispatch desk. Hearing them gave him conflicting emotions. He was very pleased that he had shot the preacher and seemingly got away with it. He also was happy the voices were not condemning him like they usually did.

*I have been waiting over a month to kill that guy,* he thought. *Oh, it tastes so sweet.*

He walked to the little refrigerator in the break room, grabbed a bottle of Corona, popped the top and took a long drink. He smiled.

But then, a frown chased down his face.

Ezekiel was also confused. He had hoped that by killing the pastor the voices would stop. But they kept shouting in his head, just as loud as ever, celebrating the victory.

He shook his head miserably. Angry and swearing under his breath, he pounded his fist on the desk top.

\*

*"I lift up my eyes to the mountains—where does my help come from? My help comes from the* LORD, *the Maker of heaven and earth,"* Pastor Carlos quietly read Psalm 121 to Rebecca.

"Oh Lord," Carlos' wife Freda prayed. "We look to you. Pastor Daniel's life is in your hands. We humbly ask for help."

Rebecca nodded and wiped a tear from her cheek. She looked at the old black and white clock on the far wall. The thick hand was on eleven, the long hand on seven: 11:07 AM. Daniel had been in there nearly three hours. *Oh God. Let that be good news*, she thought.

Rebecca swept her long, wavy, brown hair back with her left hand. She took a deep breath and looked up. She was very thankful that Pastor Carlos, Freda, Miss Roberta and the other ladies were with her. Their strength and faith gave her hope she did not have. Inside she was so tired and scared.

Her mind drifted. She heard herself replaying a phone conversation she had with her best friend Abigail Jenson just a few months ago.

*"To be very honest, Abbie, the seven-and-a half years we have spent in Las Vegas have been very challenging and often heartbreaking. Las Vegas is a literal, and in many ways, a spiritual desert. Ministry here feels like pouring out living water and seeing life begin to break out, only to have it quickly dry up and disappear. Often, the visible result rarely matches the amount of effort put in.*

*"Yes, without a doubt, we have seen God do more in the last seven-and-a-half years than we thought was possible. But so has the Enemy. He has constantly thrown heart-breaking challenges at us. We have poured out our hearts and souls into people only to have them turn on us or worse, turn from the Lord, or only to have them go back to their addiction.*

*"People we really thought we could count on have deeply disappointed us. Promises have been broken. Supporters dropped away without any explanation."*

*"I am sorry it has been so hard,"* Abigail had said. *"But you and Daniel are making such a difference. Do not let the Enemy discourage you."*

Roberta coughed, and it jarred Rebecca back to the reality of the waiting room. Then she closed her eyes and rubbed her temples. She wiped tears off her cheeks. Quietly she prayed.

*Lord, we have been through so much to get this ministry going in the heart of Las Vegas. And now this.... Father, I don't understand. It doesn't seem right.*

*But I must trust you.*

*

"What's wrong, Honey?" Doris Garcia asked as she came into the bedroom.

Five-year-old Titus Browning had his head under the pillow crying. Titus' eight-year-old brother, Zach, was sound asleep next to him snoring quietly. They were in Doris' oldest son's room. Trent was in the army now. The older Browning boys, Elijah and Caleb were sleeping in her son Travis' room. Travis and Caleb were classmates and good friends.

"Daddy... Daddy," Titus sobbed.

"Oh honey," she lifted the pillow off his head gently and stroked his curly brown hair.

Titus rolled over and looked at her with his large, brown eyes. "Will Daddy be ok?" he asked. "Some bad man shot him with a gun."

"Daddy is in good hands at that hospital, honey. Mommy is with him and God is with him," she said.

*Dear God,* she silently prayed. *You can't take this little boy's father from him. You just can't.*

# MONDAY, DECEMBER 21

## CHAPTER 6
### 12:17 AM

"We have done all we can do for now," the lead surgeon said as he looked around the operating room. "Good job, team. We got two of the bullets out and got the wounded lung patched and working. Let's close him up. Hopefully he'll make it through the night."

"Good job, doctor," The older nurse said quietly. "He's in God's hands now."

\*

"Browning? Daniel Browning? Are you here for Daniel Browning, ma'am?"

"Yes," Rebecca stood up. "I am Mrs. Daniel Browning." She gulped.

"Good news so far," The nurse smiled. "He made it through the surgery."

"Thank you, God." Rebecca said quietly. A chorus of "Praise the Lord" "Yeah God" and "Amen" rang from the lips of Freda, Carlos, and some of the others.

The nurse continued, "They should be cleaning him up and getting him into the Recovery Room very soon."

"Can we see him?" Rebecca asked.

"Not for an hour or two," the nurse said. "They need to closely monitor his post-anesthesia recovery. When he wakes up someone will come out and tell you. So, try to be patient. The surgeon will be by shortly to talk to you about the operation."

Then she saw the look in Rebecca's eye and added, "Don't worry, honey. It's routine for the doctor to stop in and brief you on the surgery."

"OK. Thank you," Rebecca said with a big breath. "Thank you so much!" She hugged the startled nurse.

"That's good news!" Roberta said. "Praise the Lord!"

Others offered an "amen" or a "praise the Lord" as well.

"I need to get home," a young lady said looking at her watch. It was after midnight.

"Me, too" another woman said. "Got work in the morning."

"I need to say goodnight to Mom up on the fourth floor and get home too," Maria added.

"Is she ok?" Rebecca asked.

"She's fine. This always happens when she does not take her medicine," Maria said. "They will probably let her go home in the morning."

"Well, thanks so much for being here and for your prayers. Why don't *all* of you go home and get some rest," Rebecca said. "Hopefully the worst is over."

"Shoo, all you girls get on home to your families," Roberta said waving her hand.

Then she turned to Rebecca. "Don't worry. I'm not leaving you," Roberta said. "Not until I see Pastor Daniel for myself and know he is ok." She squeezed Rebecca's hand.

"Thank you," Rebecca said quietly. Roberta, the seventy-year-old leader of the Prayer Force was like a second mother to Rebecca and to lots of other young women. She had hard-earned wisdom and a faith that was unshakable.

"I'm not leaving either," Pastor Carlos said. "Freda's got to get Jared and Jessica to school tomorrow, but I am here for the night."

"Are you sure? Rebecca asked weakly.

"Sure, I am sure?" he said.

"Thank you so much." Rebecca said quietly.

# CHAPTER 7

## 1:45 AM

Something swirled out of a huge black cloud.

Daniel was dreaming again, but this felt very real.

*Giant ants,* he thought. Hundreds of ants crawling all over Daniel's chest. Big red and black ants. *Just like the ones on my dad's boxers,* he thought.

No wait. It was no longer ants. They were morphing.

"Oh, no!" Now it's scorpions, massive menacing scorpions. They had red eyes and wicked smiles. Dozens of them swarmed over him and they began stinging his chest.

"Stop! Please stop! It hurts. It *really* hurts."

But they didn't listen. Pain shot like electricity through is chest. Over and over and over again.

Then it all went black.

*

*1:45 AM. It's about time to pack up and head home.* Zeke thought.

It had been quite a night. His well thought out plan to kill the preacher had gone off without a hitch.

*I shot the preacher in front of his whole church and got away with it.*

*That man won't mess up my family any more.*

Since Maria had been going to that church, she was no fun anymore. Even worse, she had all their boys deeply involved in church. Especially the younger ones. "Church, church, church. Jesus, Jesus, Jesus." Ezequiel was sick of it.

He knew firsthand what God and church and Jesus would do to you: Kill your dad. Ruin your family. Make you poor.

Tonight, he had finally stuck it to God.

But inside something didn't feel right.

*

"No Mom. The doctor still has not been in yet," Rebecca said into the phone.

"Yes, I know that it is almost 2:00 AM."

"Oh wait, the doctor just walked in. I got to go. Love you, Mom. Call you later."

"Mrs. Browning?" A thin, handsome, Asian man with excellent posture strode into the room.

"Yes. I am Rebecca Browning," Rebecca said as she sat up, running a hand through her hair and straightening her blouse.

"Nice to meet you. Please sit down. I am Doctor Kim. I am the one who operated on your husband," he paused and then began to recount the situation.

"Your husband came in with three significant gunshot wounds. Fortunately, the shooter used a .22 caliber handgun, so the bullets did not do as much damage as they could have," Dr. Kim continued. "We are also very fortunate that none of the bullets hit his spine or any major organs. Of the three bullets, one bullet was in his shoulder. We removed that one easily. Fortunately, it did no significant damage. He should recover quite quickly from that one."

Rebecca sighed.

"Another bullet was in his upper abdomen. Fortunately, it missed every vital organ. That is a miracle," he said with a smile.

"The third bullet is the problem. It grazed and perforated his right lung causing it to leak," the doctor frowned and continued. "That is why he was having such a hard time breathing. We had to separate two ribs, go in and repair and re-inflate that lung as best we could. He should breathe much better now. Although the lung will need more repair when he is much stronger."

Rebecca blinked, swallowed and took a deep breath.

Dr. Kim continued, "He was barely breathing when he came in and, as you no doubt saw, he lost a lot of blood. We almost lost him when he first went under the anesthesia, but he is quite a fighter and miraculously rallied enough for us to continue."

"That's because we were praying!' Roberta chimed in. "The Lord heard our prayers."

"Even if the patch does not hold, he can live with one working lung. We will know more in a few days."

Rebecca's head was swimming with this recent information. *Three bullets. One lung with a temporary patch on it.*

Dr. Kim continued, "When the third bullet penetrated his sternum in the center of his chest, the bullet partially fragmented. Part of that bullet is currently lodged next to his heart. For now, we can't risk removing it without causing greater damage to his heart. So, we will leave it there for now and watch it closely. When your husband is ready, we will need to remove it. But he is not ready now."

Rebecca frowned trying to fight back the tears and take it all in.

"I understand that your husband is a pastor," Dr. Kim said with a brave smile. "I am also a Christian. I was born in South Korea in a pastor's home. We came to America when I was a boy, so my father could get his degree from an American seminary. I have seen the work of God." He smiled reassuringly at Rebecca. "Like you, God sent me to this city to make a difference."

"Mrs. Browning,' Dr. Kim continued. "You need to realize that it truly is a miracle that that your husband survived the shooting and made it here to the hospital still breathing. Beyond that, it is a miracle that he survived the surgery. We need to thank God for His mercy."

Tears filled Rebecca's eyes.

The doctor continued, "The next several days are critical. I will watch him very closely."

Then he looked at Pastor Carlos and Roberta. "I know that your church has been praying. They need to continue." Quietly he stood up and walked out.

Roberta put a large arm around Rebecca's shoulders and held her tight.

Pastor Carlos grabbed his phone to send out a group text to the Grace City Prayer Chain.

# CHAPTER 8

## 2:28 AM

"How is our patient?" Dr. Kim asked as he walked into the recovery area. "How is his breathing?"

"His breathing is very labored, but consistent," the nurse answered.

"Good," Dr. Kim smiled. "He should be waking up by now."

"Sir, he shows no signs of waking up."

"What do you mean?"

"He has shown no sign of stirring."

"It's been an hour-and-a-half since he left the operation," he said. He felt a shot of adrenaline race through his tired body.

"Yes, but he is still out," the nurse said.

"Did he stir at all?"

"Not a muscle, except to breath."

"Did you try to wake him up?"

"Yes. I used both light and verbal stimulation, but there was no response."

Dr. Kim frowned. "Let's try again using manual stimulation."

He pulled a pen out of his pocket. Then he grabbed Daniel's finger and poked the nail bed closest to the finger with the end of the pen.

"No response," he said to the nurse frowning. She marked the chart.

Next, he grabbed and twisted Daniel's trapezoid muscle of his right shoulder.

He shook his head. "No response."

Then he pressed his thumb into the indentation above Daniel's right eye, near the nose. He frowned. "No response."

*

Daniel was dreaming again.

He saw and smelled the high school wrestling room. Wrestling practice had not begun yet. Coach was not yet in the room. Big Jack, the giant heavyweight wrestler, was holding court and making fun of the other guys. Daniel, just a skinny freshman, tried to slip in unnoticed.

"Hey, freshman," Jack yelled, spotting him. "You think you are pretty special winning that match against that junior last week. Don't you?"

Daniel meekly shook his head.

"Come here, let me show you how special you are."

With surprising quickness and agility, Big Jack reached out and grabbed Daniel's ankle. He jerked Daniel's ankle and pulled him close. Then Jack jumped on top of him, crushing Daniel's chest and face under his massive chest.

*I can't breathe,* Daniel thought. *Help, I can't breathe.*

Then the wrestling room grew dark.

The big evil cloud of darkness came back and filled the room. Yet, it could not touch his body. Something was holding it back.

Then everything went black.

*

"Where is he?" Rebecca asked as the clock read 2:53 AM. "Why is he not out of recovery yet?"

She had been doing pretty well, but the horrific events of the evening were beginning to weigh on her. She was exhausted. Her adrenaline was gone. She was irritable. But worse than any of that, her old nemesis, fear, was like a dark shadow that was creeping steadily toward her.

*Jesus, you've got to help my husband.*

She put her head in her hands and blinked back tears.

Having Roberta and Pastor Carlos there was great, but she really wished her dad was there.

Her mind wandered to a recurring frustration. One of the hardest thing about being in Las Vegas was being so far from family. Her parents lived in Ohio, where her dad led a small church and taught some Intercultural Studies classes at Mission University. Her parents had been missionaries in Brazil for fifteen years before coming back to the US to get her younger sister better medical attention and so Dad could teach. Her older brother had married and lived up by Lake Erie. Her grandparents lived in Pennsylvania, as did her aunts, uncles and cousins.

Daniel's family was also from Ohio. His mom, a recovering alcoholic, had gotten saved after Daniel led her to Christ. His older brothers had not become Christians yet, but they were getting closer. But none of them had the type of job that allowed them the time or money to travel. So, they hadn't seen much of them since Rebecca and Daniel moved to Las Vegas.

Daniel and Rebecca tried to get back East once a year to see their families, but it was expensive with the four boys. Her parents did not have much money and tried to come out to visit them in Las Vegas at least once a year. But it never seemed like they stayed long enough.

She looked back at the clock- 3:11 AM.

"Where is Daniel?" Rebecca thought. "Why is he not out of recovery yet?"

*

Zeke was staring at the television. He was still keyed up and not yet ready to fall asleep, so he was watching a movie, *The Shawshank Redemption* about a man who is trying to escape from a miserable old prison in the 1940's and 50's.  Watching a prison movie was a bad idea. Guilty thoughts dogged Zeke's mind.

*What have I done? I shot a man ... in his church ... in front of several hundred people ... in cold blood ... as he was preaching a sermon.*

*Why did I think I would not be caught?*

*I don't want to go back to prison.*

*What will happen to my wife?*

*What will happen to my kids?*

# CHAPTER 9
## 3:24 AM

At 3:24 AM Dr. Kim came through the door of the waiting room. Rebecca was pacing on the far side of the room.

"Rebecca," Roberta said. "It's the doctor."

Dr. Kim walked across the room to Rebecca. "Mrs. Browning, good news: Your husband has survived the surgery. I am pleased that he is breathing on his own. It is very labored, but consistent."

"Thank God," she said. "Can I see him?"

"Yes, shortly. But let me prepare you."

"Prepare me?" She asked, her eyes getting very large as she shot an anxious glance at Roberta.

"Yes," Dr. Kim said slowly. "He has not awakened yet, and he is in a coma."

"What? A coma?" Rebecca asked slowly, struggling to say the word.

Dr. Kim continued, "He is unconscious. We have been attempting to awaken him, but have not been successful. He currently is unable to consciously speak, hear, or move."

Rebecca gasped. The blood drained from her face. Gathering herself, she asked, "Why is he in a coma? What is causing this?"

"We don't know for sure." Dr. Kim said seriously. "There are three probable causes. It may be that after he was shot and was struggling to breath, he did not get enough oxygen to his brain. Or possibly, the coma is the result of the excessive blood loss he experienced before we stopped the bleeding. Or the third possibility is that the coma is his body's response to the extreme trauma he experienced by being shot repeatedly in the chest."

"Will he wake up?" Rebecca asked meekly.

"We hope so. But, to be honest, we don't know for sure yet."

"How long will he be like this?"

"Again, we do not know for sure. He may come out of it in a few hours, or it could last a few days, or even a few weeks. Unlike in the movies, the patient will usually come out of it gradually."

Rebecca nodded, then asked. "What will he be like when he comes out of it?'

"That depends on what caused it and ... if there is any brain damage," Dr. Kim paused and looked at Rebecca tenderly. "I am sorry, but again, we do not know right now. But, I have a colleague, Dr. Mitchell, who is an expert in this area. I will consult with him later today and he will assess the situation. Hopefully, he can answer our questions." Dr. Kim said. "Trust me, we are doing all we can to keep him alive."

Rebecca nodded and silently sat down.

"I think this coma may be a blessing in disguise," the doctor said.

Rebecca looked up at him skeptically.

Dr. Kim continued, "He needs every bit of strength he has to heal up from all he has been through. By being in a coma, more of his strength can go toward his healing. That's a good thing."

Dr. Kim sat down next to her and took her hand.

"Listen, God has your husband's life in the palm of his hand. God has seen him through a terrible ordeal tonight and somehow he is still breathing, so there is still much hope." Dr. Kim smiled reassuringly. "I guarantee you that he will receive the best care I can give him. But more important than that, I guarantee that God has got this under control. We must trust Him."

Rebecca nodded her head numbly.

"Remember, with God all things are possible," Dr. Kim said.

"Let's pray," Roberta said, grabbing Rebecca's and the doctor's hands.

# CHAPTER 10
## 4:17 AM

"Oh my," Rebecca gasped when she saw Daniel lying in the hospital bed.

*He looks like a dead person in a casket,* she thought. *So white and pasty.* His skin was pale and his eyes had dark circles under them. He had tubes everywhere and a large mask over his mouth giving him oxygen. His chest heaved up and down roughly with each breath.

"He looks so bad because he lost so much blood," Roberta said quietly. After forty years of nursing, she knew what she was talking about. "As they get more blood in him, he should start to look a little better."

Rebecca nodded and took her husband's limp hand. It was cool to the touch. He did not acknowledge her presence. Up and down his chest heaved.

"Well, Lord," she sighed and prayed in a firm but quiet voice, "I choose to be thankful that my husband is still alive. Thank you for seeing him through last night. Thank you for giving him a Christian surgeon. Thank you that he is still breathing." She wiped a tear off her cheek and continued.

"Please help him heal. And please, please help his brain be whole. Our church needs their pastor, our boys need their father and ... and I need my husband." Tears were dropping off her cheeks. "I refuse to give in to fear. Father, I choose to trust you."

*

Grace City Church had two people assigned to pray every hour of the day. They had been on full alert since the shooting.

From 4:00 to 5:00 AM Timmy Hill in Henderson, just on the edge of Las Vegas, and Dorothy Dreyfus, who lived near the Flamingo campus in Paradise, got on their knees in their respective homes. They had both seen the text from Pastor Carlos about Daniel's operation and that he still had a bullet in his chest. They prayed with much greater urgency than usual as they focused their prayers on Pastor Daniel.

At 5:00 AM they stopped to get ready for work. Their place in the prayer chain was taken by Martha Washburn and Rufus Johnson. Martha was one of the ladies who had been at the hospital with Rebecca and the others until late the night before. Poor Rufus battled guilt that he had been the one to let the shooter in the door. He knew that he hadn't done anything wrong, but kept wondering "what if" he had known not to let the shooter in the door. But he had learned that God was not condemning him. He was secure in the grace and wisdom of God. The joy of this knowledge fueled his heartfelt prayers for Pastor Daniel.

Early this morning, many others in the Grace City family were waking up and dropping to their knees in prayer for Daniel. Many were asking God for a miracle.

It was needed.

*

Daniel was dreaming again.

The sun was shining bright and it was hot out. There was a small, blue lake surrounded by large, green hills. The sky was rich royal blue with just a few beautiful fluffy white clouds. The air was clean and sweet.

Daniel was a skinny four-year-old. He hung onto his dad's back with his arms wrapped around his father's neck as his dad swam to the pier.

They were at Pike Lake State Park on vacation.

They had been having a rare, happy time.

They arrived at the pier and his dad sat him down on the edge and joined him. Young Daniel wanted to dangle his feet in the water, but his legs weren't long enough. He watched as his older brother and the rest of the big kids jumped off the board into the deep part of the lake.

Then they turned back toward the beach. He could see his mom waving at him. She had her swimming suit on and looked pretty he thought. She never went swimming because she never learned to swim.

His dad looked at him with an odd grin. "I think you are ready," he said. Then he stood up and dove off the pier into the water swimming underwater back toward the beach.  Soon he popped up. The water grew more swallow nearer the beach and he was standing up. He turned, looked back at Daniel, and waved. "Come on, Daniel, you can do it," he said. "Just jump in and swim to me."

*I don't think I can do that. I am just a little kid. I don't know how to swim.*

"Come on, you can do it," his dad insisted as he smiled and beckoned with his arms.

Hesitantly Daniel stood, joined his hands over his head, and bent at the waist like the big kids diving off the board. He paused.

*I can't do this.*

*But I don't want to disappoint my dad. I don't want him to yell and cause a scene.*

Daniel re-clasp his hands, took a deep breath and dove in.

Immediately he was surrounded by water. He took a deep breath and swallowed a mouth full. His head went down under the water and he felt himself sinking.

*I am drowning!*

His lungs ached. They were being mercilessly squeezed by the pressure of the water.

*I can't breathe. I can't breathe. Help me!*

# CHAPTER 11
## 5:31 AM

Rebecca and Roberta followed the small army of nurses and aides that transported Daniel from the recovery room to the ICU on the top floor. Daniel had almost a dozen tubes and machines attached to him. Some put fluid into him. Others took fluid out. Some measured his vitals and others helped keep him alive.

Roberta had sent Pastor Carlos home to get some rest as he needed to be ready to lead the church in Pastor Daniel's absence. Roberta said that she wasn't leaving until reinforcements came later in the day. Rebecca was not leaving as long as Daniel's situation was still so uncertain.

The ICU had 16 rooms and was staffed with six nurses and three aides. Every room was taken and Daniel was fortunate to be able to get in.

Daniel's room had a window that looked west toward the Las Vegas Strip. Even though the sun would not be up for another hour, the Strip was fully illumined in all its glory. Las Vegas Boulevard is one street, four miles long, that houses over 40 hotels and 35 casinos, many of them the largest and most famous hotels, resorts, and casinos in the world. Beyond that, it is home of over half a dozen large amusement rides and an amusement park. There is also nearly a dozen large clusters of expensive shops, including the Miracle Mile. There are a variety of restaurants and many well-known lounges, theaters, nightclubs, residential high-rises, and a few massive venues for large events. Open 24 hours a day, 365 days a year, the Strip is packed on weekends, especially from 1AM-4AM. People say that "Southern California and the rest of the world comes to Vegas to party."

As Rebecca looked out on the Strip, her mind wandered to their first conversation about Las Vegas, nearly nine years earlier. Daniel had urgently grabbed her after campus church and said, "I have to talk to you when we get home." He had preached that Thursday night on Matthew 16:18 where Jesus said, "I will build my church and the gates of hell will not prevail against it."

For nearly a year prior to that, "they," but mostly Daniel, had been restless. His ministry as Campus Pastor at Mission University was fruitful and fulfilling, but he felt that they were too comfortable. For months, his prayer had been, "Lord, either call us to put down roots here or send us to a tough place to do a hard thing so you will get all the glory."

That semester, Daniel had preached on the hard sayings of Jesus. He boldly spoke about "denying yourself and taking up your cross," "leaving father and mother," "selling everything you have and giving it to the poor," and the toughest one, loving Jesus so much that you choose Jesus above "father and mother, wife and children, brothers and sisters—yes, even your own life."

Rebecca loved their life in Ohio. She taught art at the high school part time and focused on raising the two little boys they had then. Plus, she was pregnant and ready to deliver their third. Her parents lived an hour away and they got to see them frequently. They had college students in their home often and she loved mentoring the college girls.

Rebecca already felt stretched and that she was giving all she had just to do what they were doing. But if Jesus demanded more, then wouldn't she have to give it? Plus, she knew her husband listened to God, and if he felt as though God was calling them out of their comfort zone to something else, who was she to resist it?

"Honey, I think I know where we are to go and what we are to do," Daniel said eagerly that night when they were home from church and had put the kids in bed. They sat on the couch and he took her hands.

"Remember tonight in the sermon I said, 'I believe that if we would cooperate with Jesus we can go anywhere and start churches that would kick down the gates of hell?'"

"Yes," she said tentatively.

"I felt as though the Lord spoke to me when I said that," he said.

"What did the Lord say?" she asked sincerely.

"I think He said, 'Find the gates of hell and plant a church.'"

"Ok," she said slowly. "So where is that? Thailand? Washington DC? Hollywood?"

Daniel smiled. "Maybe, but not for us." Then he continued. "Drake, one of the freshmen guys I have been mentoring, brought a guy with him tonight whom he met while doing ministry at Ohio State."

"Yes," she said. "So?"

"At the invitation at the end of the service, he brought the guy forward for me to pray with him. Guess what the guy's shirt said?"

"What?"

"It said, 'Sin City! Las Vegas, Nevada.'"

"Okay," she said slowly.

"When I saw his shirt, I felt as though God spoke to me. I think He said, 'Doesn't that sound like the gates of Hell? Where sin abounds, grace abounds that much more (Romans 5:20). Go to Las Vegas and help turn Sin City into Grace City.'"

When Daniel said it, Rebecca got goose bumps, or as Daniel liked to say, *God* bumps.

"Well, that would be a tough place, and starting a church there would be a hard thing. So, I guess God would get all the glory," she said slowly nodding her head. In her heart, she knew that he was right. This probably was God calling them to Las Vegas.

*Yes, but at what cost?* She had thought. *At what cost?*

For the last seven years since they had been in Las Vegas, they had given all they had to starting a church in a part of urban Las Vegas ironically named Paradise. They were trying to raise children in a place that celebrates itself as Sin City. Some of her children's Sunday school teachers were former prostitutes, gang members, and drug addicts. It all was so hard.

Now, here she was in Las Vegas. They were in Paradise Hospital in the ICU. She was watching her husband lying in a bed fighting simply to breathe. Daniel had been shot three times in their own church while he was preaching a Sunday night sermon … and he still had a bullet by his heart.

She put her head in her hands as a huge wave of weariness washed over her. She wanted to curl up and cry.

"Oh, excuse me," a young aide said as she bumped into Rebecca on the way into the room. "I need to check his IV's."

"It's okay," Rebeca said numbly. She blinked back tears, stood up stiffly and ran her hands through her hair.

## CHAPTER 12
## 6:32 AM

*Dear Lord, you have been so good to us. I thank you for your grace and mercy,* Maria prayed quietly as she put her Bible down and knelt by the chair in the family room.

*Please be with Pastor Daniel today. This is a very important day. Help him.*

*Please protect my boys as they go to school today. Help them all to grow up to become strong men of God. Especially work in Miguel and Pablo's hearts. It is hard to be a Christian in that high school they attend. They are surrounded by darkness, dirt and temptation. Help them be strong, especially Pablo. He is wavering."* Her eyes were getting moist as she prayed.

*And Lord, I know you must be tired of me asking you this, but please speak to Ezekiel today. You know that there was a time in his life when he knew your voice and followed you. Break through that hard heart of his. He is a good man on the inside. Speak to him, Lord. Please speak.*

She sniffed and blew her nose. Tears were rolling down her cheeks as she dabbed her eyes with her handkerchief.

*Speak, Lord. Speak.*

# CHAPTER 13
## 7:13 AM

"Come on, boys, hurry up. Can't be late for school." Doris Garcia said as she loaded the Browning boys and her son Travis into her large SUV.

"Can we pray for Dad all the way to school?" Fourteen-year-old Elijah asked. "Mom said he is still sleeping and has not been awake since the operation."

"Absolutely," Doris said. "Elijah, you go first."

"Dear God, we ask you to watch over our dad today," he started. "Thank you that he made it to the hospital okay and made it through the operation. Thank you that he had a good surgeon. Please be with him in a super special way and heal him."

His voice rose as he prayed more boldly. "Our church needs him, and Mom needs him....and...," his voice cracked, "... we need him."

Doris son, Travis prayed next, "Dear Lord. Pastor Browning is hurting today. Help the doctors and nurses know just what to do to take good care of him. Get him back to coaching baseball real soon."

"God, help Dad." It was eight-year old Zach Browning. "Help Mom too because she must be tired."

"Heavenly Father, we come to you in the strong name of Jesus," Caleb Browning prayed with passion. "Surround our father with mighty warrior angels. Protect him from the devil. Win the battle. In Jesus' name, amen."

"Jesus. I want to see Daddy," said Titus in a weak voice. "I want to see Mommy too. And watch over Thunderbolt as Mrs. Meadows takes care of him. Amen."

"Amen," all the boys said.

Doris wiped the tears off her cheeks as they stopped at a light. *Oh God, you got to hear the prayers of these children. You just got to.*

*

"What are they thinking?" Roberta asked laughing. "The poor man is in a coma and they bring him breakfast! I worked for hospitals for twenty-three years and I can't tell you all of the silliness I have seen."

Rebecca smiled. It was so good to have Roberta with her. She could not imagine going through this alone.

Roberta shoved the plate in front of Rebecca. "Here, honey, you eat these eggs and toast before they get cold. I don't think Daniel has much appetite right now."

Rebecca poked around at the food. Not much taste. But at least the coffee was hot.

"His vitals are not good, but they are better than when he came in here," Roberta said looking at the lighted screen. "We can thank the Lord for that."

Rebecca nodded.

*Oh, God let his nightmare end soon. Please wake me up in my own house and in my own bed with my husband snoring beside me. May this experience be nothing more than a very bad dream.*

# CHAPTER 14
## 8 AM

"Put the word out on the street. Find out who shot Pastor Daniel," Captain Zanic told his officers as they prepped to start the morning shift. "We will give a reward for information leading to the arrest of this shooter."

They nodded in agreement.

"Press every lead and turn over every stone. This pastor was one of the good guys. He and that church of his have done a lot of good around here," the captain continued.

Zanic was angry. He really liked Pastor Daniel. The young pastor and his church had brought everyone in their office donuts numerous times. He often stopped in the captain's office to solicit prayer requests. He had his church fix a great breakfast every year for the officers. Pastor Daniel had even stopped in to pray with Zanic when he heard that his wife had breast cancer. This pastor really was a good guy... and some scum bag had the audacity to shoot him in cold blood during his church service in Zanic's precinct. They had to bring that shooter to justice.

*

*I feel like I need another shower*, Zeke thought as he got up. His wife and kids had already left for school, so he had the house to himself. He had really needed a shower when he got home last night because he had sweat a lot wearing that big coat and extra hoodie. Now, he felt he needed a second shower because of the dirty nature of last night's *business*.

But it was more than sweat that needed washing off this time. It was guilt. Years of guilt, bitterness, anger, and shame. Yet, he knew that no amount of hot water would ever wash it all away.

Zeke came out of the shower and put on some sweat clothes. He walked into the kitchen and noticed that his wife, Maria, had made him a breakfast burrito and had written him a nice note. *What a good woman*, he thought.

He looked at their wedding picture hanging on the wall. They both looked so young then. She was such a beauty. Long black hair, flawless olive skin, bright brown eyes, and that amazingly big and beautiful smile.

Even after all these years, she still was beautiful and looked much younger than her age.

Now she worked at the elementary school where seven-year-old Carlos was in second grade and nine-year-old Emilio was in fourth. Miquel and Pablo were in high school.

The gap in the kid's ages occurred during the five years Ezekiel was in prison for selling drugs. When he and Maria linked up in high school, he was already gang banging. She was in her own rebellion and had gone along with it. But when he got sent to prison, she'd had to get a job to make ends meet.

Unlike many of the guys' wives, Maria had stayed faithful to Zeke while he was in prison. She visited him as often as she could and wrote to him almost daily. When he got out of prison, she welcomed him home.

But while he was in prison, Maria had really changed. She had started going to church all the time and praying. She didn't want to party anymore. Even though she didn't make a big deal out of it, she clearly did not approve of his "current business practices." That church was affecting her.

"You are so smart Ezekiel, you could be successful at so many jobs. You don't have to commit crimes to make money," she would say.

"How do you know that I 'commit crimes'?" He would always ask. "I run a legitimate limousine business."

She would just shake her head and walk away. She knew his drivers sold drugs out of their cars to the tourists they took to the strip clubs at night.

*Now that her preacher is dead, she won't go to that church anymore,* he thought. *Her preacher is dead. What will she think of her God, her church, and her preacher now?*

*

"Our pastor got shot last night," Maria told Stephanie, the other school secretary at Jack Daley Elementary School. The typical morning chaos in the school office had just calmed down.

"Oh my God! I heard about it on the news this morning," Stephanie said. "I thought it might be your church. Were you there?"

"No, not last night. My mom had another small heart attack over the weekend, and I was with her at the hospital."

"Oh my God! Is your mom ok?" Stephanie asked.

"Yes, the doctor thinks she should be fine and will be able to get out as soon as later today. But she has got to keep taking her medicine."

"They said that the shooter came right into the church and shot your pastor while he was preaching," Stephanie said excitedly.

"Yes, my friends were there," Maria said. "When I heard, I joined them and the pastor's wife in the waiting room for prayer."

"I would have guessed that you'd be at a prayer meeting. Maria, you sure have changed in the last few years." Stephanie said.

"Praise the Lord," Maria said. "He is changing me from the inside out."

Stephanie wanted to distract Maria before she got going on the Jesus thing. "They said on the news that the preacher got shot three times in the chest and that he is still alive."

"Yes," Maria replied. "They told me that when the pastor lay on that stage covered in blood, that it looked hopeless. But the Lord saw him through. With God, all things are possible. God is not finished with Pastor Daniel yet."

# CHAPTER 15
## 9:08 AM

"Let's all lift our voices together to the Lord on behalf of Pastor Daniel. He survived the night, but is in a coma," Pastor Matthew said as the guitar played quietly in the background. On cue, two dozen voices cried out to God in a beautiful concert of prayer for Pastor Daniel's healing and protection.

Pastor Matthew was leading the daily "Worship and Prayer service" at the Grace City House of Prayer. Usually about two dozen people gathered each day to practice what the website referred to as "Word-fed, Spirit-led, worship-based, corporate prayer in the city for the city." The morning group was usually a mixture of staff, interns, UNLV college students, homeless guys, and retired folks. Another fifty-people met one night a week, which included a wider demographic of adults, teens and children.

Earlier that morning, as he prepared to lead the morning prayer service, Matthew reflected on the fact that the very first ministry that Pastor Daniel and Rebecca established when they got to Las Vegas was the daily House of Prayer. They believed that everything God wanted to do with them and Grace City flowed out of their times of prayer.

Today, they did what they had done so many times before. They sat in a large circle on folding chairs, and worshipped and prayed through a couple of worship songs. Next, they read through a passage of Scripture stopping to pray for issues that the text prompted. Then they stood side-by-side and interceded for the ministries that were going that week, for people they were ministering to, for other churches in the city, and other things as they felt directed. At this point, they worshipped more and prayed specifically for each other.

One thing he loved about these prayer meetings was the frequent, tangible display of the presence of God. It was not unusual for people to weep as God touched them deeply.

Another aspect of these prayer meetings is that they had seen so many answered prayers. There were days when God miraculously healed people. Several times deeply demonized people had been delivered. Many, many times people had been freed and healed from painful emotional wounds.

Every day it was slightly different as the Word of God highlighted different issues. Of course, today there was unusual intensity and urgency. They focused most of the prayers on Pastor Daniel and his family. Daniel needed a miracle.

# CHAPTER 16
## 9:50 AM

"Mrs. Browning?"

Rebecca was startled as a young nurse entered the room. The nurse's eyes were big and she wore a silly smile. "There are reporters out in the waiting room and they want to talk to you about your husband's shooting last night."

"Reporters?" Rebecca asked.

"Yes, reporters. Not just the local ones either -- Fox, CBS, NBC, CNN and others. There are at least a dozen of them out there."

Rebecca's eyes got wide as he looked over at Roberta. "What do I do?" She asked.

"The way I see it, you have two choices," Roberta said. "Either you send me out to chase them away or..."

"...or *what*?" Rebecca asked.

"Or you go out and tell them about Jesus," Roberta said. "Tell them how God is seeing your husband through this. Tell that God is good. I think that is what your husband would do."

"I know he would." Rebecca took a deep breath and stood up. She quickly ran a brush through her hair and smoothed her outfit. "Pray for me," she said as she squared her shoulders.

"Wait a minute," Roberta said. "I have a plan."

\*

Five minutes later, short yet, formidable Roberta marched into the waiting room ahead of Rebecca. She knew how to enter a room with authority, and she used every bit of it as she lifted her hands and shushed the crowd of reporters. "Mrs. Browning has had a long, difficult night. She won't be answering any questions today, but she will make a brief statement."

Rebecca ducked her head in the waiting area, and looked directly at the reporters. She walked to the front of the room and lifted her phone where she had made some notes. Keeping her eyes fixed on the notes she began:

"Last night my husband was shot in our church as he was speaking from the platform. Yes, it was a great shock to see him covered in blood and barely breathing. Yes, it was a shock when they told us he had been shot three times in the chest. Yes, it was devastating seeing him carted away to be operated on when he was barely alive. But God was with him and with us.

"We are grateful that he survived the shooting and the operation. He is currently in a coma. We believe God is using this coma to allow his body to focus its strength on his healing. We do believe that God has this all under control.

"If my husband should die as a result of this shooting...," at this Rebecca stopped and took a deep breath. She took another big breath and continued. "...if Daniel dies in this way, he will be happy. Because he often said that we must love Jesus enough to take a bullet for him.

"We do pray for the man who did this, that the Lord would forgive him and touch his heart before he hurts anyone else. We also ask that all of you please pray for my husband."

"Mrs. Browning! Mrs. Browning!" Rude reporters lifted their hands and began to ask questions. Rebecca ducked out the room and Roberta stepped up.

"I said there would be no questions," Roberta growled in a way that let them know she meant business. She raised her hands and then in a sweet, yet commanding voice said, "Mrs. Browning asked us to pray, so let's pray." She bowed her head somewhat dramatically.

The reporters were stunned into silence. Then like sheep, many of them bowed their heads as Roberta's big voice boomed, "Dear Father in Heaven, we cry out to you today on behalf of our brother and pastor Daniel Browning. Thanks for taking care of him so far. We need this great man Father, his family needs him, and this city needs him. Touch his body and heal him, we pray. In Jesus' powerful name, Amen!"

At that, a few reporters crossed themselves and couple even murmured "Amen."

## CHAPTER 17
### 10:18 AM

Zeke was in his black SUV driving back to the office. Monday afternoons were often busy days in the Esquire Limousine Company office. Weekends were big in Vegas. Over forty million visitors came to town last year. Many left the airport in one of Zeke's limousines headed to a night of partying.

On Mondays, Zeke and his assistant, Javier, counted the income from the weekend, ran by the bank for the deposit, and put out the drivers' schedules for the week.

"Zeke, did you hear the news?" Javier asked as Ezekiel walked in. Javier was always stylish in his hipster clothes and haircut. Zeke often made fun of him for his tight pants. However, he greatly valued the way Javier kept up with details.

Zeke never listened to the news. Javier was addicted to it. He told Zeke everything he needed to know.

"No," Zeke replied. "What news?"

"About the pastor getting shot last night? "

"No," Zeke smirked subtly. "Tell me about it."

"Some guy comes in during the church's worship service, pulls out a gun and shoots the preacher as he is standing on the stage."

"Really?" Ezekiel asked innocently. "What happened to the shooter?"

"He got away," Javier said.

"Too bad," Zeke said sarcastically. He was enjoying this moment.

"Want to know what's crazy about the whole thing?" Javier asked.

"What's so crazy?"

"The pastor took three bullets right in the chest and is still alive!"

\*

"Captain, we are receiving emails and the phone keeps ringing with calls from nuts and from terrorist groups claiming responsibility for the Preacher shooting."

"Thanks Huffman," the Captain said to the young officer behind the desk. "Check them all out and note any good leads. Downtown has assigned Detectives McCauley and Marino to investigate this case."

\*

"As we open chapel this morning," Mr. Newkirk, the principal of Coronado Christian School, began. "Let's pray for the Browning family. You all know Pastor Daniel Browning. He spoke to us in chapel last month," Newkirk continued. "He was shot last night. He is in critical condition. God has been watching over him, but we need to pray. Let's bow our heads."

\*

When Ezekiel heard that the pastor was still alive, he made an excuse and went into his office. He threw himself into the chair behind his desk. Swearing, he pounded his fist on the desk.

*Loser.*

*Mess up.*

*Fool.*

*Failure.*

The voices in his head railed against him. He could not make them stop. *What am I going to do now?* he thought. *What am I going to do now?*

\*

"I can't believe you got all those reporters to pray!" Rebecca said laughing. All the pent-up emotions and exhaustion of the last fifteen hours was coming out.

"It wasn't me," Roberta said gleefully. "It was the Lord!"

"Yes, and it was amazing!" Rebecca said. "Did you see that guy from CNN? He didn't know what to do. He looked around, saw everyone else was praying and frowned and dropped his head."

"I can't believe the guy from MSNBC who got down on his knees," Roberta chuckled shaking her head.

"That was so great. Yea, God!" Rebecca said.

"Yea, God!" Roberta agreed.

But as they turned the corner into Daniel's room the laughter stopped. As they saw his nearly lifeless body in the bed, reality punched them in the gut, blow by blow.

*Daniel looked like a corpse in a science fiction casket.*

*He was covered with wires and tubes.*

*He was fighting for every single breath.*

*He had been shot three times.*

*He still had a bullet next to his heart.*

*He was in a coma.*

*They did not know if he would ever wake up..*

*They did not know what he would be like if he did come out of it.*

In silence, they both sat down and dropped their heads.

\*

Mike McCauley and David Marino were drinking coffee at the Blueberry Hill Diner on Flamingo Ave. It was just down the street from the

Grace City Church Flamingo campus where the shooting had occurred the night before. McCauley had his iPad open and was reviewing the notes they had on the case.

"We interviewed the witnesses at the church. Nothing much there." McCauley said as he began to read down the notes on his iPad.

*A man in a dark hat, a large, dark overcoat, and hoodie slipped in after the service began. The lights were down low. When the preacher started his talk, the man stood up and shot him three times. A man from the church knocked the guy off balance on the last shot. The shooter stumbled but got away out the side door.*

*Not one got much of a look at his face. A young lady saw his eyes and said he had "devil, evil eyes."* Whatever that means.

*He was possibly middle-aged; on the short side; strong; athletic; dark; possibly Hispanic.*

*He left no fingers prints; no DNA. Almost all of the lights are out in the parking lot of the office complex where the church meets. No one saw which way he went.*

"Not a lot to go on," Marino said.

"Out of two million people in this valley, half of them are male. That narrows it to one million men," McCauley continued.

"Twenty-five percent of the men in this city are Hispanic. That narrows it down to 250,000 men," Marino said.

"Let's say ten percent fit that description. That narrows it down to 25,000," Marino continued shaking his head. "Not very good odds."

"But," McCauley added. "Don't forget that he wore a dark ball cap, a dark hoodie, wore a large coat and had devil eyes. That should narrow it down to about 5,000."

"Let's go talk to more neighbors," Marino stood. "This story is all over the news today. Maybe somebody saw something last night that will help us."

# CHAPTER 18
## 11:25 AM

"Mrs. Browning?" the nurse said as she entered Daniel's room. "The mayor is outside. She wants to see you in the waiting area if you can."

"The mayor?" Rebecca asked. "For me? Are you sure?"

"I am sure," the nurse said with a bemused smile.

"Go see what she wants," Roberta said. "I got it here."

Rebecca straightened her blouse and smoothed her hair with her hand.

"Honey, you look beautiful as always," Roberta said. "She knows that you have been sitting here all night. Go see what she wants."

Rebecca walked slowly down the hall, not sure what to expect.

"Rebecca Browning!" the mayor, a sixty-year-old, bleach-bottle-blond-bombshell, grabbed her up in a big hug as she entered the room. "I am so sorry. Honey, we are all torn up about what happened to your husband last night."

She held Rebecca at arm's length and looked in her eyes. "Your husband is a good man. And you know, the Man Upstairs looks out for good men."

Rebecca nodded. She felt like a little girl.

"I want you to know that we've got our some of our best men working on your husband's case," the mayor continued.

"Thank you," Rebecca said meekly.

"Honey, we will have an officer stationed on this floor all day and all night making sure that the shooter cannot bother you," At this the mayor waved her arm in the direction of a nervous, young officer in a tan uniform guarding the door.

Rebecca nodded.

"Please let me know if we can do anything for you. Anything at all."

"Thank you," Rebecca said.

"Be assured that you and your husband are in our thoughts," the mayor said. Then she stepped back away from Rebecca and opened her purse. "Okay then, Honey, I need to get back to work. But this is my card. You call me if you need anything. Got that?"

"Yes," Rebecca said trying to take it all in. "Thank you."

With a flourish, the mayor turned and marched out of the room.

\*

"Are you scared to go back to your church?" Stephanie asked Maria at lunch.

"At first, I was," Maria said. "But then I remembered that God has a plan for everything that happens. I have seen it before. Good is going to come out of this. You wait and see."

Stephanie nodded.

Maria continued. "When my son Miguel was six, he was dying with cancer. That was bad," she said. "But because of it, I met Pastor Daniel and Rebecca and the people at our church. They prayed for him and God healed him. Because of that bad thing, I met God personally, and it changed my life."

"I know, I know," Stephanie chuckled. "You have told me a hundred times."

"Well, I'll tell you a hundred and one if I need to!" Maria said, laughing.

\*

"Mrs. Browning, I am Dr. Mitchell. I believe Dr. Kim mentioned me last night."

"Hello, Doctor," Rebecca said. She had only been back to the room for only ten minutes when she had dozed off. Now she was trying very hard to wake up and pay attention. Staring intently at her was a short, round, pink-faced man with a well-groomed, white beard.

"Your husband sustained tremendous shock last night," the doctor reviewed the situation. "He lost a great deal of blood. He also might have lost some oxygen to his brain." He frowned. "The good news, of course, is that he is still with us. But, as a result of all he has been through, he is in a coma."

Rebecca nodded. For the second time in the last half-an-hour she felt like a little girl. But this time it was as a very scared little girl.

"Although, it happens on television rather frequently, being a coma like this is rather rare." The doctor continued. "Right now, his vitals are pretty good, which is a very good sign," he said. Then he smiled. "What questions do you have?"

"How long will he be like this?" Rebecca asked meekly. Fear was pushing to control her mind.

"We don't know. Maybe a few more hours, maybe a few days, maybe a few weeks. There is no way to know. "

"I see," Rebecca said. "What will he be like when he comes out of the coma?"

"I am sorry," the doctor frowned. "But we don't know."

*

"Mrs. Browning?"

"Huh?" Rebecca was sitting in the chair next to Daniel's bed trying to concentrate on her Bible. She was startled by the two men in suits who had just entered Daniel's hospital room.

"I am Detective McCauley and this is Detective Marino," the shorter one began. "We did not get to speak with you last night because you came over with your husband to the hospital. We have been assigned to your husband's case. Could we ask you a few questions?"

"Okay," Rebecca said. Roberta had gone to get them something to eat from the cafeteria.

"What can you tell us about the events of last night?"

"I was not in the auditorium because I was back with the four-and five-year-old children's class. About fifteen or twenty minutes till seven, I heard gun shots. Rufus came running in and told us that Daniel had been shot. I ran into the auditorium and saw Daniel covered in blood." She paused, looked down, and took a deep breath before continuing.

"You are doing fine ma'am," Detective McCauley said.

"The next thing I knew the ambulance was there and they were loading him up to come here."

"So, you did not see anyone or anything suspicious?"

"No."

"Did your husband have any enemies that you know of?"

"No," Rebecca said shaking her head. She frowned in concentration. "Nothing recently that I know of. When we first came to start the church, he had made certain people upset. They made some threats."

"What people?"

"Some drugs dealers and a couple of pimps," Rebecca said. "God delivered several addicts from drugs and their dealers did not like it. The pimps were angry because we got some of their girls into a safe house."

"When was this?"

"Oh, probably over six years ago. Zach was just a baby."

"Zach?"

"He's one of our sons."

"I see," McCauley said. "So, what caused them to cease being angry at him?"

"We held our annual beginning of the year week of prayer. At the same time, a story about my husband and our ministry came out in the Las Vegas Magazine. As a result, he ended up meeting with the mayor and some men who "ran things" in our neighborhood."

"Who were these men?" Marino said.

"Daniel didn't say. But, the mayor promised to give him protection and 'the men who ran things' -- whoever they were -- put the word out to leave him alone. A few of them didn't want to get God mad at them, I guess. Daniel didn't tell me much about it."

"I see," McCauley said.

"I remember that article," Marino said with a look of realization on his face. "So, your husband is the guy who was feeding the homeless, and praying with the addicts, and seeing them get off drugs?"

"That's him," Rebecca said proudly. "So, who shot him?"

"Right now, we don't know. It's our job to find the answer to that question," Marino said.

"Thanks, Ma'am. If you can think of anything give us a call," McCauley said, handing her his card.

As the detectives walked down the hall, Marino's phone rang.

"Ok, Dominguez, slow down," Marino said answering. "You say we got a lead on the case," he looked over at McCauley. "Uh, huh." Marino nodded his head. "Uh huh... Thanks."

"What is it?" McCauley asked.

"It's a lady who was at Von's grocery store on Twain and Maryland last night. She saw a man who matches the description of our suspect. He was coming out from behind the dumpster."

*

*Oh no,* Daniel thought. *It's returning.*

The evil black cloud was back. It seemed as if it were hovering outside the hospital. It was cold and dark and sinister.

Slowly it began to draw closer.

*No. No. Go away.*

It seemed to grow larger and more menacing as it got closer.

*Stop. Don't do that.*

*Stop!*

# CHAPTER 19

## 12:54 PM

"Look at this, Rebecca," Roberta said looking up from her phone. She was looking at an article that has just been posted on the online version of the *Las Vegas Review-Journal*. "News travels fast."

Rebecca took Roberta's phone and looked at the article.

### *Las Vegas Pastor Takes a Bullet for Jesus.*

*Las Vegas, NV December 21, 2018 (AP)*

> *Last night during the Sunday evening worship service of the Flamingo Campus of the Grace City Church, Lead Pastor Daniel Browning (Age 37) was shot three times by an unidentified gunman as Browning preached the sermon. No one else was targeted or hurt. After shooting the pastor, the gunman escaped through a side door of the sanctuary.*

> *Police and prosecutors have no suspects in the shooting.*

> *The lead prosecutor, Tom Fanner, told the Associated Press early Monday that "the shooter clearly wanted to kill the pastor. We do not yet know the shooter's motives. The possibility of a terrorist attack has not been ruled out, although it is unlikely as only the pastor was targeted."*

> *Detective kept the congregants for two hours after the shooting for interviews. While waiting, the church members held an impromptu prayer vigil.*

*After a lengthy surgery to remove the bullets, the pastor remains in a coma.*

*This morning his wife, Rebecca Browning, told the press "If my husband should die as a result of this shooting, he will be happy. Because he often said, we must love Jesus enough to take a bullet for him."*

*She also said, "We do pray for the man who did this, that the Lord would forgive him and touch his heart before he hurts anyone else. We also ask that all of you please pray for my husband."*

*Those with information about the shooting are asked to notify the authorities with any information.*

Rebecca was stunned to see that the lead article was about her husband. Embedded in it was a picture of Daniel that was obviously taken from the church website. What really shocked her was the picture of her taken when she spoke with the reporters in the waiting room.

"Wow," Rebecca sighed, handing the phone back to Roberta. Then Rebecca took her own phone and Googled "Daniel Browning." She immediately saw a large number of articles about the shooting.

Some called Daniel a hero. Some, a victim.

Some called her a hero. Some called her a victim.

"Well, at least you got to talk about God and they printed it," Roberta said, "Praise the Lord!"

\*

*Still alive? Still alive? How can that preacher still be alive?* Ezekiel thought. *I shot him square in the chest several times. There is no way he is still breathing after that.*

Then the voices began. *"Loser!"*

*"Failure!"*

*"How could you mess this up?!"*

The voices kept taunting him.

*I've got to do something.*

\*

McCauley looked at the petite, elderly woman sitting in the chair next to the desk. She was all dressed up like she was going to church. In her lap, she had a small purse with white gloves lying on top under her folded nervous hands. Her hair was pulled back and she even wore pearls around her neck. "Are you Mrs. Muriel Slater?" McCauley asked looking at the notes in front of him.

"Yes sir," she said anxiously.

"Thank you, ma'am, for coming down here today. This won't take long. We just need to ask you a few questions."

"Yes sir," she nodded.

"So, what did you see?" McCauley asked

"Last night, I was coming home from visiting my sister and stopped at the grocery to get food for my Mr. Peepers."

"Is Mr. Peepers your husband?

"No, he is my cat."

McCauley shook his head and said, "Anyway, where does your sister live?"

"Over by Nellis Air Force base."

"I see. About what time was that?"

"Around 7:15 PM."

"And exactly what did you see?"

"I had not gotten out of my car yet, because I had to reach down for my purse. When I looked up I saw a man walking from the parking lot to the park. He had a dark ball cap pulled down low over his face. He had a sweat shirt with a hood pulled up and he wore a large Army overcoat. I thought the coat was a bit excessive because it was not that cold out. But you know some of those homeless people wear all the clothes they own all the time. Bless their hearts."

"So, you saw the man go into the park?" McCauley asked.

"Yes sir. But before he did, he looked around. Then he threw something into the dumpster. It looked like a brown paper bag. But it must have been heavy because it made a thump."

*

"Don't cry, honey," kindergarten teacher Karen Culver said to five-year-old Titus Browning as she put her arm around him. "I know that you are scared about your father. We all are. But God is big and strong and he is taking care of your daddy right now. Okay?"

Titus nodded his head slowly, but his upper lip still quivered. He had not been able to leave his class room and go see, but he had heard the people say that his daddy had been shot. People who got shot on the TV died. His daddy was going to die. What would he do without a daddy?

All the Browning boys had a difficult day keeping their minds focused on school work. They had heard people talk about what had happened to their father.

Eight-year-old Zach had always been the tough guy. He rarely cried. He was determined not to cry today.

But he wanted to.

The older boys, Elijah and Caleb, had seen the ambulance drive off with their dad and had heard the frightened chatter of the people who were in the auditorium when the shooting occurred.

Eleven-year-old Caleb was determined to not think about it. He knew that if he did, he would cry. His grandpa always said, "No news is good news." Other than the news that his dad was still alive, they had no news. *So that was good news, right?*

Fourteen-year-old Elijah would normally have been in the worship service on Sunday night. But someone who was scheduled had not shown up to work with the kids and so he ended up in the back helping the teacher in the third and fourth grade class

Elijah was scared. His dad had been shot. Sure, living in Las Vegas, he had seen an ambulance almost every single day of his life. But this time his dad had been in one, fighting for his life.

His mom had been at the hospital all night. They had had to stay overnight with the Garcias.

His mind was flooded with questions. *What if Dad died? How would they pay the bills? Who would pastor their church? What would they do?*

He could not wait to get out of school and hopefully get to go to the hospital to see his dad for himself.

## CHAPTER 20
## 1:47 PM

Ezekiel had been planning this assassination for several weeks. He had everything in place except finding the right time. Then it happened. His wife got the call that her mother had gone in the hospital. Fortunately for him, the call had come that Sunday afternoon, meaning that he could shoot the preacher in church and his wife would not be there.

*Perfect.* He leaned back in his chair behind his desk and smiled.

For several weeks, he had been convinced that if he could only shoot the preacher in his own pulpit, in his own church, during a worship service, *then* the voices would be silent. It was the only way. Nothing else will work.

This was the only way he could put to rest the anger that surged inside him every time someone mentioned God. That was the only way he could pay God back for killing his father.

His mind kept rehearsing the facts.

*My dad was 36 years old when God killed him. The same age that I am now. About the same age as that preacher.*

He had told himself the story every night in the middle of the night as he tossed and turned and could not sleep.

*My father, Pastor Luis Cruz of the Iglesias Pentecostales, was the best man in the whole world. My father worked tirelessly trying to help people. Everyone loved him.*

*But for no reason, God let him die with that awful, painful cancer when he was still young, and we still needed him. Even though I prayed for God to heal my dad, God let him die.*

*My father left no money in the bank. My mom had to go to work to support six kids. Then she got sick and lost her job.*

*So, I, Ezekiel Cruz, as the eldest son, had no choice. I had to bring in money somehow, so my family could eat.*

He then asked himself the same question he asked himself every single day.

*How was a thirteen-year old boy supposed to earn the hundreds of dollars of week needed to care for a family of seven?*

The answer was always the same.

*The only way was working for the gang carrying drugs.*

\*

While sitting, watching Daniel breathe, praying, reading her Bible, and responding to the many texts from family and friends, Rebecca memorized Daniel's ICU room.

Daniel's room in the ICU had a high sliding glass door and a curtain. Sitting inside on the left, Roberta manned her post and watched the door. Like Rebecca, she had been there since last night and was tired. She planned to go home and get some rest and then come back to the hospital from 6 AM to 6 PM every day until her son and his family arrived on Christmas eve.

Next to Roberta, sitting closer to Daniel's bed was Rebecca. She was not tall, but she was slender, athletically built, with beautiful, long, wavy, chestnut brown hair and eyes. She had high cheek bones and delicate features. She wore jeans and white blouse that looked good against her light brown skin.

Behind Roberta, the east wall of Daniel's room was painted ugly institutional hospital green. It had a large white front cabinet about three feet high that held a keyboard and computer screen on top for nurses and aides to check and log in information. The screen saver scrolled with announcements for the nurses. Above the cabinet was a white board with the date, and the names of the RN and Aide. A few other notes were scrawled over it with a purple marker.

Higher on that wall near the door was a basic clock with a white face, block numbers and black hands. Below it was a plastic rack holding three boxes of the thin, sterile gloves the nurses and doctors used whenever they touched Daniel. Next to it was a plastic bin holding a red box labeled with neon sign marked "Biohazard Waste."

The north wall was a bank of high windows that started two and a half feet off the ground and stretched to the ceiling. Each window was slightly tinted and had built in blinds which helped shield them from the burning Nevada sun. Under the windows was a window sill wide enough for a person to sit on.

The west wall is where the head of Daniel's bed was nestled underneath a shaded light that was mounted about six feet high and ran almost the length of the wall. Beneath it was a bank of outlets in to which the machines were plugged.

Rebecca had a love-hate affair with the mobile machines that were keeping her husband alive. The rack on Daniel's left contained flashing dispensers that monitored various IV drips, fluids, pain killers, blood, antibiotics, and several others. The various IV bags and bottles hung about six to seven feet off the ground and dripped into the dispensers a few feet below them.

The rack on Daniel's right held a high monitor with "the numbers" -- heart rate, blood pressure, temperature, respiratory usage, and bladder pressure, among others. Each was its own color - royal blue, dark red, golden yellow, and bright green. Rebecca felt as though her whole life was now focused on staring at those numbers. If they went too high or too low, her husband could be in real trouble. Every fluctuation was important.

To the far right of the south wall was a sink with a toilet underneath. Hanging from the ceiling was a curtain to be pulled when Daniel could get up and use the rest room.

*When Daniel could get up...* she thought.

*If he could get up...*

*When...if.... Would he ever get out of that bed?*

## CHAPTER 21
## 2:30 PM

Mr. Newkirk, the principal of Coronado Christian School, had let the Browning boys leave school early so Doris could take them to see their father. Doris had brought the three oldest Browning boys to the hospital with her to see their dad. Little Titus had stayed home with Doris's husband Mark. Titus was having a difficult enough time as it was. No one thought he was ready to see his dad like this.

"You boys can only go in one at a time," Roberta told them as they arrived at the lobby waiting area of the ICU.

"You will spent about five minutes each with your dad and then come out and let one of your brothers go in. Remember, even though your dad is not moving, he feels your prayers and will get stronger having you there."

"Let me warn you," Roberta said looking at the boys, "He has been through a lot, between the shooting and the operation. Plus, he lost a lot of blood. So, he looks weak, and he is. When you walk in, no matter how you feel when you see him, smile bravely. Be strong for your mom. It might be easier for her if you don't cry."

They nodded solemnly.

"You can cry later when you come out if you need to," she continued.

Elijah and Zach both looked at eleven-year-old Caleb. He was the sensitive one. Caleb dropped his head. He had refused to think about his dad all day out of fear that he would cry. Now, he would have to go in to face the awful truth.

"Come with me" Roberta said, taking dark-haired Elijah with her. *He looks so much like his father,* she thought.

Inside the ICU, sitting on a folding chair just outside of room 414 was a young police officer. His name tag said "Officer Borland." He stood up briskly as they approached the room.

"It's ok, Jim," she said looking at the policeman. "This is Elijah Browning, the pastor's son. The pastor has three boys here and I'll be taking them in one at a time to see their dad."

Borland nodded stiffly and sat down.

"Go ahead, Elijah," Roberta said, pulling open the door so he could enter.

Elijah walked deliberately. He held his head high, went straight to his mom, and gave her a big hug.

"We will get through this," he said. "God is with us." Rebecca held him tight. He was no longer her little boy. He was a young man. *Daniel would be so proud,* she thought.

Next to visit was Caleb.

He tried to be strong, but it always tore him up to see anyone hurting. Seeing his dad lying like a corpse on the bed and his mom with dark circles under her eyes, and her face blotchy from tears, was too much. He did not stay long. Tears began to form in his eyes. He turned his head away and hurried out of the room.

Curly-headed Zach was a tough eight-year-old. He rarely cried or showed emotion. Like his dad, he was fearless, often to a fault. When his turn came, he walked in, looked around and sat down next to his dad. "What's that thing in his nose?" he asked Rebecca.

"That helps him breathe," she said.

He nodded his approval. "What about them?" he asked pointing to the IV's in his arms.

"One of them is putting fluids and antibiotics into his veins. That one is giving him blood. The other one is giving him pain killers."

Again, Zach nodded his approval. Then he looked straight at his mom. "He doesn't look so bad," he said. "Can't wait till he gets out of here."

\*

After talking to Muriel Slater, McCauley and Marino drove over to Molaskey Park. They parked in front of the dumpster in the Von's parking lot. The taller Marino lifted the lid of the dumpster and looked in. Fortunately, it had been emptied recently and had only a small amount of garbage in it. It was not hard to see the brown paper bag in the corner. The tall Martino leaned over the edge and part way into the dumpster. He pulled on a latex glove, reached his long arm down to the bag, and gently picked it up.

It was heavy.

He pulled it out of the dumpster and slowly opened it.

"Bingo," he said, holding up a .22 caliber pistol. "We have a murder weapon."

\*

Except to call her mom, Rebecca had not even looked at her phone in hours. When she picked it up, she was stunned to find that it was exploding with texts and her Facebook page was erupting with notifications. Sometime early this morning, Rebecca had allowed Roberta to make a post on Rebecca's Facebook page. Roberta posted a picture of a battered Daniel lying in the recovery room after his surgery along with this message.

"PLEASE PRAY! My husband, Pastor Daniel Browning, was shot in the chest three times while preaching in church tonight. The doctor said it is a miracle that he made it to the hospital. He is in emergency surgery now. PLEASE PRAY FOR A MIRACLE!!"

In less than eight hours, the simple post already had over 1,500 responses, and had been shared over 500 times. Reading the responses made Rebecca cry. They were from people she had known as a child in Brazil, people she had not heard of since high school, college friends, former college students she and Daniel mentored, members of their supporting churches, people from all over the world who were friends of her missionary friends, and people they knew in Las Vegas. With the shares, messages were flooding in from people she did not even know.

*Praying for a miracle!*
*Asking God for complete healing.*
*Believing God is Big Enough!!*
*Praying for you in Brazil*
*Fighting with you on our knees.*
*Storming heaven on your behalf in South Korea.*
*Praying right now.*
*Sharing this with our prayer chain.*

But one especially touched her heart. It was from a girl she had known in high school. After Rebecca came back to the Lord, she had witnessed to this girl repeatedly with seemingly no progress. After graduation, they had lost track of each other. But apparently, God had worked in the girl's heart. The girl posted six simple yet, powerful words:

*"With God all things are possible!"*

Those were the same words that the doctor had said. With all her heart, Rebecca was wanting to believe them, but it was so hard. Just two feet in front of her, filled with tubes, covered with monitors, attached to machines, Daniel fought for every breath. The other words the doctor had said had pierced her deeply:

"Three bullets in the chest. One still lodged by his heart. Fighting for his life."

"Oh God, I believe. Help my unbelief," she quietly prayed. "Help my unbelief!"

# CHAPTER 22
## 3:48 PM

On the northwest side of the park, were a group of homeless people camped out under the trees. Quick observation told the detectives that none of these people matched the description of the shooter.

"I am Detective McCauley, and this is Detective Marino," McCauley said to the little group gathered around a picnic table. "Have you heard about the preacher that was shot?"

"Pastor Daniel," a tired looking woman wrapped in a blanket said. "It's so sad."

"I sure hope you guys catch the scumbag who did it," said a man with bright, red hair sticking straight up. He sniffed as he puffed on a cigarette.

"Yeah. Can you imagine shooting a pastor, especially a pastor like Daniel?" the first lady said shaking her head.

"So, you know the pastor?" Marino asked.

"Yes, people from his church come by on Tuesday nights here in the park," the tired woman said. "They fix us hamburgers on that grill, and sing some songs, and have a little Bible talk."

"Real nice," said a very short, black man in a neon, green sweat suit.

"He also has that place over on Flamingo where they give out food and clothes," a thin woman added. "Real nice people."

"Any more homeless in this park?" McCauley asked.

"Yeah," the thin woman said. Her teeth were worn and dark. "Tom stays over there," she said pointing to a few trees nestled by the far corner of the park.

"How come he's over there and not with you guys?" Marino asked. "Safety in numbers you know."

"He's crazy, that's why," the redheaded man said.

"And mean," the thin woman added. "He does not like anybody or anything, except whiskey."

"Thomas Morgan Hawthorne II," the redheaded man said in a mocking tone. "Thinks he's someone special."

"He's certainly not very sociable," the tired lady said, grinning a mostly toothless grin.

"He's a grumpy SOB," the redhaired man added.

"Likes to be left to himself," the thin lady added. "He does not like anyone or anything."

"Except whiskey," the lady with the bad teeth added.

"He does love his whiskey," the red-head agreed.

*

Rebecca's phone rang. "Josh Jenson" was the name that flashed on the screen.

"Hey, Josh," she said, comforted to hear from an old friend.

"Hello, Rebecca."

Josh was Abigail's husband, an up-and-coming author and travelling preacher, and one of Daniel's best friends from college. Something about hearing his voice, an old friend from the past, gave Rebecca hope. "Thank you," she said meekly.

"I believe the Lord is not finished with him yet," Josh said confidently. "Rebecca, let me encourage you to look at this through the lens of faith, not fear. God kept him alive this long. Let's believe that God will bring him all the way through to total healing."

"Thanks, Josh," Rebecca said meekly.

"Remember: With God all things are possible."

*There it was again,* Rebecca thought. *With God all things are possible.*

"Please let us know if you need anything," he continued. "I spoke at a large pastors' conference this morning and led them in a time of prayer for Daniel. They also took a love offering. Will $3,268 dollars help?"

"Josh," she paused. "I don't even know what to say." As self-funded missionaries with lousy health insurance $3,268 would certainly help. "Thank you. Thank you."

"Rebecca, you know that you and Daniel would do the same for us. I am so glad that it encourages you," he said.

"It does," she said. "Trust me, it does."

"I also mobilized my Blog followers to pray," he continued. "I wish we could do more."

"You have done plenty."

"We love you guys." Then he said. "Abigail has all the kids praying for Daniel."

"Tell her thanks."

"I will. I am sorry, but I have to go and get on an airplane. Hang in there and let us know if there is anything we can do."

"Thanks Josh."

*

"Interesting bunch," Marino said as he and McCauley walked across the park away from the little homeless group. Sure enough, sleeping under a tree on the south side of the park was a man wearing a large, dark, Army coat, a dark hoodie, and a dirty ball cap.

"Wake up, buddy. We need to ask you some questions," Martino said shaking the man.

"I ain't got no money," the man slurred as he sat up and raised his hands in surrender.

"We aren't here to rob you," Marino said showing the man his badge. "We are just here to ask a few questions. Tell us your name, pal."

"Tom," the man said.

"I need your full name," Marino said.

"Thomas Morgan Hawthorne II," the man blinked his eyes awake and threw back his shoulders proudly.

McCauley punched the name into his IPad. "Sounds like a big society name. How'd you end up here?"

"Long story," the man said dropping his shoulders. "My mom died when I was two. My dad remarried the enemy. That she-devil stepmother threw me out when Dad died," Hawthorne explained.

"How old were you when she threw you out?"

"I had just turned 16. Somehow, she cut me out of everything. I bounced around awhile and ended up here."

"How long have you been in this park?"

"This park? Oh, off and on for about four or five years I guess. They run us out once a year, but in a few months, we come back," he smiled, and Marino noticed that several teeth were missing.

"So, where were you last night, Mr. Hawthorne?" Martino asked.

"Right here in this park, where I always am."

The man reeked of alcohol, body odor and urine. It was obvious that he was very hung-over. He also seemed to have some mental challenges.

"Are you sure you did not go to Grace City for church last night?" Martino asked.

"Grace City?" The man frowned. "I am done with that place."

"What do you mean 'done?'"

"Those people say they love you and stuff, but one little mistake…"

"What do you mean 'one little mistake?'"

"One little mistake and they throw you away."

"So, you know the church?" The detective asked.

"Know it? I used to work at that outreach center. I helped Pastor Daniel renovate that building. I was on staff there."

"You were 'on staff'? Why are you no longer on 'staff'?"

"One little mistake…" he said looking sad.

"So, what was your mistake?"

"I was not going to hurt her," the man said with a faraway look.

"Hurt who?" Marino asked

"That little blond girl."

"You hurt a little girl?" Marino asked.

"No! I did *not* hurt her!" Hawthorne yelled. "They said I did, but I didn't. I shouldn't have followed her into the bathroom, but I was not going to hurt her."

"Your record says you were arrested for molesting three children twelve years ago," McCauley said looking at his iPad.

"This conversation is over," Tom said standing up. "I'm done talking." Then he turned a little green and bent down.

"Hey, those shoes were new!" Marino yelled as Thomas Morgan Hawthorne II sprayed them with vomit.

Hawthorne wiped his mouth with the back of his sleeve.

"Feel better?" McCauley asked sarcastically.

Hawthorne squinted and nodded. Then he frowned. "But, I got a big headache."

"Let's go down to the station and get you some coffee," Marino said as he grabbed Hawthorne's arm.

"Hey," Hawthorne protested.

"Look, pal, we need to ask you some more questions. You are under arrest for suspicion for the shooting of Daniel Browning," McCauley said, pulling Hawthorne wrists behind him and putting him in handcuffs. "Let's go."

# CHAPTER 23
## 4:42PM

"Can I *PLEASE* have some coffee? And some aspirin? My head is pounding," Hawthorne whimpered meekly. They were in the Metro Police Station on Spencer Ave. Thomas Hawthorne sat at a table in the small, gray, interrogation room facing Detective Marino. Hawthorne looked like a tall, thin skeleton compared to Marino. The ex-UNLV linebacker was 6'3" inches tall and weighed a trim 235 pounds.

"And some toast, I could really use some toast," Hawthorne whined.

"Ok, I'll get you some coffee in just a minute. But answer a few questions first," McCauley said impatiently. He was standing near the door.

Marino leaned forward and glared into Hawthorne's face. "Where were you last night?"

"I told you. In the park," Hawthorne said. "I did *not* go to the church and I did *not* shoot the pastor. I never left the park. I was there yesterday afternoon and evening with two of my old friends, Jim and Jack.

Hawthorne took a breath and relaxed a little. "Let me tell you, I was very pleasantly surprised by their visit. Yesterday was a day of wonderful surprises."

Marino looked at McCauley and shrugged as Hawthorne continued, "I had not seen either of them for a while, but to see both on the same day! It's a miracle." Then he got a quizzical look in his face, "Hey, wait, it this Christmas? Maybe the presents were a Christmas miracle!"

"Yesterday was not Christmas," Marino said. "Christmas is this coming weekend."

Hawthorne frowned.

"Tell me more about Jim and Jack," Marino said.

"Oh," Hawthorne brightened. "I found them hiding by my bed roll when I came back from using the Porta-John in the park.

"Jim and Jack? Do you know their last names?"

"Of course, I do." He looked offended.

"So, what are their last names?" Marino asked impatiently

"Jim Beam and Jack Daniels," Hawthorne said smugly.

"Okay, now we're getting somewhere," Marino smiled.

"He's talking about bourbon," McCauley said dryly.

"Of course, I'm talking about bourbon," Hawthorne said with a huge grin. "Jim Beam's straight Kentucky Bourbon whiskey! And Jack Daniel's sour mash Tennessee whiskey. Two of the very best friends a man can have."

"So, you came back from the Porta-John and the whiskey was by your bed roll?" Marino said.

"That is correct."

Marino looked at his notes and continued. "You said 'a day of surprises.' Were there any other surprises?"

"This coat and sweat shirt," said Hawthorne proudly showing his clothes.

"What about them?"

"After visiting with Jim and Jack a while, I fell asleep. When I woke up, and it was dark, and I was cold," Hawthorne said. "Some punk stole my winter coat last week. Well, lying next to me when I woke up was this coat, and sweat shirt, and a hat."

"So, you are telling me that somebody left you two bottles of whiskey, a coat, a sweat shirt, and a hat?"

Hawthorne smiled and nodded. Then he continued. "Not just *somebody,* but probably an angel. Or maybe the rich lady who sometimes comes by the park and has her driver hand out sandwiches." But, he paused, "You don't think she'd give me whiskey, do you? Are you sure that this is not Christmas?"

Then Hawthorne belched, dropped his head on the desk, and went to sleep. A minute later, he was snoring.

# CHAPTER 24
## 5:54 PM

*"Pastor Daniel needs us now. Our prayer group will be gathering with others in the lobby of the ICU at Paradise Hospital at 7 PM for prayer,"* Roberta typed into the text on her phone. Then she pushed "Send."

\*

"Oh," Maria said after looking at her phone. Maria was seated at the kitchen table with her husband and four sons. She turned toward her husband. "I am sorry, honey, but I need to go to the hospital tonight. Ezekiel, can you *please* watch the kids?" she asked sweetly.

"I thought your mother was better?" he asked, frowning.

"She is and they let her go home with my sister, Gabriella, today. But the church is having a special prayer meeting for Pastor. He is still in the ICU," Maria said, as she got up and put her dishes in the dishwasher. "I'll try to be back in time to tuck the younger boys into bed."

"Hrmph," Ezekiel groaned. He was not happy. The problem was that the pastor was still alive. "I'll watch them," he muttered as he got up and went to another room. He had to think of another way to kill that preacher.

\*

As she drove to the hospital, Maria's mind went back to when she first got to know Ezekiel. She was a mature ten-year-old and he was a shy twelve-and-a-half-year-old.

"You should come to church with me," her older sister had said. "The pastor's son is so cute."

And she was right. Ezekiel was cute, and shy, but witty. He had a killer smile and he was strong. His brown eyes had that beautiful, golden cast. He was the dutiful older brother in his family. Maria started going to youth group every week, just to be close to him.

Maria's parents were never very committed to church. Her father worked most Sundays and her mom rarely came because she felt guilty for not going to the Catholic Church. It was mostly Maria's older sisters who took her to church.

But then Ezekiel's dad died and several families left the church. The youth group lost momentum, and Ezekiel changed. He got angry and moody. Maria found a boyfriend who did not go to church and she stopped going.

After she left the church, she did not see much of Ezekiel until they met up again at a party when she was in high school. They began to see each other often. At the start of her senior year she decided to drop out of school and move in with Ezekiel. For a short time, they thrived on the adrenaline of living "the gangster life" together.

After a few years, she became pregnant with Miguel and slowed down. Two years later, baby Pablo came along. Then to the surprise of many, Ezekiel asked Maria her to marry him and he slowed down his lifestyle even more. He had worked his way to a position that allowed him to be home more often. Unlike most of his peers, Ezekiel was a surprisingly devoted husband and father.

They were happy in their own way until he went to prison. He said he had been set up for the crime and took the fall for a drug deal that went wrong and a man who got shot. She believed him.

Maria knew she needed to do something to provide for the family, so she got her GED. Then she got a job in the office at the local elementary school. She also stayed faithful to Ezekiel.

Then Miguel got so terribly sick. The doctor said it was cancer and that he was going to die. Her friend introduced her to Pastor Daniel and Rebecca. Maria started attending Grace City Church. At the end of the worship service one Sunday night, Pastor Daniel said he felt led to have the entire church gather around Miguel and pray for healing.

She remembered that night clearly.

Pastor Daniel said, "With God all things are possible. God does not always heal in our timing, but I feel as though God wants to heal this boy at this time."

When they prayed, Maria cried deep tears of repentance and joy. Then she felt as though electricity went through her body. Miguel told her later that he felt a wonderful heat flowing through his body while they prayed.

The next day, when she took Miguel in for his doctor's visit, his tests came back clean. The doctor ran more tests and was shocked.

The cancer was gone.

But Ezekiel was in prison, he did not see how sick Miguel was. He did not see God heal him. When he got out, he was glad that Miguel was healthy, but he still wanted nothing to do with God. When God was mentioned, he got angry and left the room. In his mind, she was disrespecting him by giving her heart to Jesus and her church.

"Oh, dear Father, please speak to my Ezekiel," she prayed. "Please, melt his hard heart and bring him back to you. I am asking that you would increase your activity in his life. All I want for Christmas is for my Ezekiel to find you again."

# CHAPTER 25
## 7:07 PM

Matthew looked at his watch. 7:07 PM. He hated being late. As he and his wife Chelsey got on the elevator, he pushed the button for the third floor. They were running a little late because they had difficulty finding someone to watch their kids on such short notice. They hoped at least a few people would be there to pray for Pastor Daniel.

As the elevator came to a stop on the fourth floor, they heard the clatter of voices. The door opened and they saw familiar faces. The lobby was filled with over fifty Grace City members. In one corner, a blond, young man was quietly playing the guitar and gently singing a worship song. Pastor Carlos stood next to him directing the prayers as they prayed through various Scriptural promises. The people were calling out to God in a beautiful concert of intercession.

*One thing Pastor Daniel has taught us is to pray*, Matthew thought.

He smiled as he thought back to the first prayer meeting he had attended with Pastor Daniel back in Ohio. Daniel was the Campus Pastor of Mission University. Matthew and Chelsey were seniors. One of her friends had told them of Pastor Daniel's vision to start a church in Las Vegas and about the afternoon prayer meetings that were being held at the White Chapel in the heart of campus.

Out of curiosity, they went to the prayer meeting. Inside, Pastor Daniel, Rebecca, and at least a dozen students were gathered in a circle praying through a chapter of the Bible verse-by-verse in a very orderly, yet intense season of prayer, like he had experienced in Kenya when he went there on a mission trip.

Matthew looked at Chelsey and shrugged. She sat down and motioned with her head for him to sit next to her. Within a few minutes, they were in the rhythm of corporate prayer as they prayed through key verses in Luke chapter 14.

Then Daniel led them to pray for laborers for the harvest in Las Vegas and through the church he was going to start – Grace City.

Afterwards in the car ride back to their apartment, Matthew asked her what she thought of the prayer meeting. Chelsey said that she "loved it!"

They went back the next day and within two weeks were committed to going with the team that was selling everything and moving to Las Vegas in May to plant the new church. They planned to be in Las Vegas for one year. That was over seven years ago.

And now we are praying that Pastor Daniel will make it through the night.

*

Freda Johson shooed Rebecca out of Daniel's room to briefly go down and join the prayer meeting taking place in the lobby waiting room of the ICU. As she neared the lobby, Rebecca was delighted by the sound of worship music and voices in song. She drank it in as refreshing water that soothed her parched soul.

When she walked into the room, people came up one by one and hugged her. Several paused and asked God to give her strength.

*I am so glad that I don't have to go through this alone*, she thought. *Thank you, Lord!*

After a song, Pastor Carlos' deep voice boomed out, "While Rebecca can be with us for a few minutes, let's gather around her, ladies, and ask the Lord to give her and her children supernatural grace and strength."

Quickly, Rebecca was surrounded by ladies who extended their hands to gently rest on her hands, arms, shoulders, back, and head. Sweetly their voices cried out on her behalf. The tenderness of it touched her and she began to cry.

*Such love, such sweet, family affection poured out in sincere prayer,* she thought.

*Thank you, Lord!*

Their voices reached a crescendo and then gently died down until the only sound was the guitar.

Then Pastor Carlos' deep voice boomed out again, "Please get with a partner and go back and forth taking turns praying that God would spare Pastor Daniel and heal him completely. Let's pray!"

Someone handed her a handkerchief and Rebecca wiped her cheeks. Quietly she turned and headed back to the ICU. The weariness had lifted. She felt as if she were floating, carried along by their prayers.

*

Daniel saw that the evil, darkness had stopped. There seemed to be a barrier of light holding it back. The light seemed animated as though it had a life of its own.

For that matter, the darkness pulsed as though it were a living thing as well. It throbbed as if it was angry, very angry.

# CHAPTER 26
## 9:35 PM

"Help! Help!"

Rebecca awoke with a startle. She had been sleeping in the chair beside Daniel's bed.

"Help! Help!"

A man was yelling, sounding as if he was being killed. But she had learned that it was just Charlie in the room next door. He was heavily sedated and every time he awoke, he yelled for help even though he was just fine.

Other sounds punctuated the air throughout the ICU, even though the floor was to be quiet after 9 PM. Various machines beeped, other machines whirred, people were talking at the nurses' station, automatic doors opened and closed. The noise was relentless.

Sitting there, Rebecca was hit with a monstrous wave of fatigue, frustration, and fear. Just a few feet away from her lay her husband fighting for every breath.

She knew that he even though he had come a long away, the odds were overwhelming that he still probably would never come out of this hospital alive. Even if he did, would he be able to work? To play with the boys? To preach? To hold her in his arms?

*Stop thinking like that*, she told herself. *Right now we are walking by faith, not fear. Faith, not fear.*

It was easier said than done.

# CHAPTER 27
## 11:57PM

Just before midnight, the thirteen witches of the Coven of the Sisters of the Bloody Heart had convened a special session in the backroom of the Seeing Eye Metaphysical Bookstore on the corner of Tropicana and Eastern Avenue. Of the many new age bookstores in Las Vegas, the Seeing Eye was the largest and most active. It had a big coffee shop, a healing arts and herb store, and thousands of books, CDs, DVDs, videos, healing crystals, candles, jewelry, and gifts. They held various types of workshops, lectures, concerts, films, psychic readings, community forums, meditation, and yoga every night of the week and on weekends.

The coven room was dark except for candles. The floor was carefully marked in blood with a pentagram within a circle. The coven's thirteen witches were united in their belief in the art of practicing energy manipulation. They were positioned in the nine-foot circle with over a dozen initiates standing behind them around the edge of the room.

Rose Deadwood, the high priestess of the Sisters of the Bloody Heart, stood up with a flourish. She was a successful business owner running the bookstore by day and was one of the top high priestesses in the Southwest United States by night.

Rose loved a full house and playing to the audience. She had at one time been a singer on the old Las Vegas strip in Fremont at the Golden Nugget Casino.

Rose created quite an intimidating picture and she loved it that way. She was very tall, nearly six feet. She had flawless, nearly white skin with only a few winkles around her eyes. She wore ruby red lipstick. Her long, black hair had a few, blue silver streaks. She had teeth that reminded people of vampire fangs. Her long legs were still shapely and athletic. Her pointed, black boots were visible under her long, silky black cape.

Around her, also in black capes, were the Sisters of the Bloody Heart. Mostly women in their late fifties and early sixties, these women loved the comradery and power they felt being part of this coven. There was excitement in the air for this special session of the coven.

Miss Rose stood and eloquently lifted her hands. In her dark, dramatic voice she began, "The hated pastor was shot in the heart in his own church by one of our friends on Sunday night!"

The assembled ladies murmured their obvious approval.

"The human deceiver should have died."

"Yesssss," several of the ladies hissed their approval.

"But the Hated One has somehow been able to keep him alive," Rose continued.

"Ssss," the ladies hissed their displeasure.

"Many of you have been cursing this man and his church since he arrived. Yet, in spite of constant obstacles, he has somehow survived."

"Tonight, we come together to say a united 'no' to any further survival. The Pastor goes down and so does his church. Our combined strength will break apart the enemy's protection and cause him to finally die."

"Yessss," the black robed women hissed more loudly. "Yessss!"

At exactly midnight, Rose began a series of short ceremonies. She started with the Lighting of the Sacred Candle. "I light this candle in the name of the ancient presence, which is, was, and ever shall be, male, female, all-knowing, all-powerful, and present everywhere…"

Then she knelt before the altar and placed the sacred Water Bowl upon the Pentacle. "I exorcise thee, O Creature of Water…"

Rose then replaced the water with the sacred Salt Dish. She touched the salt with the sacred blade of the Athame. "Blessings upon thee, O Creature of Salt…"

She put the salt on the blade and dipped it into the water saying, "As the salt and water purify the body, the scourge purifies the soul…"

Next, Rose drew a circle with the sword, "I conjure thee, O Circle of Power… a rampart that shall preserve and contain the power that we raise within thee…."

## TUESDAY, DECEMBER 22

## CHAPTER 28
## 12:15 AM

With the preliminaries finished, Rose was ready to get down to business. "All stand and salute the East," she commanded. The ladies of the Bloody Heart immediately stood as one and faced east. With the black-handled Athame dagger Rose made three circles, then traced the pentagram saying, "Ye Lords of the Watchtowers of the East, I summon, stir and call thee up…."

She repeated the same ritual to the south, west, and north. She then called upon her gods, "Oh, Powerful god and Gentle goddess, We invite you to our meeting. We gather before you to curse the hated pastor and cry out for his death."

With that, the assembled coven erupted in violent cries for the death of the pastor and the destruction of his church.

When the coven session had begun, unseen by human eyes, dark spirits from out of the shadows were gathering around the witches. The dark spirits seemed to grow in size, strength, and anger as the coven meeting progressed. More and more of the vile spirits arrived as the witches addressed the gods of the four directions, east, south, west and north. Then with military precision, wave after wave of the energized demons extended their wings, lifted off, and in a black flock of raging warriors flew off to the hospital.

Rose commanded her witches, "Fix the image of the pastor in your mind. Concentrate on it." Her red lips curled cruelly around her white teeth as she barked out instructions.

"Now see that image of the pastor burning in eternal flames."

Then Rose twirled around, the cape of her black robe flowing behind her. "Burn! Burn! BURN!" she cried, her voice rising with each word. "Burn! Burn! BURN!"

"Burn! Burn! BURN!" the witches echoed.

*

Roberta had gone home to sleep. Carlos' wife, Freda, was staying with Rebecca on her second night in the hospital. Exhausted, Rebecca had gone in to the waiting room and stretched out to sleep about an hour earlier. But when the automatic doors of the ICU opened loudly, the noise jointed her awake.

*I'll just check on Daniel,* she thought as she pushed the button to the doors of the ICU. It opened, and she went down to Daniel's room and sat down next to Freda.

"How is he?" she asked.

"I'm a little concerned," Freda said pointing at the monitor of Daniel's temperature. In the lower right, in angry amber numbers Rebecca saw 102.1. When she left it had been 101.3.

*Oh, Lord, help him,* she thought. "When did it go up?" she asked.

"Midnight. Just after midnight it started rising."

"It jumped a degree in half-an-hour?"

"Yes," Freda replied. "Look!"

It now read 102.4.

"I'm going to get his nurse," Rebecca said as she jumped up and dashed out of the room.

Sherri, the night shift RN, came in and looked at Daniel's vitals, touched his skin, and looked at her computer screen. "I'm going to get some ice. We'll see if that helps."

She was back in just a few minutes with two large ice bags. By then, Daniel's temperature read 102.6.

Carefully, she covered one ice bag with a wash cloth and packed it next to his ribs on his right. Then she did the same to the other side. "We'll see if that helps."

It didn't.

Twenty minutes later, she was back. "I just lowered his room temperature," she said. "Also, the doctor on call told me to order a fan and a cooling blanket. Hopefully this will turn very soon."

The temperature on the monitor now read 103.

About half an hour later, Sherri burst into the room. She turned to Rebecca, "The cooling blanket is here."

She was followed by a large lady with a huge nose who pushed a cart that held a vented box-like machine. The machine stood about three feet tall by a foot-and-a-half wide and a foot-and-a-half deep. On top of it was a small keyboard and monitor.

There was also fan in a box on top of the cart. Carefully, Sherri unpacked the fan and hooked it up. She pointed it right at Daniel.

Daniel's temperature now read 103.4.

Then Sherri opened a thick, crisp, white blanket and put it on top of Daniel. By the time she was done, Daniel's temperature read 103.9.

Freda grabbed Rebecca's hand. "We need to pray."

# CHAPTER 29
## 1:38 AM

Martha Washburn mumbled in her sleep as she twitched with an intense dream. In her dream, she had seen four golden, mighty spirit warriors standing guard over the four corners of Daniel's bed. She also saw four other angels standing between the guardians. Each angel extended his hand and proclaimed in a beautiful, antiphonal chant proclamations from the throne of grace: *Healing, peace, rest, hope, life.*

But then the dream turned. She saw a deep, black cloud rising on the horizon speeding toward the window of Daniel's room. As the cloud neared, she saw that it was made up of an army of bats, ravens and vultures. The creatures morphed into grotesque, black demons, with shiny, snake-like skin and muted black armor with silver trim. They had swords and torches extended.

The dark host vastly outnumbered the eight angels around Daniel's bed. Bravely the guardian angels braced for the attack.

The sound of rushing wings changed to that of clashing swords as the fierce onslaught began. The eight angels were valiant warriors, but there were only eight of them and dozens of demons.

Then a sinister flame exploded around Daniel's bed. Quickly, fire swallowed up Daniel's body.

\*

"104.1," Rebecca said anxiously reading the monitor. "Daniel's temperature is now 104.1!"

"We must try to pray this fever down or… anyway… we need to pray," Freda said.

*

Daniel's disturbingly, dark, dream paralleled the dream of Martha. Initially, the ghoulish flock of vultures turned into enraged hellish demons as they violently slammed into his guardian angels in ferocious combat. Despite the best efforts of the angels, the flaming swords of the demons were occasionally slashing into Daniel. Each cut shot pain through his body. They also swung torches down at him. Every time they hit him he felt intense heat.

Then the colors of the dark, dream turned deep red and then exploded into violent amber. Suddenly heat swallowed him from every angle as flames shot up around him.

*

All of the blood drained out of Rebecca's face. *Oh no, Lord, oh no. Don't let him die.*

Daniel's blood pressure had rocketed up to 165/103. His temp did not move off 104.4.

She looked again and the red numbers on the monitor shouted a second time as Daniel's blood pressure jumped even higher – 179/ 115.

## CHAPTER 30
## 2:52 AM

Feeling as though their job was complete, the coven dismissed.

"Good job, sisters," Rose said confidently. "I think we did some very good work tonight. There is no way the deceiver pastor can survive what we put on him tonight."

The others hissed their agreement and approval. They were tired from their long, late-night ceremony of casting spells and curses on Daniel and his church. They were weary but satisfied after their night of beseeching the Gods of Darkness to bring death to the minister of the Hated One. Several of them had to hurry to their homes so they could get ready to go to work soon.

As she got into her car, Rose hummed happily and switched on her radio. She expected to hear the good news proclaiming the death of the hated pastor.

\*

Finally, Dr. Kim arrived and assessed the situation. He pursed his lips, shook his head, and signaled Rebecca and Freda into the hall.

Dr. Kim spoke intensely, "You need to understand that this situation is very, very serious. We must not wait. We must operate right away."

Rebecca nodded and asked, "But, is he ready for another operation so soon?"

Dr. Kim shook his head, "No, he's not. It's a very big risk. But we have no other options. If we don't operate right away, he will die probably very soon."

"Will the operation save him?" Rebecca asked,

"There is a chance it will.

"How good is that chance?"

Dr. Kim sighed, "Maybe twenty percent, if that. But if we do not operate, he has next to no chance and will die very soon."

Tears stung Rebecca's eyes.

Then Dr. Kim took her hand, "But remember, with God all things are possible."

Numbly, Rebecca watched Dr. Kim go back into the room. She felt a huge wave of fear crashing into her. Freda reached out to her and she melted into Freda's arms. "Freda, I am so scared," she whispered. "So very scared."

"Honey, remember: with God all things are possible," Freda said.

*

*"Daniel is in real danger. He is going into emergency surgery soon,"* Freda's mass text explained. *"His life truly is in the balance. Pray!"*

Martha looked at her phone, and like others all over the city, she intensified her prayers.

"Oh, dear God. I do not believe that you spared Pastor Daniel the other night, just to let him die today. Please guide the surgeon and others involved. Please give them unusual grace and wisdom. May your will be fully accomplished in Pastor's body right now. In Jesus' name touch him with healing power."

Matthew had also received Freda's mass text and when he saw it, he got out of bed. He stood up and walked outside on to his tiny back porch so as not to wake the kids as he pounded Heaven on behalf of his mentor.

"Dear Father, you are a good Father. Pastor Daniel is your dearly beloved son. I know that his life must please you. Please, please get him through this surgery safely."

He wiped tears off his cheeks. "Lord touch him. He has meant so much to me. He and Rebecca have meant so much to Chelsey and me, and to our family. He has blessed so many people. All over this country people have been praying. Please touch his body with great power and strong mercy. Raise him up and heal him."

"Father, your Spirit is a river of living water in those who believed in Jesus. May the river shoot up from within Pastor Daniel right now, in Jesus' name! May that river of living water also pour down upon him now in cool refreshment in Jesus' name, Amen."

*

Freda had also posted an update on her and Rebecca's Facebook about Daniel, his need for surgery and the need for a miracle. Her post was hitting the East Coast at an opportune time. It was just after 7:20 AM there. As people were waking up, getting ready for work, and starting their day, they saw the request and began to pray. One after another, responses began to flood in.

"We continue praying."

"Praying for another miracle for Daniel."

"Praying in NYC."

"Asking God to touch him right now, in the name of Jesus."

"Praying for the Lord to raise him up."

"Asking God to guide the surgeon's hands."

Freda showed Rebecca the phone as it was exploding with responses to the Facebook plea for prayer. "There is a tidal wave of prayer on behalf of your husband," she said to Rebecca. "I believe that in the name of Jesus, Daniel is going to make it."

*

As his dream continued, Daniel saw himself lying in a hospital bed. He noticed a positive shift in the battle as the eight original angels in his room were joined by some other angels. Together the reinforced angel force beat back the demon hoard.

The evil warriors were in retreat... for now.

But the hoard did not leave. In his dream, Daniel they regrouped like hungry vultures waiting for a wounded animal to die, circling the hospital menacingly.

Suddenly, a massive golden warrior arrived on the scene. He easily shook off the vulture-like demons that tried to hinder him. He inhaled a massive breath and puffed up his cheeks. Then with a long blast, he blew out a mighty breath of life over Daniel. Daniel saw and felt a gentle snow shower of silver and golden flakes blanket his body. The flames died. His body cooled. And he felt refreshed.

*

As quickly as possible, a crew headed by the anesthesiologist busied themselves loading up Daniel, his eight IVs and various pieces of attached equipment. Then they wheeled him to the Operating Room.

Usually the trauma of moving would throw the vital signs of someone in Daniel's perilous state into the danger zone. Dr. Kim was worried what he would see when they were all set up in the OR.

"Look at that!" the anesthesiologist said pointing to the monitor. Remarkably, Daniel's temperature had dropped to 101.1 degrees. His other numbers, while still not good, also were improved as he went into surgery.

"Praise the Lord," Dr. Kim said to himself. "With God all things are possible. Lord you must not be finished with this man yet."

# CHAPTER 32
## 5:08 AM

Martha was worn out from her battle in prayer. She was not as young as she used to be. Her 78th birthday was last week.

As she prepared for her prayer chain shift at 5AM, she remembered back to Daniel's first week in town seven years earlier.

Martha was the widow of Barnabas Washburn, a poor Pentecostal street preacher. She had met Daniel when her husband was preaching fire and brimstone to all "the sinners" who were "drinking, gambling, and whoring" on the Strip at Fremont. Even though Daniel's approach was much different and more effective than her husband's, she thought, he had never condemned Barnabas. Instead, Daniel was respectful and kind to them and often bought them lunch.

Barnabas died six months after they met Daniel. He left Martha with a small GI pension and a tiny, yet well cared for house near the Stratosphere Hotel and Casino at the north and older end of the Strip.

After Barnabas died, Daniel raised money to pay for the funeral and to help Martha. Reluctantly, at first, she became a part of Grace City. The music was too loud. The prayers, too quiet. The girls' skirts were too short. And they did not even use the King James Version of the Bible. But the Lord was obviously very present and very active in that church.

Martha became part of the prayer ministries when she could. Not being able to drive at night was a real limitation. She also loved working with the children on Sunday mornings and working with the homeless at the outreach center during the week.

But her new delight was mentoring some of the younger ladies. Twice a week they'd pick her up and take her to the morning House of Prayer session. Then she'd meet one-on-one with a different girl each day. She'd listen to their hopes, hurts, dreams and discouragement. She would offer a few words of encouragement and pray with them.

They called her "Momma Martha" and she loved it. She missed being a momma. She and Barnabas had no daughters and only one son, Nathan. He had been a fine young man until he was killed in Iraq during Desert Storm.

*

Since the night before, Officer Darrell Jackson had sat outside the door of the ICU guarding Daniel from a return of the shooter. Now he sat outside the door of the Operating Room. He seriously doubted that anybody would be crazy enough to attack a hospital. But the shooter did have the guts to shoot a pastor during the sermon and the smarts to escape. So, it could happen.

Darrell thought back through the events of his shift. Several people had come in and out of the room during the night. As he screened them, it was obvious that none of the pastor's visitors were assassins. Instead, they were some of the nicest people he had ever met. They were obviously very concerned for the welfare of the man in the room, but they also took time to be interested in other people. They had brought Darrell coffee and a donut and offered to pray for him.

He had grown up in church back in North Carolina but got out of it when he went in the military and never really went back. He was "too busy for church" he told himself. But, the way these people dealt with this tragedy made him consider at least visiting the pastor's church one day.

Earlier that night, the Grace City people had held a prayer service in the family waiting area and sang some really nice songs. During that worship thing, they didn't just pray for their pastor. They prayed for everyone in the waiting area and for their family members who were in ICU. After that, Darrell had even seen the pastor's pretty, young wife stop and pray with an older lady whose husband was very ill.

Darrell recalled meeting the pastor at the precinct a few times. He had also read the newspaper report about the pastor and saw what the internet had to say about him. This pastor was quite a guy. He helped the poor and homeless, the addicts and alcoholics. He trained college kids. He mobilized people to pray for God to bless the city.

Pastor Daniel and his church had even been by the precinct several times. They made an amazing breakfast for the officers twice a year. The preacher also had been by the precinct last February to help when two of their officers were shot while they were simply eating lunch.

"*I hope this guy somehow pulls through,*" Darrell thought. "*If not, a lot of people will be disappointed.*"

## CHAPTER 33
### 6:34 AM

*Dear Lord, thank you for the many blessings you have given us. Thank you for always providing for our needs. Thank you for plenty of food, good clothes, and a safe place to live.*

Maria prayed quietly as she put her Bible down and knelt by the chair in the family room.

*Thank you for my boys. As always, I especially thank you for healing Miguel. Thank you so much.*

*Today, I join with many others and I ask you to please help Pastor Daniel. Pastor Daniel and the church prayed for Miguel when he was healed. Today, we are praying for Pastor Daniel that he might be healed.*

*Dear Father, please get Pastor through this surgery successfully.*

*And Lord, I know I say this every day, but please speak to Ezekiel today. Somehow soften his hard heart. All I want for Christmas is for him to have a new heart. Whatever it takes. Whatever it takes.*

Tears were rolling down her cheeks as she dapped her eyes with her handkerchief.

*Please, Lord, please.*

# CHAPTER 34
## 7:05 AM

"Hurry up boys," Doris said. "We don't want to be late for school."

One-by-one the boys piled into Doris's SUV.

Once they were all inside, Elijah shushed the other boys. "Shut up, guys. We need to pray for Dad. He is in surgery right now."

"Let me go first," Caleb said. He began, "Dear Father in Heaven, please be with our dad right now. We don't know what all is going on in that operating room, but you do. Help them to help dad...," he began to sniff, and his eyes teared up. "Please keep him alive. We really want our dad back."

"Dear Jesus, help daddy. Help him a lot and help mommy too and...," Titus prayed "... and help us."

*

"Good morning sweetie," Roberta said coming into the OR waiting room. She brought coffee, two bananas, and a bagel. Handing them to Rebecca, she said, "Here, you need to keep your strength up."

Then turning to Freda, she said, "Freda, honey, you go home and get some rest."

"Carlos already got the kids to school," Freda said. "I don't need to be at home. I am going to stay here until Daniel comes out of surgery."

*

"So how is the pastor today?" Stephanie asked Maria as she sat down at her desk at the school office.

"He is in surgery right now," Maria frowned and shook her head. Then she looked at her office partner. "Stephanie. I know you have a kind heart. Would you help me pray for Pastor? *Please.* He has four little boys."

"Ah... urr... I am not much at praying," Stephanie said.

"God loves to hear your voice and Pastor really needs all the help he can get. Just ask God to help him and I'll take over from there," Maria encouraged her.

"Okay," Stephanie said and took a deep breath. "God, Maria sure thinks that you are good and strong. Hear her prayers for her pastor," she took another deep breath and exhaled. Then she wiped a tear off her cheek. "Save his life for the sake of those little boys."

*

"Mrs. Burton, can we take some extra time today and all pray for Elijah's dad? My mom said that he is in surgery right now," said Ashley McGuire, a girl who attended to Grace City and who also happened to be in Elijah Browning's first period English class at Coronado Christian Academy.

"I think that is a good idea," Mrs. Burton said. Before she could say anything else, Ashley stood up and turned to face the class. "Ok, guys," Ashley said. "Let's get in groups of two or three and pray for Daniel's dad. He is in a very serious surgery today."

Quickly the students gathered into groups and began to call out to God.

"Let's pray, buddy," Travis said as he draped his arm around Elijah's shoulder. Elijah nodded meekly. He was really struggling to avoid fear about his father and was deeply touched by the concern being poured out by his classmates.

*

"God, where are you in all of this?" Rebecca prayed quietly as she sat in the waiting room. "We were hoping Daniel would come out of the coma today and now he is back in surgery and the doctor is giving him a very small chance of making it through. I can't see what you are trying to do. "

Rebecca felt her phone vibrate. It was a text from Josh Jenson.

"God is too good to be unkind. He is too wise to be confused. If I cannot trace His hand, I can always trust His heart." C. H. Spurgeon

*

The darkness that had surrounded Daniel earlier had retreated. He even felt as though sunshine was peeking through the heavy clouds overhead and was shining right on his chest. It made him feel better than he had felt in a while.

# CHAPTER 35

## 8:50 AM

Yolanda, the young Cuban nurse's aide, burst into the OR waiting room excitedly. "Mrs. Browning, I am sorry to bother you. As you know your husband's story has caused quite a stir," she continued. "The local new stations are covering it as are several newspapers and a few magazines. Your Facebook post went viral. It has even been shared by others with two of our nurses," she gushed and took a deep breath.

"There are a bunch of reporters outside in the hallway waiting for you to make a brief statement. Someone said you would make a statement at 9:00 AM."

"Who told them she would make a statement?" Roberta asked gruffly.

Anxiously, Rebecca looked at the clock. 8:50 AM. "Oh my God, Roberta. What will I say?"

"Don't worry, honey, the Lord will help us with this," Roberta said reassuringly. She grabbed a small notebook and a pen, "Let's see what we can do."

Ten minutes later, Roberta marched into the hallway and raised her arms. She hushed the reporters and began, "Mrs. Browning will make a brief statement. Please no questions."

Rebecca walked into the hall, less confidently than before. Nervously, she unfolded a piece of notebook paper and began to read.

"By the Grace of God, my husband, Pastor Daniel Browning, has survived a violent attack on his life and an emergency operation. The prayers of God's people locally and globally have been keeping him alive."

Rebecca paused, took a deep breath, and continued.

"Now he is in a second emergency surgery. We expect him to come out soon. We are asking God to let him live and to fully restore his health."

She stopped and looked down at the paper as she fought back the tears. She took a deep breath and concluded. "Please, please pray for him. Also, join us in asking God to touch the heart of the man who shot him. Thank you."

Then she dropped her head, turned and walked back into the OR waiting room.

Roberta stepped up, "Let's pray!" She demanded. Then she began to pray, "Dear Father God. Thank you for all you have done the last few days. Right now, in the mighty name of Jesus, we ask you to walk into that operating room with power and strength. Touch Pastor Daniel," she continued. "And Father, this poor man who shot him. He needs your love. Hound of Heaven, please hunt him down and show him how much you love him. In Jesus' name, amen."

Roberta turned and marched out of the waiting room. Rebecca followed her back to Daniel's room. She looked unusually pale and weak. Dark circles were beginning to form under her eyes. She sat meekly in the corner with her head in her hands.

*The poor girl is exhausted and scared*, Roberta thought. *Lord help her.*

\*

Immediately after Roberta finished praying, the reporters were posting parts of Rebecca's statement to their twitter and Instagram accounts. The pastor was still alive, and his wife was still talking about Jesus.

"Rose, Rose," Mary Ellen, the plump, round-faced assistant at Rose's bookstore, broke into the store office carrying her phone. "Look at this."

"@#$%^ &*%$#*, I can't believe this." Rose said jumping up from behind her huge mahogany desk. "That preacher is still alive?" She growled as she venomously spit out the words.

"Get the word out to the ladies. Coven meets in the back room at ten AM. Tell them to get here as quickly as they can. There is no time to waste."

"Yes, High Priestess," Mary Ellen said, making a note in her spiral notepad.

"And, get on the hotline. We must spread the word to the other covens."

"Got it," Mary Ellen said marking it down in her notebook.

"Call Victor, see if he and any of his coven can join us at 10:00. Tell him that if he can make it, I need him to take point on this."

"Yes, High Priestess," Mary Ellen wrote everything down while nodding approvingly.

"Now get out of here and get going," Rose barked to her assistant. "I have an important session to prepare for at 10:00."

## CHAPTER 36
### 9:20 AM

As Ezekiel was getting ready to go to work, he saw Maria's Bible and some of her Christian books on the table in next to her chair. The book on the top caught his attention, *How to Love Your Husband When He Hates Your Jesus.*

He frowned. He had never quite thought of it that way. He opened the book and thumbed through the pages and read some of the chapter titles.

*Seeing Your Husband as Jesus Sees Him*

*Understanding that Hurt People Hurt People*

*Continuing to Pray Even When You Don't See Progress*

*When He's Mad at God, He May Take it Out on You*

*Prompting Him without Pressuring Him*

"What a bunch of @#$%^&*%!!" Ezekiel shouted as he hurled the book at the wall. Snarling, he stomped out of the room.

\*

"Let's all enter His gates with thanksgiving," Pastor Carlos said. The room was immediately filled with voices thanking God for various blessing. Carlos was leading the morning edition of the Grace City "House of Prayer" meeting. There was a larger crowd than usual, nearly thirty people of a variety of ages gathered in a circle. Most were either retired senior adults, young adults, people without jobs, people how worked second shift, or UNLV college students. There was a song leader, a keyboard player and a guitarist. Carlos stood next to them leading the prayer meeting.

In between worship songs, Carlos stood and spoke. "Today, I feel especially drawn to Mark 11." He paused a few moments and allowed the others to find the passage in their Bibles or on their phones.

"Notice the context as Jesus had cursed fig tree and spoke of the faith to move a mountain into the sea. I am going to read Mark 11:20-25:

> In the morning, as they went along, they saw the fig tree withered from the roots. [21] Peter remembered and said to Jesus, "Rabbi, look! The fig tree you cursed has withered!" [22] "Have faith in God," Jesus answered. [23] "Truly I tell you, if anyone says to this mountain, 'Go, throw yourself into the sea,' and does not doubt in their heart but believes that what they say will happen, it will be done for them. [24] Therefore I tell you, whatever you ask for in prayer, believe that you have received it, and it will be yours. [25] And when you stand praying, if you hold anything against anyone, forgive them, so that your Father in heaven may forgive you your sins."

"Notice that Jesus concluded this section on prayer and faith with the encouragement to forgive others. Let us start there. Examine your hearts and choose to forgive any and everyone who you need to forgive."

After several quiet minutes with only the guitar strumming quietly in the background, Carlos continued. "Notice in verses twenty-two through twenty-four, Jesus told them to 'Have faith in God. He spoke of having the faith to speak mountains into the sea. They he gave a promise that 'whatever you ask in prayer, believe that you have received it, and it will be yours."

"Today, the mountain we need to see moved is on behalf of Pastor Daniel. He is in surgery right now. Let's pray that God will move the mountain

of sickness, pain, respiratory failure, and death away from him even as we pray."
Again, a chorus of voices erupted in passionate prayer. Some were bold, some
meek, some with tears.

"Please be very present in that Operating Room right now dear Lord!"

"Guide the surgeon's hands."

"Please release healing, health and hope."

"Bring great glory to your name, King Jesus."

Then Pastor's Carlos' voice rang out above the others. "Lord, we ask
you to roll up your sleeves and place your strong right hand on Daniel. Together
we ask you to push sickness and death into the sea. Jesus died to defeat death,
hell, and the grave. The gospel tells us that you have conquered death. We
believe that you are working while we are praying. Work now as only you can.
Please bring Glory to your Son. In His name, the name of Jesus, we pray!"

Two dozen "Amens!" rang out through-out the room.

Then Carlos continued. "Let's go back to Mark 2:1-12."

Around the room the pages of Bibles began to turn.

"Here the context is that of Jesus teaching in a home that is incapable
of holding the large crowd of those who wanted to get to him. I am going to
pick the story up in Mark 2:3

> *Some men came, bringing to him a paralyzed man, carried by four of*
> *them. ⁴ Since they could not get him to Jesus because of the crowd, they*
> *made an opening in the roof above Jesus by digging through it and then*
> *lowered the mat the man was lying on. ⁵ When Jesus saw their faith...*

Fortunately, this lame man had some good friends. They knew that man
needed Jesus to touch him. Unfortunately, the room Jesus was in that day was

too crowded. The man could not get to Jesus. So, they carried the man up on the roof, tore open a hole in the roof, and lowered the man to Jesus. Jesus said that the man was healed because of *their* faith. It was the faith of his friends that made the difference.

"Look at the rest of the section. I'm going to read Mark 2:5-12

*When Jesus saw their faith, he said to the paralyzed man, "Son, your sins are forgiven." ⁶ Now some teachers of the law were sitting there, thinking to themselves, ⁷ "Why does this fellow talk like that? He's blaspheming! Who can forgive sins but God alone?" ⁸ Immediately Jesus knew in his spirit that this was what they were thinking in their hearts, and he said to them, "Why are you thinking these things? ⁹ Which is easier: to say to this paralyzed man, 'Your sins are forgiven,' or to say, 'Get up, take your mat and walk'?¹⁰ But I want you to know that the Son of Man has authority on earth to forgive sins." So, he said to the man,¹¹ "I tell you, get up, take your mat and go home." ¹² He got up, took his mat and walked out in full view of them all. This amazed everyone and they praised God, saying, "We have never seen anything like this!"*

"Pastor Daniel is in coma. On top of that, he is in surgery. *He* can't have faith right now. But *we* can. We can bring him before Jesus right now in our prayers. We don't have to get to Jesus through a roof. We can get to Jesus on our knees. We must have faith *for Pastor Daniel*. Let's ask God to touch him and make him whole just like Jesus did for that paralyzed man."

At that, the worship leader began quietly to sing, *"Give me faith"* as the others began to pray.

## CH 37

## 9:50AM

At about ten minutes to ten, a distinguished man with a neatly trimmed goatee, a handlebar mustache, a very expensive tailored tweed suit with striped vest, a colorful paisley handkerchief, and a stylish silk tie got out of a small, silver Mercedes Benz. He carried a black cape casually lying over his arm, a black leather bag over his shoulder, and a shiny black walking stick with a small skull on top. Knowing how to make an entrance, he strode into the Seeing Eye Bookstore with a flourish. Victor Laurent had arrived.

Victor was the high priest and Warlock of the Midnight Circle. The Midnight Circle was an even larger coven that the Sisters of the Bloody Moon. It was mixed with both men and women. He also was the Chief Warlock over the entire Southwest Region of the United States.

It was unusual for him to be making an appearance at the Seeing Eye. Rumors were that Victor and Rose had been lovers in the past. After a dispute, Rose's coven had broken off from Victor's a few years earlier. But they had made peace and were still friendly. They joined the two largest Las Vegas covens together a few times a year for big events like full moon ceremonies.

"Where's Miss Rose?" he asked with a slight European accent.

"The High Priestess is already in the back getting ready," Mary Ellen said.

"Excellent," he said with a wicked grin. "Many others here yet?"

"Yes. About five or six from your group and several of ours," Mary Ellen answered. "I think we now have thirteen, counting you."

"Perfect," he said rubbing his hands. "Most excellent, indeed," Victor said. Regally, he strode toward the back of the store.

*

Pastor Matthew walked to the center of the room, "As some of you saw on Facebook," he said, "we are going to extend our Grace City House of Prayer meeting a second hour today because we want to spend some extra time praying promises over Pastor Daniel and his surgery. So, I will quote the verse and the promise and you guys turn it into prayers:

Matthew 7:7 *Keep on asking and you shall receive, keep on seeking and you will find, keep on knocking and the door will be open to you.*

Pastor Lester Steed of Faith Missionary Baptist Church had come by to join the special prayer time. He stood and prayed: "Father, today, we are going to keep on asking on behalf of our brother, Pastor Daniel Browning. We come again beseeching you to touch his body with life, health and healing."

Then the combined voices of the others added in their prayers for Daniel.

When their voices died down, Matthew spoke out again. "James 5:16 *Confess your sins one to another. Pray for one another that you may be healed. The effectual fervent prayers of the righteous man avails much.*"

Thomas Richardson, Director of Youth with a Mission who was a regular at House of Prayer on Tuesdays, stood and prayed, "Father, the only righteousness we can claim is through Jesus. But he has made us righteous with His blood. Therefore, we claim this promise and ask that indeed our prayers will avail much and that you will heal Pastor Daniel."

In a sweet concert of intercession, the combined voices of the others added their prayers for Daniel.

*

Rose had started the coven session by following the usual practices and procedures. As she did, the room was quickly filling up. There were thirteen gathered around the circle of the pentagram and about twenty others standing around the outside. Everyone was excited to have the two covens joined together.

Miss Rose had mixed feelings about having Victor leading a session in her shop. They had history, some of it sweet, some of it, well, not so sweet.

In some ways, it would be good to have their two covens joined together on a mission. But since Victor had been her mentor and outranked her, she would have to give way to his leadership. She wasn't so sure how she felt about that.

Majestically, Victor took center stage. Rose could not help but notice how impressive he looked in his black cape with red lining. In his right hand he held a large candle and dramatically used it to light the candles of those around the circle.

*He certainly has not lost any of his amazing charisma and authority,* she thought. Then closing her eyes, she began. "We call upon the warrior gods of the East, South, West and North to come."

"Come, come!" the combined coven echoed back.

"I repeat, we call upon the warrior gods of the East, South, West and North to come with power, and with might."

"Come with power, and with might," the coven began to chant. "Come with power, and with might. Come with power, and with might."

*

After the brief reprieve, the battle resumed. Daniel felt weak as he saw four, massive, muscled, majestic, malevolent warriors appear, one from each direction. The dark spirits wore ornate helmets and shiny armor. One had black armor highlighted with silver. Another's black armor was highlighted with crimson. The third's armor had golden highlights. The fourth's armor had rainbow colored highlights like the skin of a snake, changing between purple and green and blue as the light hit it.

In horror, Daniel watched them advance forward and begin to slice their way through the small angel contingent. Viciously the dark spirits fought their way toward him. As they got closer, they began to morph and grow until each had become huge fire-breathing, dark, dangerous, dragons.

## CHAPTER 38

## 11:18 AM

Victor had successfully whipped the Coven into a frenzy. With great dramatic oratory, he began to beseech the dark forces. "Prince of Death we beseech you to also come with great power and might."

The coven echoed back. "Come with power and might."

"Come with power and might!" He said louder.

"Come with power and might!" They responded with equal vigor.

"Come with power and might!"

"Come with power and might!"

"Do not delay," he demanded with authority.

"Do not delay," they yelled.

"Do not delay!"

"Do not delay!" They all yelled in unison. "Do not delay!"

\*

"Stephanie, would you mind if I took a short break?" Maria asked her friend. "I need to pray about something before the break room fills up for lunch."

"No problem," Stephanie said. "What is it?"

"I have this overwhelming feeling that I need to pray for our pastor right now."

"Well, okay... good luck I guess," Stephanie replied.

"This feels like it is bigger than luck."

\*

Rebecca, began to feel weak. Her head pounded. Then her stomach began to cramp and she was nauseated.

*What is going on?* she thought. *Why am I suddenly sick?*

*

As the Grace City House of Prayer meeting ended, Martha left feeling vaguely uncomfortable. It was as if the job was unfinished. She drove a few blocks over to Flamingo Avenue and pulled her battered, 2003 Honda Accord into the parking lot of the Grace City outreach center. She usually volunteered there on Tuesdays. She enjoyed interviewing and praying with the ladies who came in for assistance. But today, as she turned off her car, something was very uneasy in her spirit.

*Daniel is still in trouble. We should not have stopped praying.*

When she closed her eyes, she saw it. Four, large, dark dragons were descending upon the hospital from the four corners of the earth.

*

Dr. Kim had been fighting off a monstrous headache. Now he felt an awful wave of nausea hit him. The same thing must have happened to one of the nurses. She doubled over with a cramp and then she ran out of the room. They could hear her retching in the hall.

*What is going on?* Dr. Kim wondered.

*

Victor placed a large candle in the center of the pentagram.

Then, he held up an 8x10 color picture of Pastor Daniel that his assistant Jason had taken from the church website. He had enlarged it.

"Picture this man in your minds," he said. "Fix his image in your heads."

Then, with a grand flourish, he raised the picture over his head, took the sharp blade of the Athame and stabbed the eyes in the picture. The coven members hissed their approval.

"God of darkness, come and take the light of life from the eyes of this weakling," he intoned.

"Yes, yes," they hissed.

Victor raised a red rose. Theatrically he picked a petal and smashed it into the picture with a snarl. The coven hissed their approval.

He pulled out the largest thorn from on the stem of the rose and held it for all to see. Then in a grand gesture, he drove it savagely into the heart of the man in the picture.

"Prince of Death, pierce his heart."

"Yes! Yes! YES!" the crowd shouted.

"Prince of Darkness, burn this man until he is consumed forever in your flame."

"YES! YES! YES!" the crowd screamed. "YES! YES! YES!"

With impressive, dramatic flair Victor extended his arm and held the picture of Daniel over the flame of the large candle. The flame quickly enveloped the picture.

"YES! YES! YES!" the crowd screamed. "YES! YES! YES!"

*

As the menacing darkness neared his bed, Daniel was paralyzed by terror. First, he had blinding pain in his eyes. Then it was piercing agony in his chest. If only he could move, he would run and hide.

Daniel was helpless as the four giant, hideous, black dragons swooped down upon him. One after the other, they opened their mouths and breathed out a jet of fire toward him. The four waves of fire swept over him, burning his entire body. The smell of sulfur filled the air.

Then, as if in slow motion, Daniel saw an even larger, black demon warrior flying determinedly toward him. He was more ornate, more decorated, and more sinister than the others. In a smooth, powerful gesture, the demon lifted up a massive black bow and released a flaming red arrow.

Daniel watched helplessly as the arrow landed deep in his chest.

He wanted to scream in agony, but he couldn't. The arrow sliced through him and a menacing red flame rose high out of it.

The huge demon with the bow tilted his head back and roared in celebration.

*Jesus help me! Make it stop!* Daniel yelled. Or at least he wanted to yell. He could not open his mouth.

*Jesus help me! I am on fire!!*


\*


"Doctor! Doctor! The patient's temperature is going through the roof. Five minutes ago, it was 101. Now it's 104.7 and rising. He's burning up!"

\*

There were times when the voices in Zeke's head were louder than at other times. Right now, they were screaming with unusual glee and happiness.

*The preacher's going to pay.*

*The preacher's going to burn.*

*The preacher's going to die.*

Usually, it made him feel happy when the voices were happy. It was a nice relief from their constant condemnation and abuse.

But this time his feelings were conflicted. A few days ago, every cell in his body wanted that preacher to die. But now, deep in a corner of his heart, he felt guilty for what he had done. He felt dirty for *all* the bad things he had done.

A tiny little part of him even felt sorry for the preacher. People said the preacher was a good man. Remorse hit Zeke like a wave. *Maybe I had him all wrong.*

But what really hit Ezekiel was not sorrow for the man so much as for the man's family. Maria had told him that the preacher had four sons. Zeke knew how devastated his family had felt when his dad died. That wound was so deep that it never healed, and would never heal. Never.

Suddenly anger swelled up inside him. "Serves them right," he snarled out loud. "Let them know how hard it was for us. Let someone else feel that pain." He leaned back, crossed his arms behind his head and smiled.

*

"I am sure that we succeeded this time," Victor said smiling at Rose. "Let's bring our efforts to a close. Then we can all go celebrate the death of the preacher."

"Are you certain?" Rose asked. "We must succeed this time."

"No one can survive what we just unleased on the preacher. No one"

*

"Doctor! Doctor!" The head nurse shouted to Dr. Kim. "His vitals are crashing. I think we are about to lose him."

*Hold on!* Dr. Kim silently prayed. *HOLD ON!*

He reached into Daniel's chest to massage his heart.

"Beep....Beep.......      Beep..........      Beep............ Beep....................... Beep................................ Beep," the steady beep of the heart monitor was slowing

"He is going into cardiac arrest!"

"Doctor, he is coding."

"BEEEEEEEEEEEEEEEEEEP!"

"Code Blue! Code Blue!"

## CHAPTER 39
### 12:33 PM

"My heart," Rebecca cried as she lifted a trembling hand to her chest. "Something is going wrong in that operation. Very wrong!" she said. "I can feel it."

"I feel it too," Freda said frowning. "I feel darkness. Heavy darkness."

"Me too!" Roberta said. "Let's pray and pray hard!" she commanded, urgently dropping to her knees. Matthew, Carlos, and about ten others who were now gathered in the waiting room all hit their knees and began to cry out in passionate prayer.

"Touch Pastor Daniel, Jesus!"

"Please heal him, Father!"

"Fill that room with angels!"

"Help those doctors. Please give them supernatural wisdom!"

"Move with power!"

"Be the breath of life in his lungs."

"Be the Great Physician!"

\*

"Oh Lord!" Martha yelled out grabbing her chest. It was on fire. Suddenly she was burning up and sweat began to pour out of her skin.

"Father, I humbly ask you to move and move quickly on Pastor Daniel's behalf. In the strong name of King Jesus, cancel any Enemy assignment against him," she prayed firmly. "I cry out for his life."

She paused and wiped her sweaty forehead with a white handkerchief and continued. "Jesus. You are the river of living water. Please pour down cool water over Daniel right now. Holy Spirit, divine breath of the almighty God, blow the cool, refreshing breath of life into Daniel Browning's lungs right now, in the name of Jesus. Jesus, you raised Lazarus from the tomb, please raise Daniel up. Please, Lord Jesus. Please raise him up. Please do it now. Do not delay. He needs you now!"

*

The blackness was darker and heavier than Daniel had ever felt. The pain was more intense. The heat was overwhelming. The end was near.

But, suddenly there was something… a tiny opening in the darkness. A tiny beam of blindingly, brilliant, white light shot out of heaven and widened as it streaked to earth heading for the hospital.

"KAA BOOM!" It crashed with tremendous force into the giant demon warrior with the bow and arrow. The resulting shock wave threw the evil warrior far out of the picture and cast the entire evil horde back in every direction.

Yet, strangely, the golden, guardian angels were completely unaffected and stood their ground. Their backs straightened and faces broke out in huge smiles. Golden light again filled the room.

Daniel saw a massive bronze warrior standing in the light, emanating pure goodness. He wore golden armor on his chest. He held a massive silver sword. His hair was snow white. His eyes blazed with fire.

The bronze warrior opened his mouth and with great authority decreed, "LIFE. River of Life!'"

When he spoke, his words rumbled, sounding like Niagara Falls, except every syllable was unmistakably clear. But beyond that, it also *felt* like Niagara Falls. Daniel felt as though he was being doused in cool, crisp, clean water.

Then the golden warrior simply said, "BREATHE!" At this, he puffed up his chest, reared his massive head back, and blew directly at Daniel's lifeless body.

Instantly, Daniel inhaled. Breath filled his lungs. The blazing heat was gone. A cool breeze refreshed his burning skin. Color came back to his skin.

*

"Save him, Father! Save him, Father" Dr. Kim prayed desperately under his breath.

*Whoosh!*

A strong gust of wind blew unmistakably through the room. The sheet covering the lower half of Daniel rose and fell as the breeze swept through.

"What in the world was that?" the assisting doctor asked.

"Beep... Beep...Beep...Beep..."

"Doctor, he... he's breathing again," the nurse said staring at the monitor in disbelief.

"His vitals are all looking better," she paused, staring in disbelief at the other monitors as the numbers climbed. "They... they are improving. They look really good!"

"Thank you, Jesus!" Dr. Kim said aloud with a small chuckle. "Thank you, Jesus!" He had the paddles of the electric defibrillator in each hand ready to deliver an electric shock to Daniel as a last-ditch effort to restart his heart. "I guess I won't be needing these," he said, putting them down.

"What just happened?" the other doctor asked.

"It's called a miracle. With God all things are possible!" Dr. Kim said. His eyes twinkled over his surgical mask.

# CHAPTER 40
## 12:35 PM

"Amen," Roberta closed the waiting room prayer meeting.

A wave of sweet peace had swept over each of them. Somehow each of them knew that Daniel would make it through the surgery.

"Thank you, Lord," Roberta said what they all felt. "Thank you, Lord. Thank you for saving Pastor Daniel. We give you all the praise and glory."

\*

Martha took off her glasses and wiped her wet face with her handkerchief. She was slumped in the driver's seat of her car worn out from prayer. The vision, the burden, the compulsion to pray had passed. She felt peace. It was so thick as to feel tangible.

"Thank you, Lord," she said. "Thank you, Lord!"

\*

As Dr. Kim walked out of the OR waiting room, he mentally replayed the events of the surgery.

*I have never had a surgery quite like this one,* he thought.

*Last night the patient's temperature went sky high and his vitals were plummeting. Emergency surgery was his only hope. Yet, the patient seemed to revive unexplainably as the operation began. All went really well during the first part of the surgery as we re-patched the lung and took another fragment of shrapnel from the abdomen.*

He stopped, puzzled.

*In my twenty years as a surgeon, I can never remember a patient's vital signs fluctuating so wildly. About ten o'clock, stuff got bizarre. I got that blinding headache and felt nauseated when I began to put in the patient's wound vacuum. One of the nurses had to leave with severe cramps and vomiting. The assisting surgeon was sweating profusely for no reason. Everyone in the room got unusually tense and angry.*

*Then the patient's vitals crashed and he coded on the table.*

*But just before I tried to shock him back to life, a wind blew through the room. My headache left. My stomach settled. The cloud of uneasiness in the room vanished.*

Then it hit him. *Something must be going on that is bigger than what was happening in that room. Was that spiritual warfare? It must have been.*

*

"12:45," Rebecca said looking at the large clock.

*12:45 and Daniel is still in surgery,* she thought.

Rebecca was never good at sitting still very long. Now, after over forty hours of constant vigilance in the hospital, Rebecca could not just sit there anymore. "Excuse me for five minutes. I'll be just down the hall if the doctor comes," she said to the ones with her in the waiting room.

*A little cool water on my face might help.* She thought.

When she had left the room and started down the hall, the awful reality hit her like a wall. Even though they had just prayed their way into a place of peace and victory, she felt too weak to resist the voice of fear playing in her head.

*My husband is fighting for his life. He is still in an operation that he has little chance of surviving.*

*His assailant is still out there.*

*I have been here since Sunday night. I miss my house and my kids. I desperately want a hot shower and a quiet meal at home with my family. I want to sleep next to my husband.*

*But I am stuck in this ugly, old, hospital while they try to keep my husband alive.*

*I get it. This is my calling right now.*

*So, Lord, give me the grace, give us the grace to get through this.*

Then she turned and headed back to the waiting room.

# CHAPTER 41
## 12:53 PM

Dr. Kim walked into the waiting room and saw Mrs. Browning and a few others gathered in the far corner.

"Mrs. Browning," he said with large smile. "I have good news."

Rebecca stood up and stepped eagerly toward him.

"Your husband made it through the surgery."

"Yes!" Rebecca said with a fist pump. "Thank you, Lord!"

"It was truly touch-and-go there for a while," Dr. Kim said. "Frankly, it looked like we were going to lose him. He even coded on the table."

Rebecca stared at him with large eyes.

"But…" he paused, his tired eyes growing moist. "The Lord brought him through!"

Rebecca gave a huge sigh of relief and asked, "How is he now?"

"His vitals were very good when I left him to see you. Surprisingly good. Miraculously good."

"And the coma?"

Dr. Kim looked serious. "He is still under the anesthesia. We won't know for sure about that for another half hour or so."

"And the bullet by his heart?"

"It is still there, I am afraid." Dr. Kim said. "Because of the wide fluctuation in his vital signs during the surgery, it was best not to bother with that bullet today. But, it is not a problem for now. When he is stronger, I can take it out."

Then he brightened, "The good news is that he is still alive."

# CHAPTER 42
## 1:20 PM

Pastor Carlos and Pastor Matthew were eating a late lunch at In-and-Out Burger on Maryland Avenue by UNLV. They had headed over from the hospital after hearing that Daniel had survived the surgery and decided to celebrate with burgers, fries, and milkshakes.

"That was a truly interesting prayer meeting we had earlier this morning," Matthew said.

"I know exactly what you mean, especially after ten o-clock," Carlos said. "There were times when everything flowed in a sweet symphony. But after ten o'clock there were moments, especially when we tried to pray for Daniel, that things got weird."

"I know. I got the worse headache a little after ten o'clock," Matthew said.

"Me too. I got so dizzy, I thought I was going to get sick," Carlos said.

"Ashley did get sick. Did you see her leave?"

"No, but Ben looked green," Carlos said.

"I know. I got so dizzy and there were times when my mind went blank."

"Me too. "

"You know you are right; it started right after ten o'clock," Matthew said. "I did not want to pray; I just wanted to lie down."

"Spiritual warfare. The enemy was really fighting our prayers," Pastor Carlos said. "It was a big reminder that our battle is not against flesh and blood, but against the rulers, against the authorities, against the powers of this dark world and against the spiritual forces of evil in the heavenly realms."

"Yes, I think you are right about that," Matthew said. "I could *feel* it. Thankfully, God won!"

*

McCauley and Marino parked their unmarked car in the Von's parking lot by the Molaskey Park. They jumped out and headed toward a clump of trees on the northwest side. The same small group of homeless people were gathered around the picnic table.

"Did you guys arrest Hawthorne?" the red-haired man asked.

"What is your name, sir?" McCauley asked

"George. George Roberts." the red-head replied.

"Thank you, Mr. Roberts." McCauley said. "To answer your question, we took Hawthorne in for questioning."

"Think he shot the pastor?" the tired looking lady asked.

"That cowardly jackass. He'd never shoot anyone," George sniffed.

"Did any of you see Hawthorne on Sunday?" McCauley asked

"What was Sunday?" George asked.

"That was two days ago. It's been sunny the last two days, but it rained a little on Saturday and it was cooler Sunday night."

"I remember, it was cold."

"That ain't cold. I grew up in North Dakota. Now *that's* cold," the lady with bad teeth said.

"Did any of you see him on Sunday?" McCauley asked.

"Yes, I saw Hawthorne on Sunday night about dusk," George said confidently. "Every day, about dusk I take a walk to stretch my legs," he shook his long legs and smiled.

"Hawthorne was right there under that tree," George pointed across the park. "Somebody had given that fool two bottles of whiskey. He was cuddled up with those bottles like a man on his honeymoon."

"Did you see him after that?"

"Yah. I did," the tired lady said. "About an hour or two after dark. I walked over with the people from the Lighthouse Church to find him. They had stopped by with sandwiches."

"Was he still here?"

"Hadn't moved. Couldn't really. The bottles were empty, and he was passed out cold."

*

"A blond-haired beauty wants to say 'hi!'" A plump, middle-aged lady wearing red and white striped tights, a hunter-green top, and a red Santa hat adorned with flashing lights had burst into the waiting room. Beside her, tripping over its monstrous feet, was a waist-high Golden Labrador retriever puppy.

"Sunshine the therapy dog wants to wish everyone a Merry Christmas!"

Sunshine had on a red vest and reindeer headgear. She came up and licked Rebecca's face happily. Rebecca was not really in the mood for a visit, but she could not help but smile as the big puppy licked her cheeks.

*That felt good*, Rebecca thought. *Sunshine reminds me of Thunderbolt when he was a puppy.*

Sunshine licked her again.

"Down, Sunshine," the puppy's owner commanded pulling the dog's leash.

"It's okay," Rebecca laughed.

*It has been days since I relaxed and smiled. It feels like it has been months.*

\*

Zeke sat in the break room of the Esquire Limousine Company finishing a pork burrito from his favorite burrito place, Café Rio. He was trying to look at the newspaper when his phone displayed a text from Maria.

*"The pastor made it through his surgery!"*

Zeke looked down at his phone. "@#$%^&*%!!!"

"What's wrong, boss?" Javier asked innocently.

"Oh, I lost a bet with my little brother," Zeke lied. Then he stood and ducked into his office.

When he closed the door, he was immediately consumed by a tsunami of intense anger. Then the voices began.

*You have a problem. The preacher is still alive. Can't you do anything right?*

*You have always been weak. You don't deserve anything good happening to you. You are stupid and lazy and careless.*

Zeke hated these voices. They acted as if they owned him. Maybe they did. They were always telling him what to do. They were always condemning him.

*You know you need to do something about that and you need to start now. Don't put it off like you always do.*

He hated being enslaved to these voices, but they were right. He needed to finish the job. He needed to do something about that preacher.

Zeke picked up his phone and texted his brother Ezra. Ezra worked in the maintenance department at Paradise Hospital.

# CHAPTER 43

## 2:30 PM

McCauley and Marino were back at the Blueberry Hill Diner. McCauley set down his coffee cup.

"Let's review," McCauley said looking at his iPad.

"So, we have a description of the shooter. Short to medium height, dark, wearing a large dark army jacket, a dark hoodie and a ball hat."

"We also have a witness who saw a man matching the shooter's description throw something in the dumpster at the Von's by Molaskey Park," he continued. "We also have a probable murder weapon. We should get a report from forensics today."

"It's not a *murder*. Not yet at least," Marino corrected.

"Well, we were told to treat this like a murder," McCauley replied. "Anyway, we also have a man who was found in proximity of the weapon who was wearing a coat, hoodie and hat matching those of the shooter. Plus, our suspect, Mr. Thomas Hawthorne III, has a motive. He hates Grace City enough and is crazy enough to try to shoot a preacher during church."

"Yes, but that's the problem. He's just a crazy, homeless drunk," Marino said. "And even if he was capable of pulling it off, and he's not, there are witnesses who can back up his alibi that he did not leave the park at the time of the shooting."

Marino continued, "I have been thinking, possibly the real shooter planted the whiskey Sunday afternoon and after the shooting planted the clothes in order to make us think Mr. Thomas Hawthorne III is the shooter."

McCauley nodded and sighed, "The shooter is smart."

"Not *that* smart," Marino said.

"Smart enough that we have no idea who he is."

\*

Daniel was back in his room in the ICU. Rebecca was glad to see him breathing as he slept peacefully. Gently she kissed his cheek. He looked weaker, smaller, and paler than she had ever seen him.

"I love you, sweetheart, and I am right here," she said as she tenderly stroked his wavy brown hair.

"You have been through so much the last few days," she said quietly. "I hope that you are sleeping deeply and are not in pain. You would be proud of our church. They have rallied to your side and have been holding special prayer meetings," she said as she stroked his hair.

"My phone is full of texts from people all over the country and around the world telling me that they are praying for you," she continued.

"God is using this to get his message out. They ran a story on you in several major newspapers including *USA Today*. You are 'the Pastor who took a bullet for Jesus.' Actually, you took *three* bullets for Jesus," she said.

"Do you remember?" she asked as she stroked his hair. "You got up to preach Sunday night and some guy shot you right in the chest."

"They have not caught the guy yet, so they have a police officer guarding you. He is sitting on a chair outside the door."

"When you proposed to me, you told me that we would not have a comfortable or easy life," she squeezed his hand. "You told me we would go wherever God sent us and we would do whatever God told us to do. You promised me that, even though we would face hard times and heartache in ministry, we would do it together."

"Well, I thought planting a church in urban Las Vegas was difficult and hard and heart breaking. But, the last few days take the cake," she sighed and ran her hands through her hair.

"In the last few days, you have almost died three or four times already. Even if you make it, no one knows what you will be like if you ever come out of the coma."

"Oh Daniel," she began to weep. "Daniel, I need you. Our boys need you," she sniffed. "Keep fighting. Don't quit...don't quit."

# CHAPTER 44
## 3:30 PM

"Ok, Elijah, you can go in first and see your dad. Remember, he had a long surgery and is very, very weak," Roberta said, gently pushing Elijah through the entry doors of the ICU. Yesterday when he had visited, he was in such shock that he had not even noticed the police officer stationed outside his father's room.

"He's ok," Rebecca said to the officer. "This is our son, Elijah."

"Elijah, say hello to Officer Burke."

"Hello," Elijah said stiffly. "Thank you for guarding my dad."

"It's my privilege," Burke said. "I have worked with him a few times at events for the homeless and for the addicted. He is a good man."

"We think so," Rebecca said, smiling as she led Elijah into his father's ICU room.

*It feels so good to have my boys here,* she thought. *At least they will get to see their father breathing one more day.*

Elijah walked right up to Daniel's bed and took his hand. "We miss you Dad," he said.

"I hear you have almost died a few times since yesterday, but they can't kill you. You keep breathing. You keep fighting," Elijah squeezed Daniel's hand. "I am really proud of you Dad."

*I am really proud of you son,* Rebecca thought. *And if your father could see you, he would be proud too.*

\*

"I think I'm going to be sick," the tall, athletic man mumbled as he rubbed his throbbing head. "Real sick."

After ten years of making big money and living the high life, LeRoy Broxton's NBA career as a power forward had come to an undistinguished end. After the Dallas Mavericks cut him, near the end of last season, no other team was interested in picking up LeRoy Braxton or his massive ego.

The highlight of his career was hitting the game-winning shot for the Los Angeles Clipper's first and only NBA Championship. Shortly after that he married Chastity Chastain and joined her popular reality TV world.

At first, he loved being back in the spotlight. But very late Saturday night he and Chastity had had yet another violent fight. He was tired of the constant glare of celebrity life, and he was sick of the superficial, shallow, never-ending meddling of her family.

He needed a break, so he jumped into his black Ferrari, escaped LA, and drove to Harden, Nevada. Once there, he went straight to the Romance Ranch brothel with a backpack full of cocaine and Viagra. Nevada is the only state in the union where prostitution is legal, and he was determined to party hard all week long.

When he arrived, he picked two girls out of the "line-up":- black-haired Monica Morales and Kool-Aid red-head Suzie McKay. Together the three of them headed to his private VIP suite for fun and games.

But after three days of partying, he was feeling awful. He looked around. A bunch of empty bottles littered the end table. Monica was passed out next to him on the huge bed. Suzie had left earlier. He pushed Monica out of the way, stood up slowly, and stumbled into the bathroom.

Then everything went black.

# CHAPTER 45
## 5:15 PM

"Knock, Knock," Big Tony said as he opened the door to Daniel's room. Smiling, he entered the room, followed by Rufus.

"Tony, Rufus, it is so good to see you both," Rebecca said as she stood up and gave them hugs.

"We had to come to see Pastor and you," Rufus said. "How is he?"

"He has a rough night and a very tough time during the operation. But, he is doing pretty well now, considering all of that," Rebecca said.

"Is he...a... you know... still... you know ...?" Big Tony asked.

"In a coma?" Rebecca asked trying to help him out. "Yes, the doctor said that they don't know when he'll wake up."

"Well, except for all those tubes, he looks real peaceful," Tony said.

"Don't say, 'he looks real peaceful.' That makes it sound like he's in a casket, not a coma," Rufus corrected. "Don't scare the poor girl."

"It's ok," Rebecca smiled. She was glad to have them there. Their loyalty and faithfulness the last few years had been such a blessing.

"How are *you* doing Rebecca?" Tony asked. "You look tired."

"Don't say, 'you look tired.' Rufus said.

"Well, she *does* look tired."

"That's all right, Tony," Rebecca said. "I *am* tired. Not much sleep the last few days."

"We have sure been praying for you and the boys," Tony said. "And everyone has really been praying for Pastor."

"We sure have," Rufus added.

"I know you have," she said. "We feel it."

Rufus got a very serious look on his face, "Rebecca, this is spiritual warfare. I know it. In the special prayer meeting this morning, we all sensed an outside influence trying to hinder our prayers. It would seem that there is something going that bigger than all of us."

Rebecca felt a chill go down her spine. Even though her husband was considered by some to be proficient at it, she was no fan of spiritual warfare. Too often it felt as though the Enemy knew he could not touch Daniel, so he came after her and the kids. When she thought about the Enemy attacking her boys, fear hit her like a punch in the stomach.

"But, Rebecca honey, remember God has got this," Rufus said staring into her eyes. "Now, I don't usually say things like this, but I believe Daniel is going to be fine, just fine. We got to have faith. Remember, with God all things are possible."

## CHAPTER 46
### 7:14 PM

"Rebecca, I hope I am not disturbing anything," Maria said as she entered Daniel's room.

"Oh, Maria," Rebecca said as she stood and gave Maria a hug. "Thanks for coming."

"You guys have been on my mind all day. I was so happy to hear that Pastor survived the surgery. It was strange but around 11:30 this morning I felt an extra burden to pray for him."

"I am glad that you did," Rebecca said. "We felt it here also. As it turned out, he actually coded during the operation at that time. But God ...," she paused. "God spared him."

"Coded? Oh my! How is he now?" Maria asked as she turned and looked at Daniel.

"Good. Surprisingly good. The doctor said it was a miracle," Rebecca said smiling.

"Praise the Lord!" Maria said.

"Sit down," Rebecca said, pointing to the empty chair where Roberta has been seated all day before heading home at seven. "How's your mom?"

"Mom is good, she has these flare-ups when she won't take her medicine. But hopefully the last one scared her enough so that she will keep taking it."

"How is the rest of your family?"

"The boys are good. They are growing up so fast. How are *your* boys handling this with their dad in the hospital? Where are they staying?"

They are with the Garcias," Rebecca replied. "Overall, they are okay. But this has shaken them up."

"I am sure that it has. It has shaken all of us. Are *you* doing all right Rebecca?" Maria asked. "This has to have shaken you as well."

"It has. And it probably feels worse than it really is because I am tired. Not much sleep the last few nights. But I must keep choosing faith instead of fear. No matter what happens I must trust Him."

"That's a great attitude."

"It's the only attitude; otherwise I get overwhelmed with fear," Rebecca said. "Anyway, enough about me. How is *your* husband Ezekiel, right?"

"Oh, Ezekiel. He keeps me on my knees. Funny you should ask because I have been sensing that something big is going on with him. I am praying he comes to the Father soon, maybe even by Christmas."

# CHAPTER 44
## 9 PM

Rebecca was deep in thought as she walked back to Daniel's room after stepping out of the room for a few minutes to go to the café and get a coffee.

"Rebecca, how's it going?" said a tired, sixty-year-old lady whose husband occupied the room next to Daniel's.

"Oh," Rebecca was startled by the voice. "Karen, thanks for asking. Well, as you know, Daniel had to go back in surgery this morning and for much of the day. It was rough, he was in there so long. The doctor said that he actually died on the operating table."

"Oh no," Karen said looking horrified.

"But the Lord revived him," Rebecca said, touching Karen's arm. "Daniel is doing so much better tonight. He's doing the best he's done since he has been in here."

"Good," Karen said quietly. "That's so good to hear."

"How about Glenn? Any improvement?"

Karen sighed deeply. "The doctor was in earlier. He said that it was not looking good. We had hoped he might be out by Christmas.... but..." Karen dropped her eyes. "... but, today the doctor said, he wouldn't be getting out before Christmas, and if things don't turn around soon, he ... he won't be getting out at all."

"Oh, Karen, I am *so* sorry," Rebecca said as she put her arm around the shorter woman. "Would it be all right if I prayed for Glenn and for you?"

Karen nodded her head, "Yes, please do."

"Dear Father in heaven," Rebecca began. "We come to you today on behalf of Glenn. You know all about his medical condition and what the doctor said today. But you are bigger than cancer and you are good. Would you be so kind as to touch Glenn's body?"

Then Rebecca said something she did not often feel led to pray, "Father, would you make a definite positive change in his physical condition and do it soon?"

"And, Father, would you give Karen and the rest of the family extra grace and strength as they go with Glenn through this difficult time?" Rebecca continued. "In the name of Jesus, amen."

"Thank you," Karen said as she wiped tears off her cheeks.

Then Rebecca surprised herself by saying, "Remember, with God all things are possible."

Karen smiled and nodded. She and Rebecca hugged. Then she ducked into her husband's room.

## CHAPTER 45

### 9:35 PM

Rebecca was happy that they took Daniel's breathing tube out, but she was so weary. She had lived on adrenaline for two days and now the adrenaline was gone. She was physically exhausted, emotionally drained, and spiritually stretched to the max.

Since her younger sister had collapsed and nearly died when they were children in Brazil, Rebecca had battled fear and depression. Although it had been better the last few years, occasionally she felt helpless to stop the flood of negative thoughts filling her mind and darkening her soul.

But now, there they were again, the negative thoughts running through her tired mind. It was as if there were a narrator reading the script of her life. Ever since her sister almost died, Rebecca had often handled her stress this way.

*Rebecca had loved living in the college town ministering to the college students. She loved the beauty of the farm country surrounding them outside Lincoln, Ohio. She loved their big old country house on the edge of town with the Dutchers beautiful farm spread out behind them. She loved her friends back home. She loved having her parents living forty minutes away and her older sister and her girls a little less than an hour. She liked that her older brother and his family were just an hour and fifteen minutes away. She loved the high school where she had taught art part time.*

*Truth be told, she never really wanted to come to Las Vegas. She deeply loved their quiet life in Ohio.*

*She certainly loved Jesus more than anything else. She revered God too much to come between her husband and following his calling. But did they really have to leave home to follow Jesus? Couldn't Daniel just be the campus* pastor? If they had to plant a church, couldn't they do it in Columbus instead of Las Vegas? Did it have to be so hard?

When people asked if she loved Las Vegas, she usually answered, "I love the people and the ministry."

But she did not love Las Vegas. Living in Paradise near the Strip was dirty, nasty, crowded, and ugly. Nine months out of the year it was hot. In the summer, it was painfully hot as temperatures exceeded 100 degrees daily.

Church planting was often very difficult and disappointing everywhere, but especially here in Paradise.

So many people had promised to come to church and never showed up. Even if they did come and make a commitment to God, so many seemed incapable of maintaining a commitment to anything other than themselves for more than a few weeks. So many acted like a consumer instead of a contributor, even some of the "mature" members. Relationships were often shallow and superficial.

She hated the thought of raising her kids in such a sex-soaked atmosphere. It took every penny she and Daniel had to put the boys in Christian school.

At the church, when they did find good people, or they helped someone to the point that they could help others, they often moved away. They either got transferred or they wanted to move "back home" and minister to their family.

Many of the young adults who came to serve with them just did not have the stamina to endure through the tough seasons.

Yet, God had blessed. They had seen miracles time and time again. Money came in at the last minute from unexpected sources.

*Lives had been transformed. Addicts were delivered. People had been healed. Marriages saved. Prostitutes rescued. And so many young adults trained for ministry.*

*And the church did have so many truly wonderful people.*

*But, after the first eighteen months of miracles, things changed. Then, what she and Daniel referred to as the "dark days" set in. The newness wore off. The glamor of urban ministry lost its sheen. They were exhausted.*

*Then the Enemy attacked. He hit them, and he hit hard from every direction.*

*Lies. Misunderstandings. Betrayals. Abandonments.*

*Equipment was stolen. Things broke down. Key people left.*

*In a year, they lost 30% of their donors and 40% of their members. The place they were renting for Sunday worship refused to renew the lease. Key staff members got tired of raising their own funds and left to take paying jobs at large churches. Their worship leader had an affair with the keyboard player.*

*Then a very large church in Virginia tried to hire Daniel as a teaching and young adult pastor. Mission University offered to make Daniel the Vice President of Spiritual Affairs, a larger, more prestigious role than he had before. A great church in Maryland asked Daniel to be their senior pastor. She was sure he would take one of those great offers. She hoped and prayed he would choose the college in Ohio, so they could move back home.*

*But when they both prayed together, they did not feel released from Vegas. Daniel felt that he could not abandon his calling to Las Vegas. She knew it was the right thing to do, but she was sad about it, and to be honest, was mad about it.*

*Thankfully, God turned things around the last few years. The church began to grow. Reinforcements came to serve. The blessing of God became evident.*

But now this.

Questions battered her mind like waves of a stormy sea crashing into the rocks on shore.

*Yes, Daniel survived today's surgery and the one Sunday night. But would he be able to survive any more operations?*

*How many more would there be?*

*He was hooked up to a dozen machines, what if the power went out? Would he survive?*

*What if his fever went up again?*

*What if he died in his sleep?*

*How could she provide for the kids?*

*How would their kids ever be able to go to college?*

*What if Daniel never came out of the coma?*

*What if he came out of the coma with low brain function?*

*What if he couldn't talk or walk?*

*What if he could never preach again?*

*What if he would never be able to play with the boys again?*

*What if Daniel would never hold her again?*

# WEDNESDAY, DECEMBER 23

## CHAPTER 46
## 1:47 AM

Before she left at 4 o'clock that afternoon, Suzie McKay had been instructed by LeRoy Braxton to come back at midnight and take Monica's place. But Suzie's brand-new puppy had gotten violently sick just as she was heading out the door. She sent Monica a text telling her that she would be late. But she ended up being later than she thought because it took her awhile to find someone to watch the little dog.

Now it was after 1:30 AM and Monica still had not replied to her text. *Must be busy with LeRoy*, she thought.

Suzie knocked on the door of LeRoy's room and there was no answer. All the girls who worked at the ranch had master keys to the rooms and she used hers to unlock the door. Quietly she walked into LeRoy's room and saw Monica asleep on the large round bed. But there was no sign of LeRoy.

She saw that the bathroom door was opened so, she headed that way. *Monica would have told me if he had left,* she thought.

"LeRoy, are you in there?" she called.

Susie went quietly into the bathroom and saw the huge basketball player sprawled out in the bathtub. "LeRoy... honey, wake up."

He did not move.

"LeRoy, wake up," she said a bit louder as she shook his shoulder.

He was motionless.

"LeRoy!" she said as she reached out and gently shook his shoulder. Then she saw that there was a white foam around his lips.

"Oh, my God! Oh, my God!" she screamed as she ran out of the room.

"Monica, wake up!" she yelled, shaking Monica who was stretched across the bed. "LeRoy is passed out in the bathroom. He looks like he is dead."

"He had better not be dead!" she said standing up. "Vance will kill us if anything happens to this client."

Monica walked into the bathroom and shook the large, limp man in the bathtub. "Wake up, wake up, LeRoy!"

LeRoy, still unconscious sniffed. A small bit of blood came out his nose.

"Well, at least he's still alive," Monica said, making a face. "But barely."

"What do we do?" Suzie asked.

"We need to call 911, right now," Monica said firmly.

"Shouldn't we get Vance first?" Suzie asked eagerly.

"We can get Vance in a minute, but LeRoy needs help. If he dies because we did not call 911, we will really get in trouble," Monica said.

"Ok," Suzie said, fumbling with her phone. "What do we tell them?"

"Tell them the truth. LeRoy Braxton is unconscious in the bathtub and we can't wake him up."

"It's ringing," Suzie reported nervously.

"Hurry! Hello, we need help right now!" Suzie yelled into the phone.

"Calm down, Miss. What's wrong?" the voice on the line said.

"LeRoy Braxton is unconscious and he's not waking up."

"Where is your emergency? What is the address?"

"I'm at the Romance Ranch in Harden."

"What is the address?"

"660 Rocky Ridge Road."

"Thank you. We have dispatched an ambulance," the voice said. "Is he breathing?"

"Monica, is he breathing?" Suzie looked anxiously at Monica.

Monica pressed her hand to LeRoy's chest to try to feel his breathing.

"Yes, he's breathing," she said to Suzie, "but barely."

"He's breathing," Suzie said into the phone, "but barely."

"Is there anything else?"

"Yes, he has blood coming out his nose and white stuff around his mouth. And it looks like he fell into the bathtub."

"Was he taking anything?" the voice asked.

"Yes. He was drinking a lot, and snorting cocaine," Suzie answered.

"Plus, he took a lot of Viagra," Monica said loudly toward the phone.

"A lot!" Susie added.

"The ambulance is on its way. They should be there very soon."

"Hurry, if he dies we will get in so much trouble."

# CHAPTER 47
## 2:33 AM

"Sir, I am very sorry to wake you up, but this is very important," EMT Jason Smith said into his cell phone.

"It had better be. Do you know what time it is?" Sheriff Barfield replied rubbing his eyes.

"Yes, sir," Smith continued. "LeRoy Braxton is at the Romance Ranch."

"Leroy Braxton? The basketball player?"

"Yes, he also is on that reality show with Charity Chastain."

"Oh yeah, my wife watches that junk," Barfield replied. "What about him?

"He is at the Romance Ranch. He is unconscious, and we can't wake him. He has overdosed on something. Appears to be some combination of drugs, alcohol, and Viagra."

"You can overdose on Viagra?" Barfield asked.

"Yes. We just covered that in my last continuing ed. class," Smith replied. "What do we do? Our local clinic won't do. He is going to need a hospital.

"Load him up and prep to Life Flight him. Let me make a call about the hospital and I'll get right back to you.

\*

"Yes sir. We need to know where to take him. It is LeRoy Braxton we are talking about. Not only is he an NBA star, but his wife is a TV star," Sheriff Barfield said into the phone.

*That's just great.* Captain McKnight sighed. He was sick and tired of these entitled celebrity issues. *Only three months to retirement*, he reminded himself.

He began to process his thoughts out loud. "Ok, so, there will be a circus surrounding him. The hospital that usually takes care of these cases is Paradise. It is the one closest to the Strip. Also, they have a private VIP entrance so, it will take a while before anyone knows he is there," McKnight continued. "So, take him to Paradise Hospital," McKnight said to Barfield. "I'll let them know you are coming, and I'll have some officers ready to get him inside and to secure the area."

"Thanks," Barfield said. He was relieved to have someone else taking responsibility of Braxton. These celebrity things were out of his league.

*

"Beep … Beep… Beep… Beep!" Sheriff Barfield had just gotten back into bed when his phone rang. He looked to see who it was." Jason Smith" was the name that appeared on his screen.

"Sorry to bother you sir, but we have run into a problem."

"Is it Braxton? Did he die?"

"No, but he is still unconscious," Smith said.

"So, he is still breathing?" Barfield asked.

"Yes. And we are giving him oxygen." Smith replied.

"Good. So, what's the problem?"

"He's too tall," Smith said.

"What do you mean?" Barfield asked.

"He is too tall to fit in the helicopter."

"You're kidding."

"He *is* a basketball player," Smith said.

"How about the ambulance?"

"We tried that. His feet stick out the back doors."

"Put him on his side and bend his knees. Then he should fit," Barfield said.

"Oh, yes. We should have thought of that," Smith said quietly. "Thanks, sir. Sorry to bother you."

# CHAPTER 48
## 4:15 AM

Daniel was dreaming. He saw himself seated with Rebecca in the student lounge at Mission College.

Her sleek, chestnut, brown hair hung down lazily onto her shoulders. She wore a thick, red Ohio State sweatshirt and clean faded blue jeans that fit her perfectly. Her eyes sparkled with life, intelligence and fun. But what really mesmerized him was her glow. The light of the love of God shone through her.

Daniel had long, curly brown hair and wore a blue and green flannel shirt. He had a mustache that his roommate said was "the substance of things hoped for, the evidence of things not seen."

*We look so young and happy,* Daniel thought.

They sat on a cheap couch with their Bibles opened on their laps.

*Oh yes, "Discipleship Dating,"* he recalled. Back then, he was testing her. In his heart, he knew that the girl he married would have to love Jesus more than she loved him. She would have to love prayer and discussing the Bible more than a nice dinner and a movie, which he couldn't affo4rd anyway.

\*

*"Father in heaven, thank you so very much for getting Daniel this far. But please do not stop now. Please wake him up out of that coma and give him full recovery,"* Rebecca quietly prayed after the beeping of one of Daniel's machines woke her up.

*"Also, please help me with this fear,"* she continued.

*"Ever since Sarah died, I have had such a hard time trusting you with these types of things. But I know that I must. I know that ultimately, whatever happens, you will be with us. Whatever happens, it will ultimately be best."*

*"Lord, I believe. Help my unbelief."*

\*

Daniel was dreaming again.

"Oh no. Oh no," Rebecca was holding a phone and crying. He saw a younger version of himself and Rebecca when they were dating. They had been studying in the student lounge when Rebecca got a call from her mother.

"I love you too, Mom," Rebecca said quietly, wiping tears off her cheeks, and sniffing. "Call me tomorrow with the details."

"What's wrong?" Daniel asked. He was afraid of her answer.

"Sarah... she died tonight," Rebecca looked at him, her eyes red and moist with tears.

"I am so sorry," Daniel said as he put his arms around her. "I am *so* sorry."

Rebecca sank her head in his chest and sobbed.

Sarah was Rebecca's younger sister. After a long battle with cancer, she could not fight any longer and had died.

Two years younger than Rebecca, Sarah had first gotten sick when the family was still serving as missionaries in Brazil. Her first attack of stomach cancer occurred when she and Rebecca were playing in the back yard. Seven-year-old Sarah began to violently vomit blood and nine-year-old Rebeca was helpless to do anything about it. Rebecca was further traumatized by the long months of seeing her sweet, little sister suffer in the hospital. From that point on, fear seemed to hang around her like a hungry panther waiting to pounce.

After the medical system in Brazil was unable to give Sarah any more help, the family came back home to the United States to be nearer to family. Miraculously, Sarah defied the odds and got better. But after Rebecca came to college, Sarah had gotten worse.

And now this.

\*

Rebecca had been dozing in her chair, but when the nurse came by to check on Daniel, it woke her up. Slowly, Rebecca stood up next to his bed and gently she reached over and took Daniel's hand. "You are one stubborn man," she said with a small smile.

"Although I have not always appreciated it, I am glad that you are such a fighter," she reached with her other hand and began to stroke his hair.

"You have taught me so much, Pastor Daniel. You made us read all those verses about how God loves poor people, then you showed us how to love the least of the least. You made us study all those verses about giving up everything and following Jesus. Then you made me do it by bringing us here."

A smile broke across her face, "When we first met you made dates out of reading the Bible and praying together because you didn't have money for anything else and you were testing me."

A mock frown wrinkled her brow. "You work too hard, aren't home enough, and are usually distracted when you get home. But you still love me and the boys, and we know it," she said.

"I love you Pastor Daniel Browning and I always will. Please, get well so we can grow old together," she paused and sniffed back a tear.

"Please, don't give up until you are completely well. We need you."

\*

"Monica, I can't believe you let this happen!" Vance, the Romance Ranch Director of Operations, lit a cigarette and glared at her. "I have had it with you, Monica. Get your stuff. Get out of here. You are fired. Don't let the door hit you on the way out."

"You can't fire me. I quit. Last month, Becki's Love Nest offered me more money to work there anyway," Monica said as she stomped out and slammed the door.

She hopped into the front seat of her 2006 Camry. Then she pulled out her phone and went to the pictures. *Well Vance*, she thought. *What will your boss think when these pictures of your biggest client hit the Internet? I can see the headlines, 'Go to the Romance Ranch and end up in a coma!'*

# CHAPTER 49

## 5:07 AM

"Mrs. Browning, we need to speak."

Rebecca turned to see Dr. Patel, the hospital doctor in charge of the ICU. He had been by earlier in the evening to check on Daniel.

"What is it?" Rebecca asked rubbing sleep from her eyes.

"I am sorry, Mrs. Browning, but for the next two hours you will not be able to leave the floor. Then we must move your husband," Dr. Patel said.

"What? Move my husband?" Rebecca asked. "Why? Is he ok?"

"Yes, he is doing quite well considering all he has been through. But, well...," Dr. Patel paused and gave her a weak smile. "A celebrity is coming in very soon. So, the floor will be locked down. We will move your husband and the others. A lot of reporters and photographers will try to get on the floor and he needs a secure environment."

"Who is *he*?"

"I can't divulge his name."

"I don't care about *his name*. I thought my husband *needed a secure environment*," Rebecca said, her voice rising. "He was shot just a few days ago, remember?"

"Yes, I know," Dr. Patel took a deep breath.

"What do you know?" Rebecca was tired and not in the mood for bad news.

"I know that your husband was shot a few days ago."

"Do you also know that the shooter is still out there? They have not caught him yet."

"Yes, I know that as well. But this is our protocol. If you would like to file a complaint you can do so," Dr. Patel said.

"File a complaint?" Rebecca shook her head. "I can't believe this. My husband has been fighting for his life and you are moving him out to make room for a celebrity!"

"I am sorry."

"So where are you moving him to? The cafeteria?" Rebecca was angry and fire flashed from her eyes.

"He will be in the Step Down Unit on the second floor."

"What is a *Step Down* Unit?" Rebecca spit the words out like they were sour.

"It is where we provide intermediate or transitional care between the ICU and the general medical-surgical wards."

"My husband almost died last night, and he did die briefly on the operating table yesterday. He is still in a coma! Are you telling me that he is ready for less care than he is getting now?"

"I am very sorry, Mrs. Browning. But I assure you they will give him the best care they can."

"In the ICU, there is one nurse for every two patients. What is the ratio on the Step Down Unit?"

"One to four,' Dr. Patel answered, refusing to meet Rebecca's gaze. "One nurse for every four patients."

"So, you are telling me that first, you are going to move my husband, who is in a coma and has been through major trauma the last 24 hours *and* died on the operating table? *And* second, you are moving him to a unit where he will receive *half* the attention he is receiving now? All because some *celebrity* is so popular that he needs the entire ICU to himself?" Rebecca's eyes blazed and her hands shook.

"I am sorry. But this is our protocol. If you would like to file a complaint you can do so."

"I am! Right now! With you!"

## CHAPTER 50
### 6:34 AM

*Dear Lord, thank for the many blessings you have given us.*

Maria was kneeling by the big recliner chair in the family room. Her head was bowed in humble submission.

*Thank you for providing for our needs. Thank you for plenty of food, good clothes, and a safe place to live.*

*Thank for my boys. As always, I especially thank you for healing Miguel. Thank you so much.*

*Today, I thank you for getting Pastor Daniel through another operation safe. Make him stronger today.*

*Also, Lord, Pastor is in a coma. Please wake him up soon. And when you do. Give him all his abilities back. Make it be as though he was waking up on a typical morning.*

Maria shifted slightly and lifted her face to the heavens.

*And Lord, I know I say this every day, but please speak to Ezekiel today. Somehow soften his hard heart.*

Her eyes moistened.

*He came home from work so angry last night.* A tear rolled down her cheek.

*His anger comes from the hurt he has. Please heal his hurt, please heal his heart.*

*Please help him drop his anger at you, oh Lord. Please free him of the awful anger.*

*Increase your work in his life and deliver him from the evil of his pain and anger. Do whatever it takes.*

*Please Lord, Please.*

\*

Daniel felt himself dreaming again. This time it was different. Everything turned brown and sepia like an old movie. He saw a Hispanic family seated around a table eating a meal together. Everyone in the image is laughing and happy. There is obvious joy in the faces of the family.

At the head of the table is the father. He is a shorter man in his mid-thirties. He is wearing a short-sleeved, white dress shirt, as are all three of the little boys gathered near him around the table. At the other end of the table is the mother. She is a beautiful, yet frail, woman in a lovely flowered dress. There are two little girls in pretty, pink dresses next to her.

The scene faded out. A new scene began.

As Daniel was watching, he saw the same family, all dressed up in their Sunday best. They are all crammed into an early 1980's tan Ford Granada station wagon with several dents on the side and a missing hub cap. The windows are down, everyone is sweaty, and the radio is playing Salsa music. They pull up in front of a store front church.

"Iglesias de Dios Pentecostal' is painted in bright red paint on the sign outside.

The scene shifts to a worship service in the small, storefront church. The room is packed. The atmosphere is full of anticipation. There are fans on the edges vainly attempting to cool the crowd.

The little family is seated in the front row. The father is behind the pulpit preaching and waving his arms with an excited and intense look on his face.    Daniel can't understand much of what he is saying, because it is in Spanish. But it is obvious the people are fully engaged.

The boy on the front row is attentively listening.

Then the scene fades.

\*

Ezekiel was still in bed. As he often did, he dreamed of being a boy. Today, he dreamed that he was sitting in the old, storefront church listening to his father preaching. Bits and pieces of the sermon seemed like arrows pointed right at him.

"You must forgive the ones who hurt you," his father said with that warm, welcoming smile of his.

"The person who gets hurt the most by bitterness is you!

"When you refuse to forgive, you open your heart to be tortured by bitterness.

"The only way to be free from the prison of bitterness is to use the key of forgiveness.

"Some of you have been angry at God for the hurts you suffered many years ago. The only way for his love to heal your hurts is to confess the sin of bitterness and let go of it.

"Some of you need to forgive yourselves."

## CHAPTER 51

### 7:00 AM

Rebecca happened to look up and see a figure in a white coat walking by Daniel's room.

"Dr. Patel," Rebecca said. "Please, wait."

The doctor turned slowly. His eyes widened, and he squared his shoulders when he saw Rebecca coming toward him.

"I want to apologize for my behavior earlier. I know that you don't make the hospital policy. I was angry and fearful, and I took my frustration out on you," she said.

The doctor smiled gently, relived that she was not angry. "Your frustration is understandable. You have been through so much the last few days."

"Will you forgive me?" she asked.

"Apology accepted, Mrs. Browning," the doctor answered awkwardly. "Have you been getting any sleep this week?"

"Well, not much. I get an hour or so here and there through the night. I don't think it adds up to much."

"Did you get any sleep the first few nights?

"No. We were too concerned about whether or not Daniel would make it.

"Well, he was resting very comfortably when I checked him last. You need to get some rest."

# CHAPTER 52
## 7:50 AM

Monica's posting of pictures of LeRoy Braxton being carried out of the Romance Ranch to an ambulance was going viral on the Internet already. As a result, the circus was beginning.

People were beginning to congregate outside Paradise Hospital. Some were there hoping for a look at a celebrity. Many held signs offering support for LeRoy, while others held signs bashing Chastity for driving LeRoy to drink. A few claimed that it was all a hoax to remedy the TV show's ailing ratings.

News trucks and television cameras were cramming into every available spot near the hospital. Every space with clear sight lines to the hospital was inundated with requests to set up cameras. One crew did not ask permission; they just camped out on an empty lot nearby.

\*

"Faster," a skin-headed man yelled over his shoulder. "Terri, you have to go faster." The skin-headed man and a young woman wearing army boots were running up a hill with backpacks.

"I'm trying Brian," the tired woman said as she gasped for breath. "I am doing the best I can."

"The Revolution starts in just a couple of days," he barked back at her. "We must be ready to bring down the Tyrants!"

\*

"LeRoy Braxton," Roberta said as she looked at her phone. "Rebecca, LeRoy Braxton must be the *celebrity* who made everyone get moved to Step Down so he could take over the ICU.

"LeRoy Braxton? Sounds familiar," Rebecca said as she rubbed her eyes. She had been dozing in one of the reclining chairs by Daniel. This room was much smaller than the one in the ICU. "Why is he famous?" Rebecca asked.

"Says here that he was a basketball star *and* is married to that Charity Chastain. You know her; she's on one of those reality shows," Roberta said as she peered over her glasses at Rebecca.

"Ok, I think I do know who he is," Rebecca said. "So, why does he need the ICU?"

"Says here that he overdosed at a brothel outside of town," Roberta replied.

"*What* did you say?" Rebecca gasped.

"He overdosed after spending several days at a brothel outside of town."

"You're telling me that my godly husband Daniel, who got shot for being a preacher, *and* these other very sick people all just got kicked out of their rooms in the ICU to make room for a guy who overdosed at a brothel?!" Rebecca was standing now with both fisted clenched. "Sometimes I hate Las Vegas!"

"Now, now," Roberta said. "No one said this world was fair, or just, or friendly to preachers. Our trust is not in the world, or the hospital, or the police department. Our trust is in the Lord."

"Sometimes, I wonder if the Lord knows what He is doing. Because I sure don't!" Rebecca said. "Please keep an eye on Daniel. I'm going to take a short walk," Rebecca said as she turned and walked out.

# CHAPTER 53
## 8:30 AM

"Good morning, Mayor, I am sorry to bother you, but we have a situation you need to know about," McKnight said into his desk phone.

"It had better be important, sweetheart," The mayor drummed her fingers on the desk. "I have got a ton of things I have to get done today."

"It's about LeRoy Braxton, the basketball player," McKnight said.

"Oh, the one who married Chastity Chastain? I love her TV show." The mayor softened. "What did he do? Fondle a tourist? Rape a hotel maid? Get drunk and drive his sports car into a store window?"

"No, Ma'am. He was found unconscious at the Romance Ranch north of town."

"Romance Ranch? Yes, I have heard of it. There was a problem there a few years ago right?

"That's right."

"So, what about LeRoy?" the Mayor asked.

"He overdosed on something. Seems to be a combo of alcohol, drugs and Viagra. They still cannot wake him up."

"You can overdose on Viagra?" the Mayor asked.

"It appears so," McKnight said, managing to maintain his professional tone.

"Well, will he be OK?"

"Not sure. He's still unconscious. They took him to Paradise Hospital last night. He's in ICU."

"Oh my. He'll attract a carnival of media clowns when word gets out. The paparazzi will swarm the place. Is the hospital secure?"

"Yes. For now."

"Don't we have someone under protection there already?"

"Yes, the preacher who got shot."

"Oh yes, the preacher with the pretty, little wife. How is he?"

"He is still alive."

"I see," the mayor paused. Then she looked at her watch. "Like I said, I am so busy trying to get things done before Christmas. Anyway, you called me to tell that Braxton is at Paradise," the mayor said impatiently. "Thanks for the update. Is there anything else?

"I heard that Chastity Chastain is on her way, and she will bring a huge entourage."

"Yes, she is extremely popular right now. But what is the problem? Are there many other patients in the ICU?"

"It was full. But we have already moved all the other patients without a problem. But about the preacher..." McKnight paused.

"What about him?

"At your request, we have had one of our officers guarding him 24/7."

"Why so much protection?"

"The shooter is still loose."

"Oh, that's right," she nodded into the phone. "We have not caught him yet. Well, live or die that preacher is already old news. Braxton will dominate the news cycle for the next week. He is now the priority."

"I understand. But what should I do about the preacher?"

"Did you move him along with the other patients?"

"Yes."

"Good. So, what's the problem?"

"He was moved with the others to the Step Down Unit. But, the layout of the unit makes it much more difficult to secure with only one officer. On top of that, I am already stretched for officers with Christmas coming in two days and New Year's around the corner. Because of Braxton, I had to station officers at the elevator and stairwells to keep Paparazzi out of the ICU. Plus, I had to station officers to guard LeRoy. Ma'am, I simply don't have enough good officers to guard Braxton in the ICU, let alone post an additional officer to guard the preacher."

"I bet that shooter has skipped town. If not, he would have tried something already," she pondered. "The media will forget about the preacher and move on to the Braxton story." She paused then asked, "Do you have a rookie or retired cop that could come in just for a few days to guard the preacher?"

"No. But even if I did, my department is already over budget for the year."

"Look, as I see it, LeRoy is the priority," she said. "If anything happens with him, the press will kill me."

"What about the preacher?"

"Oh, the press won't kill him," she said.

"But the shooter might," he persisted.

"Look, post quality people around LeRoy and make sure nothing happens to him. Do what you can with the preacher. Make it happen."

"Yes, Ma'am," McKnight shook his head and hung up.

## CHAPTER 54
## 9:20 AM

Maria felt a tug in her heart. Suddenly, she was overwhelmed with an urge to pray for Ezekiel.

Quietly, she excused herself, got up from her desk and headed for the ladies' room. In the hallway, she began to quietly pray.

*Father, I feel that my husband needs you right now. Please protect him.*

*Also, please speak to him. While you are at it, remind him again in some way that that he can be forgiven. Tell him that he can come back to you.*

*Get to the cancer of his bitterness and somehow cut it out. Set him free. I believe that with you, all things are possible.*

\*

As Martha was sitting in the prayer meeting at Grace City listening to the worship team sing, she felt a very strong compulsion from the Lord. As the wife of a Pentecostal preacher, she could always tell when the Lord nudged her to act. "Pray for the shooter. He needs to be forgiven."

Quietly, she sidled over to Carlos while the group sang. "We need to pray for the shooter," she said to him. "He needs to be forgiven."

Carlos burst out in a big grin, "I was just thinking that."

Then Pastor Matthew came up to Carlos on the other side, "I think we need to pray for the shooter."

Carlos laughed. Then he signaled for a pause on the singing. "Guys, it is abundantly clear," he said, smiling and glancing first at Martha and then at Matthew, "we need to focus our prayers, right now, on the shooter. He needs to be forgiven. Let's ask the Holy Spirit to go to him wherever he is and speak.

Let's pray that the enemy voices in his head will be silent and that the voice of the Holy Spirit will be clear."

*

As Zeke headed back to the bedroom to get his jacket before going to work, he felt strangely drawn back to his wife's Bible and books again. The book that was now on top, really caught his attention, *No Condemnation: How to Receive the Scandalous, Ridiculous Forgiveness of God.*

He turned and read the words on the back of the book:

*"If you are reading these words, you have hope. If you are still breathing, God is not finished with you. You can still be forgiven. No matter that you have done."*

Ezekiel paused and thought, *maybe I can be forgiven. Maybe there is hope for me. My dad used to say things like that.*

In his mind, he could see his dad: thirty-five years old, young and strong; wearing a short-sleeved white shirt; red tie; old, black dress shoes; and worn, black dress pants. Ezekiel saw his father's excited young face. His black hair was slicked down with a shiny oil. His old leather, Bible was open in his left hand. His pointed dramatically with the index finger of his right hand. A big, warm smile adorned his face.

The image was so real that it was as if Ezekiel could hear his father preaching in his head.

*"There is hope for you. All of you. God loves you. If you are still breathing, God is not finished with you. You can still be forgiven. No matter that you have done. There is hope."*

Ezekiel wanted to believe him, he really did. But the condemning thoughts were so loud.

*But I have done so many bad things. I have hurt so many people. I am a bad person. I shot a freaking preacher! How can I be forgiven?*

His eyes fell to the rest of the words on the back of the book.

*"Forgiveness is not based on what you have done or who you are. Forgiveness is based on who Jesus is and what he has done. And what Jesus has done is good enough to pay for your sins, no matter how many and no matter how bad."*

Tears swelled in Ezekiel's eyes. *Maybe, just maybe there is hope for me,* he thought.

But then the voices started in again.

## CHAPTER 55
## 10:02 AM

"Are you doing all right," Roberta asked. It was obvious Rebecca was not. She looked pale and washed out. She had dark circles under her eyes, and she was on the edge of tears.

"Roberta, I am struggling," Rebecca said. "I know I should be happy that God spared Daniel on Sunday night and that Daniel survived the surgery yesterday, but...," she paused "...but I am just *so* afraid that he's not going to make it. I start worrying about what we are going to do. How will the boys get by without a father? How will we pay the bills? I also worry about the church. You know how it is for young churches in Las Vegas. Most of them don't survive. I wonder what will happen to all the people we have reached."

"Stop that," Roberta commanded. "God never promised to give you tomorrow's grace today. You are trying to handle tomorrow's problems with today's grace and that just won't work. God will give you all you need to handle all the trouble you face one day at a time."

"But what if he doesn't get better? What then?" Rebecca's eyes were filling with fear.

"Oh, child," Roberta said quietly as she stroked Rebecca's hair. "There is a place the Lord brings us to as we go through hard times. It is that place where we can say, "Lord, *even if* this never gets better, *even if* it only gets worse, *even if* it hurts worse than ever, I will still trust you, Lord. Even when it does not make sense, I will trust you, Lord."

Rebecca nodded her head slowly.

"It is one thing to believe God for the miracle," Roberta continued. "But it is another to continue to believe even when the miracle doesn't come."

Roberta's voice grew more resolute, "Sometimes, I think that is the bigger miracle: trusting God through the pain, in spite of the pain. We have to learn to trust God through the questions, in spite of the questions."

# CHAPTER 56
## 10:31 AM

"Billy, are you sure we have talked to everyone who was working on Sunday night?" McCauley asked the little, red-headed manager of Blueberry Hill.

"I think so," Billy said. Then he paused. "Wait. Did you talk to Jose? He was out sick yesterday."

"Jose? What is his last name?" McCauley asked as he looked at the list of employees.

"Mendez, Jose Mendez," Billy replied. "He works in the kitchen."

"Nope. We did not speak with him. When does he come in again?"

"You're in luck. He's working this morning," Billy said pointing into the kitchen. "Jose is that big guy right over there."

McCauley and Marino headed for the kitchen.

"Jose Mendez?" McCauley asked as he walked up to the big cook in the corner.

"I am Jose. Who wants to know?" Jose glared at McCauley.

"I am detective McCauley and this is detective Marino," McCauley said flashing his badge. "Please come over here so we can ask you a few questions."

"Hey, I have my Green Card," Jose said.

"No, nothing like that. We're looking for the man who shot the preacher next door at Grace City Church on Sunday night. When you were working Sunday night, did you see anything unusual?

"Let me see… Sunday night… I was cooking that night and as I remember, it was slow. On my break, I stepped out behind the restaurant to back to get some fresh air and have a cigarette."

"See anything?"

"There is a homeless guy that has been sleeping at the end of the alley by those trash bins," Jose pointed. "He came over here and got in the dumpster looking for food. I personally don't care if they get food out of there because we throw a lot of good stuff out every night. But, homeless people in the parking lot is bad for business. The boss doesn't like it."

Jose lowered his voice. "Don't tell the boss this, but I called him over here, told him I'd leave the lock off the dumpster and he could dumpster dive all he wanted after we closed at eleven. Then I chased him off," Jose continued. "He went back over to those big garbage bins by the alley. Then he crawled between them and laid down. I think he said his name was Johnny or Tommy. Something like that."

*

"So, Ezekiel what brings you over to my world today?" Ezekiel's brother Ezra asked when Zeke met him at the hospital. Ezra worked as a facilities manager at the hospital overseeing routine maintenance. He was a little taller and thicker than his older brother, not as strong and lean. People said that he was the softhearted, sensitive, more gullible brother. As boys, he had idolized his older brother Ezekiel. After their father had died, he had wanted to be like his big brother and try gang life. But Ezekiel wouldn't let him. "You take care of Mom," Ezekiel had said. "I'll take care of the money." Ezra was married to a very sweet Christian lady and they had two little girls.

"I haven't spent much time with you lately," Zeke said. "It hit me the other day that I never really saw where you worked. I thought that since we are slow at work this week, and it is Christmas time, I should reconnect with my family. So, I thought that maybe on your break you could show me all around the hospital and show me what you do."

"Really?" Ezra asked.

*He is still like a big, clueless, puppy*, Zeke thought. *We are never that slow for Christmas.*

"You want to see what I do? Are you sure?" Ezra asked. "It is nothing exciting."

"Absolutely," Zeke said. "You are a big man in the facilities department and it's about time I saw what you did."

"Ok, I'd love to show you around. We don't have to wait till break. You can go with me now... all day if you want. Let's go," Ezra said eagerly.

*

Old Johnny Mulholland shrunk back between the garbage bins when he saw the men in suits flashing police badges.

"Excuse me, sir, I am Detective Marino, and this is Detective McCauley. Can we ask you a few questions?"

"I didn't do anything," Johnny said.

"No, we have questions about the shooting the other night."

"I didn't do anything."

"We don't think you did," Marino said. "Come out here and tell us what you know about the shooting."

"Why are you talking to me?" Johnny asked.

"Jose at the diner said you had been sleeping here lately," Marino said less patiently. "Look, we don't care about that. We want to know if you saw anybody coming down this alley between six thirty and seven o'clock on Sunday night."

"Maybe."

"Maybe?"

"Is there reward money in it?"

"There could be. But there also could be an arrest for vagrancy," Marino said. "So, did you see anybody come down this alley Sunday night? If so, what did he look like?"

Johnny frowned and mumbled something under his breath.

"What was that?" Marino asked.

"Ok, I saw a guy," Johnny said.

"Go on."

"He was kind of a short guy. He had a dark coat and a hat. He came down the alley from out of that old office complex," Johnny said, pointing toward where Grace City was housed.

McCauley and Marino nodded to each other.

"Go on," Marino said.

"He kind of ambled along like he was pretending to be drunk, or high, or something. But when he hit the street he looked around and quickly walked down the street and got in his car."

"You saw him get in a car?

"It was big, an SUV I think."

"Did you get the license plate number?"

Johnny frowned and raised an eyebrow, "No."

"Did you see anything distinctive about the vehicle?" Marino pressed.

"No…" Johnny paused, thinking. "… wait, yes. The car had a small, silver skull on the back bumper."

# CHAPTER 57

## 11:15 AM

"Thank you for taking my call, Most High Priestess Matilda," Rose said nervously toward the phone on her desk.

"Yes," the old witch's voice screeched. No one knew how old Matilda was, but her leathery face was ridged with deep crags and creases. Her nose was slightly hooked, and she even had a wart on her chin. She wore black lace as she sat in a Victorian-style parlor under a crystal chandelier. The walls were filled with old photographs in elaborate frames. Her thin, right hand was covered with a black, lace glove in which she held the receiver of an old-time phone whose base sat on an elegant marble-topped table.

Matilda was a legend in the world of witchcraft. Her supposed supernatural powers set her apart from the others. The moral downfalls of pastors, the stunning reversals of political elections, and even unexpected military victories or defeats were attributed to the potency of Matilda's curses and spells. She lived alone in a penthouse apartment on a hill in the heart of Rome close to the Vatican.

"Most High Priestess. I have Victor Laurent with me on speaker phone," Rose said, smiling nervously and looking at Victor.

"Hello, High Priestess, Matilda," Victor said with a loud voice and syrupy smile. "As always, it is an honor to speak with you."

"Yes, yes. You don't have to yell. I am not deaf!' Matilda replied coldly. "Let's cut the chit chat. How can I help you, my children?"

"We hate to trouble you, but we really need some advice," Rose began anxiously. "Have you heard about the preacher who got shot here in Las Vegas on Sunday night?"

"Of course, I have heard; it was all over the news."

"Well, the good news is that we got him shot."

"And the bad news?" Matilda asked.

"The bad news is, we can't seem to get him to die or stay dead."

"I see. How did you "get him shot?" Matilda asked with sarcasm dripping off her lips.

"He has been one of my assignments. My coven has been cursing him and his ministry for some time now. Eventually it broke through, I guess, and a man walked right into church and shot him."

"But he didn't die?" Matilda asked.

"No, Most High Priestess. So, my coven and Victor's met in a special session. I did the basic death curse," Rose continued. "It worked. We have a nurse on the inside who said that the preacher's temperature went sky high and his vital signs crashed. So, for all practical purposes, he should have died."

"But he didn't die?" Matilda's voice was raising.

"No, he made a remarkable recovery," Rose was flustered. "So, we asked Victor and his coven to help."

"We did the Fire and Death Curse," Victor said. "I also did the Thorn in the Heart of the Rose. That one has never failed me."

"And…?"

"He did die briefly on the table," Victor said meekly. "But he revived."

"He revived!" Matilda roared. "He revived! I would think that you two could at least kill one little preacher. Seems the Evil One is propping him up."

"Yes," Rose and Victor said in unison.

"What do we do with a stubborn one that won't die?" Matilda mused. "Let me think..." silence filled the room as the clock steadily tick-tocked the seconds.

"I got it! You two are in luck. December 25 is a full moon," Matilda said triumphantly.

"That's right..." Victor nodded.

"The one you want dead is a preacher, right? Oh this is perfect," Matilda said gleefully. "You have not done a blood sacrifice, yet. Am I correct?"

"No, or I mean yes," Rose said. "Yes, we have done no blood sacrifice."

"There is the full moon on Christmas night. While Christians celebrate the birth of the hated Nazarene, you will have a black mass and celebrate the death of that preacher," Matilda beamed in satisfaction.

"Of course, Victor, you will have to shed some of your own blood."

"Gladly, Most High Priestess," Victor said, frowning at Rose.

"And you will have to slaughter a lamb," Matilda said.

"Slaughter a lamb... I see.... Yes, yes!" Victor laughed, "Most High Priestess, it's perfect. You have done it again," Victor gushed.

"Oh Matilda, I mean Most High Priestess, I just knew you'd have the answer we needed," Rose said.

*

"What's in here?" Ezekiel asked Ezra. They were walking into a darker section of the basement of the hospital. Zeke noticed that the checkered tile floor was more worn and faded in this section.

"This is the old section of the hospital," Ezra said. "It's the first part they built.

"In there is where they keep the HVAC units for the old section of the hospital," he said pointing to a dark metal door. "They aren't used as much now, but they keep them on hand as a back-up I guess."

"We need to replace the HVAC in our offices at Esquire. Can we go look?" Ezekiel asked.

"Sure," Ezra said. "But there is not much to see. Just some heavy, old HVAC units. They kept them down here in the basement back then, before they started putting them up on the roof."

Ezra opened the door and hit the light switch. A few bare lightbulbs lit up the room.

"So, these vents still work?" Zeke said pointing overhead.

"Yes, they lead directly into the rooms."

"What rooms are over top of us?" Ezekiel asked.

"Rooms 100 to 125 on the first floor, 200 to 225 on the second, 300 to 325 on the third, and rooms 400 to 425 on the fourth floor," Ezra.

"Is the ICU above us?" Zeke asked.

"No, but the Step Down Unit is. It's on the second floor."

## CHAPTER 58

## 11:50 AM

Everyone was restless and excited in the lunchroom at school. Christmas break started in three hours, but Caleb Browning's thoughts were elsewhere. Questions flooded his mind:

*How is Dad doing?*

*Is Mom ok?*

*How will the Christmas Eve service at church go tomorrow night without Dad?*

*How'll we celebrate Christmas this year with Dad in a coma in a hospital bed?*

*Will Titus understand?*

*Is Dad going to make it?*

*What if he doesn't?*

*

"Maria, are you ok?" Stephanie asked. "You have an odd look on your face."

"Oh, sorry, I must have zoned out," Maria said. "I was just thinking that for some reason I as if this Christmas will be very, very significant for Ezekiel."

"How so?"

"I'm not sure. But I just feel like something is going on, something big."

"I would say that you are crazy," Stephanie said. "But, you always seem to be right about those strange feelings of yours."

*

"Ezra, let me buy you lunch," Ezekiel said as he slipped his arm over his brother's shoulders. They were walking into the crowded hospital cafeteria.

"Are you sure, big brother?" Ezra asked.

"Yes, I want to thank you for letting me shadow you this morning," Ezekiel replied.

"Well, I hope you weren't bored. It can't be fun for you to inspect vents, change filters, crawl around the basement, and climb on the roof.."

"It was more fun *and* interesting than you will ever know," Ezekiel said with a sly grin.

*

Daniel was dreaming. Again. he saw the old-time, sepia background. He also saw the little storefront Spanish church, but it was not filled with joy and expectancy like his last dream. The little family stood quietly across the front. The mother wore a black dress. They were lined up next to a casket.

Inside the casket, Daniel saw the father-and-pastor lying stiff and pale, dressed in his finest suit.

There was a line of people quietly giving their condolences as they processed slowly by the family.

The oldest son, who appeared to be about twelve now, was looking up into the face of a large, fleshy, man in a cheap shiny suit. The man put his hand on the boy's shoulder and looked him in the eyes. Even though the man spoke in Spanish, Daniel could understand what he was saying. "Ezekiel, you are the man of the house now. It is your job to take care of your mother and brothers and sisters."

The boy gulped and nodded.

*Poor kid looks petrified,* Daniel thought.

# CHAPTER 59
## 1:00 PM

"I got it!" Marino said with a triumphant grin. He and McCauley were back at their desks in the police station.

"You got what?" McCauley asked without looking up.

"The homeless guy said he saw the man get into a black SUV with a small silver skull on the back bumper, right?" Marino said. "Well, I knew that sounded familiar. When I used to work North Central Metro, there were several limousine companies in our precinct. I think they all had black SUVs, but only one company had silver skulls on their back bumpers."

"Good work," McCauley said looking at Marino. "So, which limo company had skulls?"

*"That* I don't remember," Marino said.

"Well, you have given us a good place to start," McCauley turned back to his computer. He quickly punched up a listing of limousine companies in Las Vegas.

"Do any of these seem familiar?" McCauley asked as he began reading. "A-1? Airport? Atlas? Ball? Best? Celebrity?" McCauley looked at Marino. "Any of those ring a bell?"

"Most of them do. There are a lot of limo companies in the North Central Metro Precinct," Marino said.

"How about Crown?" McCauley continued. "Destiny, Esquire? Executive? Excellence?

"Wait. That might be it."

"Excellence?" McCauley asked as he wrote it down.

"No, Executive," Marino said. "Oh, I am not sure. Keep going."

"Five Star? King? Las Vegas? Lewis? Luxury?"

"I don't know. There are too many."

"Just a few more," McCauley said. "Monarch?  Presidential? Queen? Regal? Star? Tip Top? VIP?"

"If I had to choose, I'd say it's either Crown, Executive, Regal, or VIP."

"Let's check some addresses," McCauley said, typing on his keyboard. As their addresses came up on the screen, he squinted.

"Are any of these addresses in North Central Metro?" He turned his screen to Marino.

"Let me see," Marino said, squinted at the screen. "Yeah, they all are."

"Let's call them and ask which one has a skull."

"Wait. That might tip off the shooter. They aren't far. Let's drive over and see for ourselves. We may just catch a shooter."

## CHAPTER 60
## 1:45 PM

"Hey, honey," Ezekiel said into his phone. The voices were driving him to action.

*You better fix this.*

*You better kill that preacher this time.*

*You are running out of time.*

"Maria, I have a quick question. Is your pastor still in the ICU?" Ezekiel asked.

"They moved him to the Step Down Unit on the second floor. Room 217. I was going by to see his wife, Rebecca, on my way home from work," Maria said.

"Did you say, 'Step Down Unit'?" Ezekiel asked trying to cover the excitement he felt.

"Yes. Why do you want to know? Are you going to visit?" Maria was puzzled by Ezekiel's request.

"No, but I thought about having my company send him flowers," Ezekiel said.

"Ezekiel. That is *so* sweet. You *must* be getting in the Christmas spirit," Maria was shocked. *Send him flowers?*

"Oh, I still hate Christmas. But it might be good for business one day."

"Oh, Ezekiel, you aren't as unfeeling as you let on," Maria said. "Will you be home for dinner?"

"Yeah. About 5:30 PM."

The one thing Ezekiel rarely did was lie to Maria. She was too good of a person to lie to. But the voices were persistent.

*If you ever want her back, you better lie to her.*

*Otherwise she will go back to that preacher.*

*He has been brainwashing her and the kids.*

*You must set them free.*

*You must kill the preacher.*

Zeke was in his office, sitting at his desk with the door closed. In front of him was a computer screen with a map of Paradise Hospital and a legal pad with a sketch of the floor plan.

"The Step Down Unit…the Step Down Unit," he said quietly as he stared at the map of the hospital. "There it is."

"Room 217. Room 217. Got it," he smiled. "Perfect!" he began writing on the legal pad. "This might not be as hard as I thought," he said to himself.

\*

Slowly, Marino pulled the dark, blue, unmarked Ford Taurus into the small parking lot outside the offices of Crown Limo. As he and McCauley got out of their car, they looked toward the shiny black limos parked across from them behind a high chain link fence. Of the various limo companies in the area, Crown had the smallest fleet. The customer had only three types of vehicles to choose from. Crown had six or seven of the ten-passenger stretch limos, several Lincoln Town Car corporate sedans, and a few luxury, Chevy Suburban SUVS.

As McCauley and Marino got closer, they could see that there was a small, golden crown on the lower right side of each bumper.

"No skulls," McCauley said "… just crowns."

"Yeah," Marino said heading back toward the driver side of the unmarked police car. "Let's go to Executive. It's just down the street."

*

"Jason, are you ready?" Victor said to his assistant, a dapper young man in his mid-thirties who was seated in a chair across from Victor. Victor sat behind a massive desk in an ornate office of Hedge Thorn Antiques. He owned a group of lucrative Pawn shops and for fun he operated the antiques store in old Las Vegas. The store also served as a warehouse for the witchcraft stuff he sold online, and a meeting place for his coven.

"I am ready," Jason said as held up his iPad.

"First, we can't meet on Sunrise Mountain since it has been thoroughly violated by that Christian group," Victor templed his fingers in thought. "I was thinking that Bucks Mountain a bit north of Sunrise is very isolated. It's mostly just Federal land that some ranchers use. You need to scout it out today, ASAP."

"Got it," Jason nodded.

"Second, as soon as we are finished meeting, you need to contact *these* people," Victor said handing Jason a small piece of notebook paper with names listed on it. "We need the A team. There will be Rose and I, plus yourself, plus these five warlocks from this coven. I also had Rose give me the names of the five top witches from her coven. And there are a few alternates."

Victor looked at Jason and raised his eyebrows and leered, "I hope the women are young enough so that we can enjoy an orgy after." Victor and Jason laughed.

"Tell them all that this is *top priority*," Victor said as he knocked his fist on his desk.

"We will meet at Rose's store at 9:00 PM and drive out in her minibus," Victor continued. Jason nodded as he recorded the instructions.

"Tell the people on this list that they need to bring their special caped robes."

"On the drive out, we will prep them for the set-up and the logistics of the Black Mass Blood Offering."

"The Black Mass Blood Offering?" Jason asked.

"Yes, Matilda suggested it. I'm glad she did. It should do that preacher in once and for all," Victor pounded his desk. "Also, here is a list of what we'll need," Victor said handing Jason another sheet of spiral notebook paper with writing on it.

Jason read through the list:

"A large goblet - check."

"The special large black candles - check.

"A lighter - check.

"The altar bell that was stolen from a Catholic church - check."

"The sacred silver saber - check."

"13 small, thin, easily breakable crosses - check."

"Sir, I can get all of that rather easily," Jason said. "But these last two items. Am I reading this correctly: a strong rope and a small white lamb?"

"You are correct," Victor smiled.

"Sir, does this mean what I think this means?" Jason asked.

"A blood sacrifice of a lamb," Victor said, raising his hands with a flourish. "It will be glorious!"

"Very good," Jason said with a huge smile. "Very good."

"Of course, you will need to drive separately with the equipment and the lamb in the black van."

"Yes, sir," Jason saluted. "I'll get right on it."

# CHAPTER 61
## 3:05 PM

All four of the Browning boys, along with Travis, piled into Doris Garcia's SUV. She had Christmas music on the radio. "It's Beginning to Look a Lot Like Christmas" played through the speakers.

*It does not feel like Christmas*, Elijah thought. He was sitting behind the driver, deep in thought as he looked out the windows at people walking down the sidewalk in shorts. He had spent the first seven years of his life in Ohio where it was cold and even snowy around Christmas. Sunny and 62 degrees, like it was today in Las Vegas, did not feel like Christmas. Then again, with his dad in the hospital, it did not feel much like Christmas anyway.

"Did you boys have a good day at school?" Doris asked cheerfully.

"Yes, ma'am," they all replied politely.

"Okay. I talked with your mom and this is the plan. First, I'm driving the Browning boys to the hospital so you all can see your dad."

"Even me?" Titus asked eagerly.

"Yes, honey, even you," Doris said. "Then we are going to get you guys something to eat."

"Where?" Zach asked. He was a picky eater.

"How about a hamburger at In-and-Out Burger?" she asked.

"Yay!" all five boys yelled.

"And a milk shake?" Caleb asked.

"Yes, a milkshake."

"Did you know they have Bible verses on their cups?" Zach asked her.

"Yes, Travis pointed it out to me," Doris said. "John 3:16 was on the bottom lip of my cup."

"Pretty cool, for a hamburger place in Las Vegas," Elijah said.

"After we eat, we are going shopping at the Boulevard Mall so you can get your mom a present. Do you have any ideas about what you want to get her?" Doris asked.

"Dad usually gives us ideas for what to get Mom," Zach said quietly. "Oh," Zach said when he realized that Dad would not be giving them any ideas this year.

The van grew silent.

*

Zeke opened his office door and walked by Javier. "I'm heading out. I've got to get a few more Christmas presents," Zeke said. He went out the back door and climbed into his black, Cadillac Escalade. A few months ago, he had upgraded several of his current SUV limos. As a result, the Cadillac dealer gave him a great price on this loaded, big, black Escalade. Technically, it belonged to the company, but everyone knew it was his.

*I love this car*, he thought as he leaned back in the rich, leather seat.

*The only way to keep it is to kill the preacher*, the voices said.

*Go kill the preacher.*

He started the engine, checked the mirrors, and carefully pulled out onto Sixth Street and headed south toward Charleston. He kept the big vehicle spotless inside and out. He rarely even let his kids ride in it. This baby was his reward for being a good business man.

*Yes, I love this car*, he thought as he turned the radio on 97.5 KEVG "Blazing Today's Hottest Hip Hop."

*You need to kill the preacher,* the voices were saying.

*You need to kill the preacher on Christmas.*

"That's why I'm here," Zeke said out loud as he pulled his SUV to a stop in the parking lot of the Home Depot. He pulled out his legal pad and checked a list of the equipment he would need Friday night.

*

"McCauley and Marino quietly got out of the car in the parking lot of Executive Limo. They headed back toward the fleet. Before they could go very far, a very big, well-muscled, man with a shaved head, a long black beard and wearing a leather vest came out the back door to greet them.

"What do you guys want?" Baldhead asked.

"I am Detective McCauley and this is Detective Marino," McCauley said as he flashed his badge. "We just need to look at the back bumper of the cars in your fleet."

"What are you looking for?" Baldhead asked.

"We'll know when we see it," Marino said.

"Look, I am a retired cop," the big man said, holding out his hand and smiling. "Name is James Tucker. I was on the NYPD for twenty years until I retired in 2005. My brother-in-law bought this company six years go, and we try to run it clean and by the book. If something is not right with one of my drivers, I want to know."

"Let me unlock the gate," Tucker continued as he pulled out his keys. "Feel free to look at all our vehicles inside and out. We also have two vehicles picking up clients right now and five getting ready to go to the airport soon."

As he pushed open the gate protecting the limos, Tucker looked at Marino, "So why are you guys looking at the back bumper of limos? Was there a hit and run?"

"Nothing like that. We are looking for the guy who shot the preacher the other night," Marino said while he and McCauley gauged Tucker's reaction.

"You don't think someone here had anything to do with that shooter, do you?"

"We don't know," Marino said. "That's why we are here."

"Like I said, we try to run this place clean and by the book. I'll do anything I can to help you. Is there anything in particular that you are looking for?" Tucker asked.

"A witness said that he saw a man fitting the shooter's description leaving the alley by the church and getting in a black SUV, possibly a Cadillac Escalade," Marino continued talking to McCoy as McCauley examined the vehicles. "The back bumper of the SUV had a small, silver skull."

"As you can see," Tucker said gesturing toward the back of his limos. "All of our cars have the word *Executive* written in gold on the *left* side just above the bumper. No skulls."

"I see that. Thanks," McCauley said.

"But," Tucker continued. "I do know who *does* have skulls - Esquire. Sometimes people get us confused with them. I have heard from some of our drivers that they are a bit shady over there."

"Esquire? Where are they located?"

"They are over on Sixth Street, about a block from the Stratosphere Casino. I bet you find your skull over there."

## CHAPTER 62
### 3:15 PM

McCauley and Marino pulled into the parking lot of the Esquire Limousine Company and headed toward the fence surrounding the fleet.

All the vehicles were parked under an overhang to protect them from the sun. The fleet was larger than Crown's, with more options. Along with ten-passenger stretch limos, they also had a couple of Hummer stretch limos, a few Lincoln Town cars, a 36-passenger party bus, and three, big, black Cadillac Escalade SUVs. The way they were parked, the detectives couldn't see the bumpers on the Escalades. But other vehicles, the ones they could see, had small silver skulls on the lower left bumpers.

"Let's go inside and see if someone will let us in to look at the back bumpers of those Escalades," McCauley said heading toward the office door.

As they entered, Javier at the front desk was packing up to leave.

"I'm Detective Marino and this is Detective McCauley," Marino said, flashing his badge.

Javier frowned and put his papers down. "How can I help you?"

"We need you to open up your fence and let us get a look at the back bumpers of your Cadillac Escalades," McCauley said.

"Why?" Javier asked.

"We think one of your vehicles was associated with a crime."

"What type of crime?" he asked skeptically. "A hit and run?"

"No," Marino answered brusquely.

"So, what type of crime?" Javier persisted. He assumed that they were referring to the drugs many of the drivers were selling to clients. He was surprised the cops were bothering them about the drugs though. Zeke had said everything was clear. The Collective had handled it.

"Let's just go look at those cars," Marino growled as he towered over Javier.

Javier reached in his desk and pulled out a large set of keys, then got up and headed to the fenced area. "How do you know it was one of our cars? Someone see a license plate?" Javier asked as he led them to the fenced area.

"Something like that," Marino said, coyly.

Javier unlocked the fence and led them around to the back where the Escalades were parked. "Here they are."

"Bingo!" McCauley said, nodding at Marino.

"I see that all of your cars have skulls," Marino said. "Why skulls?"

"Our owner likes them. He thinks the skulls look classy. Any problem with that?"

"Not for us," Marino said.

"Can you show us the drivers' records for Sunday night? We need to know where all of your cars were and at what time."

"Yes, it's on my computer back in the office," Javier replied.

After getting back to his desk, Javier punched his key board. "Give me a second," Javier said. After a few strokes of the keyboard, he said, "Here they are. These are the records for Sunday night. Want me to print it out for you?"

Staring at the screen he frowned. "It looks like all of our cars were either here on the lot or in service in other parts of the city on Sunday night," he said.

"Did you file these?" McCauley asked.

"No, Zeke did. He's the owner. Juan usually works Sunday nights, but Zeke let him have a night off. So, he covered for him."

"Is Zeke, here? Can we talk to him?"

"He just left," Javier said.

*

Titus was holding Rebecca's hand as they slowly entered Daniel's room. His little eyes were big when he saw all the machines surrounding his father, the mask Daniel was wearing, and all of the IVs running in and out of his body.

"It's okay, honey," Rebecca said. "Those things are helping Daddy."

"Is that really Daddy?" he asked.

"Yes, honey. He is very, very sick right now."

"Is he going to get better?"

Rebecca sighed. She gave him a tired smile and said, "Lots of people all over the world are praying that Daddy will get better."

"That's good. Right, Mommy?" Titus asked.

"Yes, honey, that is very good."

*

Daniel dreamed of his family gathered around the kitchen table in their house in Las Vegas. There were bowls of food on the table and the boys were filling their plates. Everyone was there, Rebecca, Elijah, Caleb, Zach, and Titus. The five of them were smiling and laughing.

Daniel saw himself seated at the head of the table. He leaned back, took a deep, contented breath, and smiled with satisfaction. He loved it when they were all together, all healthy, and all happy.

*

When Zach entered the room, he walked straight up to Daniel.

"Go ahead. Talk to him, Zach. We don't know if he can hear us, but I know that it helps," Rebecca said.

"Dad, we miss you a lot," Zach began. "My brothers and I have been staying at the Garcias' this week. It's pretty good, but we would rather be home."

He looked at Rebecca, turned his palms over and shrugged.

"Go ahead," she said softly, "you're doing a good job."

He shrugged again and started, "Mrs. Garcia is going to take us to In-and-Out Burger when we leave here. Mom said that they feed you with a tube. I don't think I'd like that. I usually get a vanilla shake, but today I'm going to get a strawberry shake in honor of you, 'cause I know you always get strawberry."

"Then we are going to get Mom a Christmas present. I wish you could talk and could tell us what to get her."

"We don't have to go to school tomorrow or Friday 'cause of Christmas. Mrs. Garcia said we could sleep in. We might help at the homeless brunch at the Outreach Center tomorrow. Then we are coming to see you."

"Tomorrow night is Christmas Eve. Elijah says it will be weird without you and Mom there. I have to sing a song on stage with Titus and the other little kids. Caleb gets to sing with the big kids."

"We're all sad that you got shot and have been sick and have to live in the hospital."

"Everyone at school keeps asking about you and they are all praying for you."

Then he looked at Rebecca and shrugged.

"Okay. Well. This has been Zach. Over and out."

*

Daniel dreamed of his house again. It was night.

He walked upstairs to the bedroom where Zach and Titus slept. It must have been Zach's night because he sat down beside him in his bed.

"So, Zach tell me something special about your day or week."

Zach's eyes got big. "Promise to not tell Mom?"

"I promise not to tell her unless it is something she absolutely has to know."

"Promise not to get mad?"

"I promise, unless it is something that I have to get mad about."

"Okay," Zach said eagerly. "I got in a fight at school."

"You did? Did you get in trouble?"

"No. If I did they would have called Mom."

"I guess you are right," Daniel said. "What happened?"

"I was in the bathroom and a fourth grader, Dex Crawford, made fun of me. He had been picking on me all year. I told him to stop it, and he shoved me."

"What did you do?"

"I smashed him right in the nose," Zach said with a grin.

"Did he cry?"

"You bet! Plus, it started to bleed," Zach said proudly.

"How come you didn't get in trouble?"

"I definitely wasn't going to tell anybody 'cause I didn't want to get in trouble. And Dex wasn't going to tell anybody that he got beat up by a third grader," Zach said. "So he told people he fell in the bathroom."

Daniel tried not to smile but he couldn't help it. He knew he should not be proud of his son for fighting, but he was proud that he stood up for himself against a bigger, older bully.

## CHAPTER 63
### 4:23 PM

"Not bad, not bad at all. This might work," Zeke said to himself as he tried on a salt-and-pepper wig in Cleopatra's Thrift Store. Cleopatra's was a used clothing and accessories store on Main Street in old downtown Las Vegas.

He put the wig in the shopping cart and looked at his legal pad. Then he looked at his watch.

*If I hurry I can still make it. Las Vegas Medical uniforms doesn't close till 6:00 PM.*

## CHAPTER 64

## 7:15 PM

As she had done all week, Rebecca gave each of the boys an extra-large hug as they prepared to leave. "You guys did a great job of talking to your dad. I know that even if he can't hear it, he feels it. I know that it helps make him stronger. I am very proud of each of you."

"We'll be here tomorrow afternoon and all day on Christmas," Elijah said.

"Yes, I can't wait!" Rebecca said

"Dad is going to wake up for Christmas," Zach announced.

Rebecca was taken aback by his impromptu announcement. She looked at Zach and said, "Yes, dear, we *hope* that he will."

"He will, Mom. You'll see," Zach was adamant.

Rebecca nodded. She was stunned by Zach's bold confidence.

After the boys left, the room felt especially empty and lonely. Rebecca's eyes teared up.

*I don't want them to leave every night*, she thought. *I just want to be a family, in our house, all together, with everyone healthy. That's all I want for Christmas.*

There was a gentle tap at the door to Daniel's room. Four young ladies stealthily tiptoed into the room. They carried simple strands of garland, strands of little white lights, red velvet bows, and a large gift bag. One-by-one they gave Rebecca big hugs.

"This room looks so sterile," said Chelsea, Pastor Matthew's wife. She had on a green, elf hat.

"So, we thought we'd give it a bit of Christmas spirit!" Danielle stage-whispered excitedly. She had silly reindeer horns on her head and was wearing a truly ugly Christmas sweater.

Rebecca noticed that they all had on ugly Christmas sweaters. "Wow! You girls are definitely styling tonight. I *love* those sweaters," Rebecca laughed.

"Glad you like them. We brought one for you," Shun-Chin grinned. She wore a Santa hat. She handed Rebecca the bag.

Rebecca reached into the bag and smiled. She pulled out a bright red, white and green sweater, with big white snowflakes randomly arranged on it. The snowflakes had glitter in the middle. She tilted her head back and laughed.

All the ladies laughed.

"I *love* it!" Rebecca said.

"We hope it is okay that we came," Destiny said. "Our Life Group wasn't meeting tonight, so, a few of us got together and thought we'd come and bring you a bit of Christmas cheer."

"I am so glad you did. It's been a long week of sitting in this room. Thank you *so* much." Rebecca said, hugging her. "I needed to laugh. I *really* needed to laugh."

*

Daniel was dreaming again. He and Rebecca were at Jennings's Dairy restaurant. It was their second or third date. They were eating crepes with strawberry filling and whipped crème. He had whipped crème on the end of his nose and she was laughing at him.

But his focus was solely on her.

*This girl is so much fun,* he thought. *When she smiles, she glows. She is smart and witty. She is confident and strong, but she is also very kind and sweet. I want to spend the rest of my life with this girl.*

He reached to wipe the whipped crème off his nose, but instead knocked over his water glass. Rebecca tilted her head back and laughed even louder.

\*

"Remarkable," Dr. Kim said. "Truly remarkable." He shook his head and smiled at Rebecca. "His breathing is excellent."

"I know you will say that you don't know, but I have to ask. Do you think he will come out the coma soon?" Rebecca asked.

"As you said, we don't know. But he looks so much better than he did yesterday morning when I was in here before his operation."

He turned slightly to walk out and then he paused to turn around. "I am going to have them take the breathing tube out of his mouth. Let's see how he does without the ventilator. That will make him more comfortable."

"Are you sure?" Rebecca asked.

"Yes," he smiled at Rebecca. "Consider that my early Christmas present."

# CHAPTER 65
## 9:37 PM

Daniel was seeing the young Hispanic boy again in his dreams. The boy stood nervously in a dark room in front of a desk. Behind the desk sat a large, heavily tattooed man in a sleeveless, white tee-shirt.

"You got just one shot. Sell this stuff and bring me the money. Every penny of it," the large man sneered at the boy. "I'll give you your cut out of what you bring back."

Anxiously, the boy nodded.

"Now get out of here!"

*

It seemed to happen every night that week. Every time Rebecca tried to close her eyes and rest, her old nemesis, fear, came rolling into her head spewing reasons to be afraid.

*You know he's going to die. No one can survive three bullets in the chest.*

*He already died in the OR and the next time he won't revive.*

*After these doctor's bills come in, you'll be left penniless. There'll be no money for Christian school for the boys, let alone college. A single mom cannot raise four active boys, especially in this city. Your mom and dad have only a small house. You can't stay with them.*

Rebecca tried to fight back in prayer, but she was too tired. "Jesus help me," was about all she could whisper.

But fear persisted. Negative thoughts kept rolling through her mind.

*The shooter is still out there. No one is guarding the door. He could walk right in here and shoot you both. Then what'll the boys do?*

*Daniel will probably wake up brain dead. You'll have to take care of him like a little baby for the rest of his life.*

For the last several years Rebecca had enjoyed victory over her fear. As she experienced more and more of God's love, she found that God's love drove fear away. As she learned to walk in the Spirit in more and more situations, she found that God did not give her a spirit of fear, but of love, power, and the discipline to control her thoughts.

But this was different.

Yes, her counselor had helped her go back to the day when her sister first got sick. Together in prayer, they asked Jesus to redeem that painful event in her heart. She told fear and all its awful friends to leave for good. That day peace had swept into her heart.

But even though she felt that fear was no longer camped in her head, it never completely left. It was always lingering around, scratching on the door of her mind and peeking in the windows.

On Sunday night, when she saw Daniel lying sprawled out on that stage in the pool of blood, she must have opened the window. Fear had come back. When she tried to close her eyes and rest at night, it rose up in her mind. She felt powerless to stop it.

As the recording of reasons to be afraid played through her mind, it raised doubts about the wisdom, power, and goodness of God. She felt anxious and tense. There was a huge pit in her stomach. Everything felt darker. Negative, hopeless thoughts kept flashing through her mind.

"Enough!" Rebecca burst out. "Freda," Rebecca called out to her friend seated on the other side of the room. "I need you to pray for me. I am struggling with fear."

*

"I'm home", Ezekiel said as he walked in the door from the garage. Maria and Miguel were seated at the kitchen table.

"Did you get Manny's car running?" Maria asked.

"Yes, it wasn't too hard."

"It was nice of you to help him, "Maria said.

"I'd rather help him with his car than give him the twenty bucks I owe him," Ezekiel laughed. Then he looked at Miguel. "You still up?" he asked.

"Just going to bed," Miguel said. "I'm tired. School starts too early."

Then Miguel gave him a big hug. "Good night, Dad," he said.

"Good night, son," Ezekiel replied.

As Miguel turned his back and walked toward his room, Ezekiel was overwhelmed with the reality that that Miguel was becoming a man. In body type, facial features and mannerisms, Miguel was just like Ezekiel.

"Maria, I need to go back out in the garage. I forgot to put my tools away," Ezekiel said. He was engulfed with thoughts about his oldest son.

*I wish I had not missed most of the first eight years of his life because I was in prison. Maria said that he was dying from cancer and that the church prayed for him. She said that he was miraculously healed. But I won't believe it.*

Ezekiel opened the hatch on his SUV and reached in for his tool box.

*When our church prayed for my dad to be healed, God killed him even though he was the preacher. That Christian junk doesn't work. Churches and preachers these days just prey on the weak minds of women and children.*

He put the toolbox in its place on the shelf.

*Miguel probably never had cancer in the first place. The preacher probably just said that to make a show. Maria is so sweet that she got duped by it.*

He paused with his hand on the doorknob back into the house.

*I hate that preacher.*

The voices started up their tormenting chant.

*Kill the preacher. You got to kill the preacher on Christmas.*

*Kill the preacher. You got to kill the preacher on Christmas.*

## THURSDAY, DECEMBER 24

### CHAPTER 66
### 4:30 AM

When the nurse came by to check Daniel's blood sugar level, Rebecca woke up. She saw Daniel sleeping and reached for his hand. She took a deep breath and sighed.

*Will you ever move again? Wil you ever open your eyes?*

*Will you get out of that bed?*

*Am I going to get my over-committed, often distracted, crazy husband back?*

Her chest began to tighten. She felt that familiar cloud of heaviness beginning to form around her.

*Daniel had always said that depression and gratitude cannot live in the same house,* she thought. *When the boys complained, Daniel used to make them tell him ten things they were thankful for before they could give any more complaints. After giving their ten things, they usually couldn't even remember their complaints.*

So, she began to give thanks.

*Father in Heaven, I thank you that you gave us Dr. Kim. They say he is the best surgeon and he is obviously a good man.*

*Thank you for the way our church people have supported us through this challenge.*

*Thank you for my boys and the way they are handling all of this.*

*Thank you for all the people around the country that have prayed for my husband.*

*Thank you that Daniel has beaten death repeatedly this week.*

*Thank you that his vital signs are really good and that he is noticeably stronger.*

She felt the dark cloud lifting. It was replaced by peace. With her other hand, she stroked Daniel's hair.

*Thank you for my husband. It is not always easy being married to him, but he is a good man.*

Then she began to speak to Daniel, "You never promised that we would have it easy, but you did promise we would have an adventure. Boy, have we had an adventure! Most of it has been good, some of it not so good."

"Before the kids came, you dragged me all over the world on mission trips. After the kids came, you dragged me all over the country so you could speak at student camps. We have not had much money, but we have had a lot of fun," she said, smiling.

"The last seven years here in Las Vegas, we have had a lot of blood, sweat, and tears. But we have seen a lot of lives changed. So *please* get better."

"I can't wait to look into your eyes again."

"I can't wait to lie in bed and laugh after the kids go to bed."

"I can't wait to watch you coaching our boys again."

"I can't wait to hear you preach again."

"I can't wait to hear you sing, loudly and slightly off key again."

"And... I can't wait until you hold me again."

\*

Daniel had begun to dream. It was one of those gorgeous spring days in central Ohio. The sun was bright, the flowers were blooming, the grass and trees were lush and green. Daniel saw himself standing in the front of the Community Bible Church in Wooster, Ohio.

The little, red brick church was full of people in their Sunday best who were quietly waiting in eager anticipation.

An acoustic guitar played expertly in the background. At the appointed hour, Benjamin Brooks, Rebecca's brother, brought Daniel's mother down the aisle stage left and seated her in the first row, in front of his other family members and friends. A few moments later, Benjamin returned with Rebecca's mother and seated her stage right, in the first row in front of the rest of Rebecca's family and friends.

Daniel and his groomsmen entered from the side of the platform and took their respective places across the front. One by one, the bridesmaids walked down the aisle and took their places on Daniel's right.

Daniel stood in the front flanked by his three best friends from Mission College - Josiah Lancaster, Micah Miller, and Joshua Jenson. All four of the young men looked quite handsome in their classic black suits. Across from Daniel stood Rachel, Rebecca's younger sister. She looked gaunt and sickly next to the other healthy, young ladies - Hannah, Josiah's wife; Abigail, Josh's fiancé; and Rebecca's cousin, Kaitlyn.

Suddenly the church's little organ pumped out Pachelbel's "Canon in D." Everyone turned and looked to the back of the church.

The first to turn the corner was Rebecca's father, the Rev. Jonathan Brooks. He looked very handsome in a dignified suit and wearing a delighted, but nervous grin. But he was very quickly eclipsed in the brilliance of what came next.

As Daniel watched, everything shifted into slow motion. He gasped at the sight of the most beautiful woman he had ever seen. Slowly, deliberately, confidently, she strode step-by-step down the aisle holding her father's arm. Rebecca's long, thick, chestnut hair lay in shiny curls on her shoulders. She wore little bright, purple flowers in her hair. She wore a white linen gown that fit her athletic figure perfectly. Her strong, tan arms and shoulders seemed to glow as they contrasted with the whiteness of the dress.

Then, the sun broke out as Rebecca caught Daniel's eye and gave him a stunning smile. He gasped at the realization that this wonderful creature walking straight toward him was actually smiling at him.

Time froze. He was caught up in her smile and the room began to spin. Then all went dark.

# CHAPTER 67
## 6:36 AM

*Dear Lord, thank for the many blessings you have given us,* Maria prayed. *Thank you for providing for our needs. Thank you for plenty of food, good clothes, and a safe place to live.*

*Thank for my boys. As always, I especially thank you for healing Miguel. Thank you so much.*

*Please help Pablo not harden his heart to you.*

*Today, I ask you to touch Pastor Daniel in an extra special way. His family needs some hope this Christmas. Please wake up Pastor Daniel this Christmas. Yes, Lord, please wake him up soon. And when you do, please give him all his abilities back.*

*And Lord, yet again I pray for my Ezekiel. The last few weeks he has been distracted and this week he has been very irritable. I thank you that he called me about getting flowers for the pastor. But Lord, something does not seem right about that.*

*Like I said yesterday. I feel like something big is going to happen to him. Make it something good.*

*Please help him drop his bitterness toward you. Please free him of the awful anger.*

*Please, Lord, Please.*

\*

Ezekiel lay in bed sleeping and dreaming of the days when he was a boy and his father was still alive. The two of them were walking out of the church. They saw that a gang had tagged the side of the building with spray paint.

"Those kids did it again," his father said. "If I didn't feel so sorry for them, I'd be really mad at them."

He then looked at Ezekiel, "Son, understand, it's not that they are bad boys as much as they are in bad situations. They are broken boys from broken families. They are looking for acceptance and status in the wrong place. A gang can never substitute for a good family."

"God loves them," he continued. "If they could only see it, the church could be a family for them. We got to love them and make them feel accepted in our church."

He looked Ezekiel square in the eyes and squeezed his shoulder, "But on the other hand, if they ever try to get you to join their gang, you run in the opposite direction. For most of these boys, being in a gang leads to a life of crime, and prison, if not an early death."

Then his father squeezed Ezekiel's shoulder hard and looked at him very seriously, "I would have a hard time forgiving you if you ever joined a gang."

# CHAPTER 68
## 8:15 AM

"Bill, is everything all right? How is MaryAnn?" Rebecca asked the small man standing in the hallway of the ICU massaging his temples and looking lost.

"Not good," Bill croaked. "Not good at all."

Rebecca noticed that he was pale and his hands shook slightly. "The doctor just left. He said that now that she has stopped eating there really is nothing more they can do for her. He said I need to call the kids and let them know that it won't be much longer."

"Oh, Bill, I'm so sorry," she said as she gave him a hug. "Did the doctor give you a time frame?"

"He said that it would be in the next couple of days. I sure hope that it's not on Christmas."

"I am so sorry," she said again.

"I don't know what I am going to do without her. We have been married thirty-three years."

Bill's cell phone rang. "Excuse me, Rebecca: it is one of the kids," he said as he answered the phone.

She nodded and continued down the hall to the machine with water bottles and iced tea.

"A quarter of our patients will not leave the ICU alive," Rebecca heard an older nurse speaking to a young trainee. "Another quarter leave here to go home briefly for hospice care before they die. So, we need to be extra kind and sensitive to our patients, as half of those here at any given time will not live much longer."

Rebecca quickened her pace to get away from their conversation as quickly as possible.

*Oh no*, she thought. *Daniel is probably not going to make it. He won't survive another night like Monday night. He is so weak that he is barely hanging on as it is.*

*Oh God,* she prayed quietly. *What am I going to do?*

She ducked into the restroom and the combination of fatigue and fear overwhelmed her. Her chest was tight and it was hard to breathe. Feeling empty and helpless, she slumped down on her knees unable to stand against the tidal wave of doubt and doom that hit her. She began to sob and it was like a dam burst inside.

"What am I going to do?" she sobbed. "What am I going to do?"

## CHAPTER 69

### 8:40 AM

Like much of Las Vegas, Zeke's company was open for business 365 days a year. Of the forty million tourists last year, a surprising number of people came to Las Vegas at Christmas. Many did not have family or did not celebrate Christmas, so they came to Las Vegas to get away. Most came to gamble and party. A few came to hike at Red Rocks or go to the Grand Canyon. Many of them were potential clients for Zeke.

He and Javier were going to work until noon. Then he'd be working from home on Christmas Day.

"Morning, Boss," Javier said brightly.

"Gramma got Run Over by a Reindeer!" came prancing out of Javier's radio.

"Turn that garbage off," Zeke growled. He hated Christmas music. "Anything important happen after I left yesterday?" Zeke asked, as he always did.

"Mack got a ticket for speeding. Rafael got a flat tire. And the police stopped in."

"Did you say *the police* stopped in?" A burst of adrenaline shot down Zeke's spine.

"Yes. Two detectives. They were looking for the guy who shot the preacher," Javier said.

The hair stood up on Zeke's neck. With studied restraint, he asked, "Why did they come here?

"They wanted to see if we had silver skulls on our cars."

"Why did they care about that?" Zeke's mind was racing as fast as his pulse.

"Someone saw a guy who could be the shooter getting in a black car with a skull."

"What?" Zeke asked a little too excitedly. "Someone saw the shooter get into a black car with a silver skull?"

"That's right," Javier replied.

"What did you tell them?" Zeke asked nervously.

"I told them that all the cars were accounted for Sunday night."

"Good. Did you show them the records?

"Yes. They said they wanted to see you."

"See *me*? When?" Zeke was about to jump out of his skin.

"I told them you'd be in this morning."

"You told them *what*?" Zeke was livid. "Why did you tell them that?"

"I thought you could straighten this out."

Zeke slowly arose from his chair. "I'll straighten you out!" he snarled. His eyes blazed with rage.

Zeke was usually very restrained. But he was known for his violent temper. Javier had only ever seen him this angry twice. Once Zeke caught a driver who tried to steal money and once he caught a driver using a company car to run a small prostitution ring on the side.

The first time he broke the driver's arm. The second time, he busted the driver's head wide open.

Javier was terrified of what Zeke was going to do to him.

Suddenly, the door from the guest parking lot burst opened. Javier was grateful that Zeke was startled and sat back down.

In walked McCauley and Marino.

*

"Pancakes! Yay! I love pancakes!" Titus shouted.

"Thank you, Mrs. Garcia," Elijah said when he saw the stack of pancakes sitting on the breakfast table.

"I thought I'd give you boys a treat for Christmas and you all need a good breakfast before you go see your dad," Doris chuckled. She had on a Christmas apron and Christmas music played on the radio.

"Can you help me put syrup on my pancakes?" Titus asked.

"Of course, I can! I can also help you put on this strawberry topping if you like, with some whipped cream."

"Yay!" Titus yelled. "This is the best breakfast ever."

*It would be,* Elijah thought. *If only Mom and Dad were here.*

*

"Good morning, I am Detective McCauley, and this is Detective Marino. Are you the owner of this business?" McCauley said, showing Zeke his badge.

Zeke glared at Javier, then turned to the officers.

"Yes, sir, I am," Zeke answered professionally. "Would you two like to come into my office and sit down?"

"Thanks," McCauley said, following Zeke in.

"Javier, get these men some coffee," Zeke barked.

"Yes, Boss," Javier replied, meekly.

McCauley started casually, "So, how long have you owned this place?"

"Seven years," Zeke said. "I started seven years ago with one car and built it up from there."

"Congratulations on your hard work," McCauley said.

"Here you go," Javier said, as he entered the office and handed the detectives two steaming cups of coffee. "You guys want sugar?" he asked as he offered them a jar stuffed with sugar packets.

"No thanks," McCauley said.

"I'll take a few," Marino said, grabbing a handful. "Thanks."

"Close the door on your way out," Zeke said. Then he turned his attention to McCauley. "So, what's this about? You know I have some ... friends, right?"

"Yes, we know about the Collective. That's not why we're here," McCauley said. "Sunday night, a man walked into a church and shot the preacher three times in the chest. The shooter escaped out a side door. We have a witness who saw a man matching the description of the shooter get into a black car with a small silver skull on the rear, right side of the bumper."

"I see," Zeke said. His pulse was racing.

"Your assistant said that all of your cars were either in service or sitting in the lot here on Sunday night."

"That's right. Do you think that one of our cars was involved?" Zeke asked.

"That's what we are here to find out," McCauley said. "So, *do* you have any black, Cadillac Escalade SUV's?"

"We have a couple."

"Where were they Sunday night?" McCauley asked.

"Let me look," Zeke said as nonchalantly as possible and turned to his computer. He typed on the keyboard and hit "Enter." He scanned the screen briefly, then turned the screen so they could see it.

"Looks like Car #14 was in service. It made a run to the airport and took clients to the Bellagio. Then it went back to the airport and took clients to the Sapphire. Then back to the airport and took clients to the Wynn. Then it picked up the guys from the Sapphire and took them to the MGM Grand."

"Car #15 was also in service. It picked up clients at the airport and took them to the Crazy Horse Strip Club. Then it went back to the airport and took clients to Coyote Ugly Saloon. Then it went back to the airport and took clients to Caesar's Palace. It picked up a few people at Harrah's and took them to the club at the Aria. Then it picked up the people at Crazy Horse and took them to the Venetian."

"What about the Cadillac Escalade I saw in the owner's parking space when we came in?" McCauley said as he leaned closer.

"That's the one I've been using," Zeke said as the sweat began to roll down his back.

"It had a silver #16 on the door."

"It was in the parking lot on this property with me on Sunday night."

"How do we know that?" Marino asked.

"It says so here in the records," Zeke showed them the screen.

"I see," McCauley said. "Who keeps the record?"

"The manager/dispatcher for that shift."

"So, who kept the records Sunday night?"

"I did," Zeke said as innocently as possible.

The room was filled with silence. McCauley and Marino exchanged glances.

Finally, Zeke broke the silence, "Look, there is also a video record of the parking lot on Sunday night," he said with a smile as he turned back to his computer. "Want to see the video? The black Escalade is parked right there in the owner's spot all night," he said over his shoulder.

McCauley and Marino looked at each other.

"Yes, we will look over the video of Sunday night," McCauley said. "Plus, we'll need to speak to the drivers of the other cars. Get us their contact information," McCauley said. "Something is not matching up."

# CHAPTER 70
## 9:00 AM

"Mrs. B., I have to go off work now," Officer Jackson said. "I need to tell you a few things before I leave."

"What's that, Darrell?" Rebecca asked.

"First, tell your people that I said 'thank you.' The last few nights, your people have brought me cookies, donuts, and hot coffee just the way I like it."

"We do have wonderful people at our church, Darrell. Like they told you, they just wanted you to know that they love you and that God loves you."

"Yes, ma'am. They told me that," Darrell nodded. "Second, thank you for praying for my older daughter. My wife called me last night and told me that Jessica called her last night and they talked for over an hour."

"That's wonderful. I'm so very happy to hear that."

"And the third one, well, I am sorry," Darrell hung his head.

"Sorry for what?"

"The Sergeant called and gave me some bad news," Darrell paused and took a deep breath. "I won't be back on this shift anymore."

"Oh no. I'll miss you, Darrell," Rebecca said, hugging the gray-haired officer. Rebecca struggled to keep her composure.

"Oh, you will be seeing me again. I'm bringing my wife and daughter to your church when your husband is back preaching there," Darrell said.

"I hope so," Rebecca said with a smile.

"But, that's not the worst part."

"Oh?"

"You know that LeRoy Braxton came in and took over the ICU."

"Yes, I know."

"And you know that his being here has created a media circus and that the Sergeant had to put extra officers on duty to protect him from the media and whatever."

"Yes."

"And with this being Christmas and all, even more of his family are coming in today, including his wife Charity and John Rich, his brother-in-law. If you ask me, I think he just wants an excuse to party in Vegas over Christmas."

"John Rich?"

"John Rich plays running back for the Browns. He was league MVP last year when they won the Super Bowl. His coming will create even more of a media circus. Plus, some White Supremacists are coming to protest the way LeRoy got special treatment, and it might get violent outside on the street."

"You have got to be kidding," Rebecca could feel her heart rate rising.

"I wish I was," Officer Jackson said, sadly. "Anyway, the department was already shorthanded since this is Christmas Eve and all. Someone higher than the Sergeant told him that there are not enough officers to post one here protecting Daniel. The sergeant wanted me to tell you that he is very sorry."

"I'd come back and protect him for you, but like I told you, my family is flying out at 11 o'clock this morning to visit my wife's mother and family in Georgia for Christmas."

"So, what does that mean?" Rebecca asked. Fear started to surround her.

"No one is coming to replace me," the sad-faced officer shook his head.

"So, no one will be protecting Daniel?"

"No ma'am. You are on your own."

*

"Ready, Terri?" asked a dark-haired man with a swastika tattooed on his neck. He energetically returned the pistols he was holding to their holsters.

"Yes, Brian. But, I'm so nervous," Terri, a stocky, brunette replied. She also had a pair of pistols on her hips.

"A little nerves are to be expected. But we are prepared. We have been training for this day for nearly a year," Brian said as he picked up a gym bag carrying ammo and other weapons. "Let's go."

Terri picked up a backpack filled with food and ammo and climbed into the passenger seat of their old green van.

"Today, we begin to strike back," Brian said. "Today the Revolution begins!"

# CHAPTER 71
## 9:30 AM

Rebecca was curled up in a big chair next to Daniel's bed. Her Bible and journal were open on the ledge of the window beside her. She quietly prayed.

*Father, I keep trying to replace my fear with faith. But, now I am not only afraid that Daniel won't wake up, but I am also afraid that the shooter will come back to kill him.*

*I know most of my fears are foolish. But this feels very, very real. It is very real that a man shot him Sunday night. It is real that Daniel is still in a coma. It is real that he died yesterday on the operating table. It is real that the man is still out there somewhere.*

*The shooter might be planning to try again. What am I to do?*

*The boys will be here soon and I don't want to make them afraid. But I am struggling with these fears.*

*Help me. Please help me.*

*I believe. Help my unbelief.*

\*

"Brian, look!" Terri said, pointing at a police car outside the Donut Hut on Desert Inn Avenue.

"Good eyes, Terri," Brian said as he turned down the volume of the vitriolic, anti-government rhetoric crying out against the tyranny of the New World Order. He calmly turned into the parking lot and pulled up next to the police car. There were no other cars in the lot. "Those cops are eating their last supper - donuts! How appropriate," he laughed.

Terri smiled nervously.

The van rolled to a stop and he leaned back to grab the gym bag. Then he paused, "Nah, I don't think we'll need it. Ready?"

Terri nodded.

"Let's go. The Revolution begins today!"

Brian jumped out of the van and Terri followed as they headed toward the small shop. Boldly, Brian threw open the front door and strode inside. Terri followed.

"Hello!" the pudgy owner called out happily from behind the counter. "Welcome to Donut Hut."

Brian ignored the man, opened his coat, drew both his pistols, and began shooting at the officers seated at the small table by the window. "Let the Revolution begin!" he yelled as he fired shot after shot into the helpless policemen.

"Let the Revolution begin," Terri screamed as she pulled a pistol with her right hand and shot the stunned owner in the head.

## CHAPTER 72
## 10:00 AM

Rebecca was waiting patiently in the family waiting room of the Step Down Unit. Doris had texted her a few minutes earlier when she arrived at the hospital with the boys to tell her that they had to go the long way into the hospital to avoid the protestors who were outside the main door of the hospital vying for attention.

"Mommy!" Titus yelled as he burst into the waiting area. He ran over to Rebecca and leapt into her arms.

He was followed by Zach, who walked in and presented his head for a kiss.

Then came Caleb, who hugged Rebecca hard.

Then Elijah, looking older every day, she thought.

"They had plenty of help at the homeless brunch, so we decided to leave early and come on over." Caleb said.

"I see. We'll I am glad you did. Did you guys bring some books so you can read?" Rebecca asked.

"We had pancakes for breakfast!" Titus said, "We had pancakes."

"Pancakes?" Rebecca said smiling.

"Mrs. Garcia makes the best pancakes," Titus said.

"I am sure she does," Rebecca said smiling at Doris.

"She put syrup, and strawberry goo, and stuff like that on them," Zach added matter-of-factly. "They are better than yours. You only put healthy honey on the pancakes you make."

Rebecca looked at Doris and laughed. "I'm sure Mrs. Garcia's pancakes are the best in the world."

"I'm sorry, Rebecca," Doris said sheepishly. But then she smiled and added, "But it *is* Christmas Eve."

"We weren't supposed to tell Mom," Caleb glared at Titus and Zach.

"It's ok. I am glad you boys enjoyed them," Rebecca said.

*

"Wow! That was amazing!" Brian yelled as he and Terri got back into the van.

"We did it. We really did it. I can't believe that we did it," Terri said excitedly.

"The best thing is, no one saw us. We are free to create more chaos!"

"Are you sure?" Terri asked skeptically. "Maybe we should wait to see if anyone else takes action."

"'December 24: The Day of Revolution.' You read the blog. One hundred and fifty years ago, the Klan began on Christmas Eve. Today our brothers and sisters will unite and rise up!"

"I know, but what if we're the only ones? It wouldn't be a Revolution if we're the only ones. Since no one saw us, maybe we should wait for some of the others to take action before we do anything else."

*

Zeke sat at his desk trying to concentrate, but the voices in his head were relentless. *Those detectives can tell that you did it. They did not buy your story, or the altered records and video.*

Zeke, clenched both his hands into tight fists. A vein in his forehead became visible.

The voices continued: *You stupid idiot. How did you let anyone see you? Why did you take a car with a skull? Stupid! That makes it easy to track it all back to you. Why did you park the car so close to the church?*

He slammed his right fist into the desk.

*You must kill the preacher. You must kill the preacher. The only way you will ever be free is to kill the preacher.*

The voices in Zeke's head were louder than ever.

Zeke groaned and put his hands over his ears. But the voices would not be silent.

*You better not mess it up. If you do, they will catch you and Zeke will go back to prison. You don't want to go back to prison, do you Zeke?*

Zeke swore. He stood up and jerked open his office door. "Going to get some coffee," he snarled to Javier on the way out the door.

"But we have coffee here," Javier said. "I brought in a special Christmas blend."

"Shut up, Javier," Zeke said. "I'll be back later." Then he yanked open the office door and stormed out.

*

McCauley pulled out his phone. "McCauley here. What is it Captain?"

"Two cops were gunned down at the Donut Hut on Desert Inn this morning about 9:30," Captain McKnight said. "The owner was also shot and killed. The killer covered the bodies with those yellow 'Don't Tread on Me' flags. The words, 'The Revolution Begins!' was written on the wall of the shop. So far we are trying to keep it out of the media."

"I see," McCauley said. He frowned at Marino. "Any witnesses, Captain?"

"No. there are no witnesses. Two of our guys went in to get a morning donut and found a murder scene."

"I see," McCauley said.

"Since the preacher is still alive and getting well, there is no sense having two of my best murder detectives on his case," McKnight said. "Get to the crime scene and find out what you can about who killed two of our men on Christmas Eve! Those Officers had families. We've got to get those killers! That is Priority One!"

## CHAPTER 73

### 10:30 AM

There was a smaller crowd gathered on the sidewalk outside the hospital than the day before. Most of those holding signs were African Americans claiming that either the hospital or Charity Chastain, the Caucasian wife of LeRoy Braxton, was mistreating LeRoy.

"Honk! Honk!" The crowd scattered as a huge, jacked-up, white Dodge Ram 1500 pick-up truck adorned with Confederate Flags drove up on the sidewalk. It was followed by several others that circled up at the entrance of the hospital. One had a horn that played "Dixie." All had men in the back of the trucks who were carrying shotguns.

"KA- BOOM!" A sawed-off shot gun exploded into the air. A thin man rose from the second truck standing next to a large yellow Gadsden flag. He lowered his shotgun and put a bull horn to his mouth.

"We will not be replaced!" the thin man yelled into his bull horn.

"We will not be replaced!" the men in the other trucks replied.

"We will not be silenced!"

"We will not be silenced!"

"Our blood, our soil!" he yelled

"Our blood, our soil!" they replied.

"KA-BOOM!" He fired the other round from his shot gun.

"BOOM! BOOM! BOOM!" The other men fired their guns into the air in reply

"Let the Revolution begin!" he yelled.

The truck took off down Maryland Avenue. The other trucks followed.

The original protesters were nowhere to be found.

*

The sound of the guns firing outside their room put terror back in Rebecca's heart.

"What was that, Mom?" Caleb asked.

"Just some guys in pick-up trucks," Elijah said, trying to reassure his family. He had been closest to the window and had looked down on the short-lived event after the first gun shot.

"What did that man say?" Titus asked with eyes wide.

"Oh, I don't know. Something about celebrating Christmas, I guess," Elijah said, looking over at Rebecca.

"That must be it," she said following Elijah's lead. "You know how people love to fire guns off at New Year's and the Fourth of July in our neighborhood."

"And for Cinco de Mayo, the Day of the Dead, and Mexico's Independence Day," Zach said.

"I hope you are right. We don't need any more shootings," Caleb said.

"That's for sure," Zach said.

They all agreed.

# CHAPTER 74

## 11:45 AM

All four of the Browning boys and Rebecca were gathered around Daniel. Christmas music was playing gently on a laptop.

"Can we all pray as a family for God to heal Dad?" Elijah asked as he looked at Rebecca.

"Absolutely," Rebecca replied with a smile. "Your dad would love it if we would do that."

"Ok, everyone, join hands," Together the family joined hands around Daniel's bed. "Let's start with Caleb, then Titus, then Mom, then Zach and I'll close. Caleb, you go first," Elijah directed.

"Dear God, please heal our dad. We miss him. He looks bad with all that stuff going in and out of him," Caleb prayed.

"Jesus, wake my daddy up and let him come home with us soon. In Jesus' name, amen," Titus said. Then he looked up at Elijah for approval. Elijah smiled and nodded at him.

"Father, thank you for these boys," Rebecca began. "I am so proud of each of them. Please hear our prayers today and heal Daniel. This city needs him, our church needs him, and we need him."

"God, you are big and strong. I only want one thing for Christmas: I want my dad back. So, how about waking Dad up for Christmas? In Jesus' name, amen," Zach prayed.

"Father in heaven," Elijah began. "This has been a hard week for all of us, but especially Mom and especially Dad. I agree with everyone else and especially Zach. The only thing I want for Christmas is to get our dad back. Please wake him up for Christmas. In Jesus' name, amen."

"Amen," everyone said.

*

Daniel was dreaming again. His family was gathered in the living room. The boys were much smaller and younger.

Then he saw that Thunderbolt, their big, golden, soft-coated Wheaten terrier was not in his usual spot sprawled out on the couch over top of Caleb and Zach. Instead, he lay lethargically in the middle of the floor.

Thunderbolt had been sick for a few days and they didn't know what to do. They didn't have the money for a vet. They boys were very worried.

"Why don't we pray for him?" Daniel had suggested. "Let's gather around him and join hands."

In wonderfully sincere and simple prayers the boys interceded for their dog.

Thunderbolt lay very still and did not move.

"I think we should do it again," Caleb said.

Everyone agreed. This time some of the boys prayed louder and more directly, asking God to please heal their ailing dog and raise him up.

Daniel went last.

And everyone said, "Amen."

Then it happened.

Thunderbolt, opened one eye, then the other. Slowly he got on his feet. Zach hugged him around the neck and the rest of them cheered. Thunderbolt tottered over to the back door and vomited all over the rug.

Elijah let him outside; the dog ran out, vomited again in the yard, and came back to the door.

Elijah let him in and he was as good as new. He bolted around the house like a puppy. He had not been sick a day since then.

*

Zeke sat in his SUV in the parking lot between Walmart and Lowe's. He had filled the back of his vehicle with extra presents for his family. Now he was replaying his plan and going over the list of items he needed to carry it out. "I think I have everything I need," he said as he pawed through his back pack.

"*&%^$!" he grunted. "I forgot to get the lighter."

*

"I think we should do it again," Zach said.

"Do what again?" Rebecca asked.

"I think we should all pray for Dad again, harder this time," Zach replied.

"Me too," Caleb said.

"Ok, Zach, you go first," Elijah said.

"Dear God, my Bible teacher said that you are the God of angel armies. Please send a bunch of angel warriors to smash the devil and his evil spirits. Please have those angels lift Dad out of that bed. Like Caleb and Elijah, the only thing *I* want for Christmas is to get our dad back. Please wake him up for Christmas. In Jesus' name, amen."

"Jesus, make Daddy better for Christmas," Titus said.

"Father in heaven, you gave us the greatest gift when you sent your Son to us on Christmas. Thank you. But the second greatest gift would be to have Daniel wake up for Christmas," Rebecca prayed.

"Lord, you made Thunderbolt all better when we prayed for him. Please make Dad better after we pray for him. In Jesus' name, amen," Caleb prayed

"Father in heaven, we come to you as a family, all of us joined together for one cause. We want to see our dad, Pastor Daniel Browning, wake up from his coma for Christmas. In Jesus' name, amen," Elijah said.

"Amen," they all said.

*

Daniel had been seeing a wonderful light arching through the sky on its way toward him. Like a knife -- or better, a laser-- it cut through the darkness lurking outside his room and shot into his chest. Warm light pulsed up and down through his nervous system. Liquid life and love flowed through every vein and artery.

For the first time in days, Daniel did not feel the excruciating pain that had pulsated through his chest with every breath. The thin cloak of darkness that had been resting over him blew off.

Then it happened.

Daniel felt Caleb and Elijah squeeze his hand. He squeezed back.

*

"Mom?" Elijah asked anxiously. "Mom?" He called louder.

"What is it, honey?" Rebecca asked.

"I think Dad just squeezed my hand."

"He did squeeze your hand," Zach said. "And he just squeezed mine too."

"What?" Rebecca asked, her voice gently rising with skeptical excitement.

"Dad just squeezed our hands," Zach said.

Elijah who was wearing a funny grin, began to nod his head up and down. "He's right, Mom!"

"Are you sure?" She asked.

"No doubt about it," Zach said. "Hope he does not vomit any green stuff on me like Thunderbolt."

Rebecca leaned closer to Daniel. She put one hand on his cheek and with the other she grabbed his hand from Zach. "Daniel, honey, can you hear me? Daniel, can you hear me?"

"Oh my!" she said. "He squeezed my hand! He squeezed my hand!"

Roberta, who was returning from the cafeteria came bustling in. "What's all the commotion about?"

"Daniel squeezed our hands!" Rebecca said, hugging Roberta. Tears were streaming down her cheeks. "Daniel squeezed our hands!"

"You got to be kidding!"

"No doubt about it," Zach said. "With God all things are possible."

"I know that, but did Pastor really squeeze your hand? Let me see," Roberta said as she took Daniel's hand from Elijah.

"Pastor Daniel, this is Roberta," she said a bit too loudly. "If you can hear me, please squeeze my hand."

"Oh, praise the Lord! Praise the Lord!" she yelled. "Pastor Daniel has come back from the dead!"

# CHAPTER 75
## 12:50 PM

"I am *so* happy!" Doctor Kim said as he stood by Daniel's bed. A huge grin that lit up the entire room covered his usually dignified face. Rebecca stood across from him holding Daniel's hand.

"I started to say that I cannot believe it, but I *can* believe it. With God, all things *are* possible," he said.

"There was a moment in the OR when it looked as though we had lost him for sure. But the presence of God filled the room and brought him back from death. Now he is waking up and has started to move. Praise the Lord!"

Then he focused on Rebecca, "Now, you need to understand that this week, he has been through a great trauma and two significant surgeries. His body is still in shock in many ways. But the Lord seems to have touched him.

"I think he will probably sleep the majority of the time. But when he is not sleeping, I expect him to become more and more awake and begin to move more and more."

"When will he open his eyes? When will he speak?" Rebecca asked anxiously.

"We don't know. Hopefully soon. It usually happens in stages," he cautioned. "But remember, as we have seen, with God all things are possible."

\*

*You must kill the preacher. You must kill the preacher. The only way you will ever be free is to kill the preacher.*

The voices in Zeke's head were louder than ever.

*You must kill him on Christmas. You must kill him on Christmas. The only way you will ever be free is to kill the preacher on Christmas.*

%^&*%$#@! Zeke exploded in a tortured scream as he slammed his fist into the dashboard of his SUV.

# CHAPTER 76
## 2:30 PM

"That's what I said, Mom: Daniel squeezed our hands!" Rebecca was standing in the corner of the room talking on her cell phone. Doris had taken the boys down to the cafeteria to eat a late lunch, so it was only Rebecca and Roberta in the room.

"I know!" she continued. "The boys were praying for a Christmas miracle and God gave it to us. With God all things are possible."

Rebecca grew quiet as she listened to the voice on the other end.

"Yes, Mom. I know that you and Dad would be here if you could," Rebecca held her phone to her ear and nodded.

"Yes, I know exactly how it is. As the pastor, Dad can't leave the church on Christmas or Christmas Eve." She smiled as she looked over at Roberta.

"Mom, don't feel bad about it. I know that money is tight and that trying to get affordable flights out here at the last minute just before Christmas is almost impossible," Rebecca said into the phone.

Then after listening some more, her face broke into a huge smile. "Great! If you guys can get out here next week that would be *wonderful!* God has had us covered this week. Roberta and Freda have been here with me. Doris has been great taking care of the boys, and Danielle loves taking care of Thunderbolt. So, everything has worked out."

"No, do *not* get a hotel. You can stay at the house with the boys. They will love being back in their own house. They will also *love* seeing you both," Rebecca said.

"Yes, we'll Facetime with all the boys tomorrow," Rebecca smiled. "Love you too, Mom. Bye."

*

"Yes, Madam Mayor, it was a good thing you were not in the office today," Captain McKnight said into his phone.

"But other than a few bullets fired at your windows, there really was no damage. Yes, we captured the assailant. Like the others, he was spouting something about a Revolution. Seems to be a white nationalist who views all government as tyrannical.

"Of course, there was that big riot down the road at Dixie State College in St. George when they tried to return the statue of the Confederate soldier to the school courtyard," McKnight continued. "There was that big riot in Richmond, Virginia. The FBI said that it all seems connected somehow to the anniversary of the KKK."

McKnight nodded as he listened.

"Yes, Ma'am, other than the officers being killed, the so-called "Revolution" that was to begin has not amounted to much here, yet. Someone started a fire at Second Baptist Church. Some crazies fired some guns and scattered the crowd that's been outside Paradise Hospital. They tried to have a march at Fremont, but we shut that down rather quickly,"

"No Ma'am, we have not yet brought in the people who gunned down the police officers," Captain McKnight said into the phone. "But we have an ID on the van they escaped in and trust me, it is just a matter of time before they are apprehended. We have the maximum amount of resources focused on bringing them in."

"Yes, Ma'am, dead or alive.

## CHAPTER 78
## 4:50 PM

"Are you sure we are safe here, Brian?" Terri asked. "It's going to get dark soon." They were both squatting by a small fire next to a small tent on the western ridge of the mountains in the Desert National Wildlife Refuge.

Earlier in the day, they had parked the van in an abandoned shed. The shed was outside of Coyote Springs, Nevada, north of the Valley of Fire State Park off Route 169. After the shooting, they had taken Interstate 15 northwest of Las Vegas and driven to the shed. They stayed in the shed until after 3:00PM before slipping out and heading into the mountains. This gave them plenty of time to get to the campsite before the sun set at 4:30. The back of the van was well stocked with water and freeze-dried meals. They brought some of them up to the campsite.

"We're safe," Brian said confidently. "According to the police scanner, we were out of Vegas before they were even looking for us. No one would think of looking for us way out here. Just in case, that shed shielded us from any helicopters that might fly overhead searching for us."

"I know I heard a helicopter when we were in the shed," Terri insisted.

"Yes, that is the fourth time you told me that," Brian fumed. "Like I told you, the shed has a roof on it and they can't see through the roof."

"Apart from a few little things here and there, it didn't seem to be a very big Revolution," Terri remarked. "You and me shooting those cops was the only real bloodshed."

"I *was* disappointed in our brothers and sisters," Brian shook his head. "But think about it. Because nobody else got their hands bloody, we are kind of like the heroes of the Revolution so far!"

"I did not get my hands bloody," Terri said, looking at her hands.

"That is a figure of speech," Brian said and rolled his eyes. "That means that we shed blood. Nobody else has done that."

"Oh," Terri nodded. "I see."

"I figure that tomorrow we steal us a truck and go back into Vegas and shoot us a few more cops. That should solidify our status as the heroes of the Revolution."

"But tomorrow is Christmas," Terri protested.

"Yes," Brian had a glow in his eye. "I can see it now -- the history books will call it the Christmas Day Massacre!"

"Oh," Terri said trying to comprehend being in history books. "I never thought of that."

Then she looked over at the little tent in the fire light. "I am afraid it'll get cold in that little tent,

"That's why we brought those sleeping bags with us," Brian said. "They're supposed to keep you warm down to five degrees. You'll be fine. Plus, I can keep you warm."

\*

The Browning family was gathered in Daniel's room eating Christmas cookies. Since Daniel stunned everyone, (but Zach), by squeezing their hands, the room had been full of joy and laughter. For the first time in a week, Rebecca felt that there really was hope.

"I brought my guitar," Caleb said. "Let's sing Christmas carols. I brought a book that my guitar teacher gave me. It's full of Christmas songs."

"Great idea," Rebecca said. "Your dad *loves* Christmas carols."

"Yeah, he sings them in the shower all the time," Zach said

"How do you know?" Rebecca asked. "You are supposed to be asleep when he showers."

"Your shower is on the other side of my bedroom wall. I hear him singing all the time. Dad *does* sing very loud, you know."

"Oh, he does love to sing," Rebecca said.

"Well, he's *not* that good at it, you know," Zach said.

They all laughed.

\*

In a dream, Daniel was with his family gathered around the piano in the family room. The room was bathed in warm, golden light. The house was decorated for Christmas with a large Christmas tree, green garland, twinkly white lights, and several nativity scenes.

Rebecca was playing the piano and Caleb, the guitar. Pastor Carlos and Pastor Matthew and their families were also there. Everyone was laughing, smiling and singing Christmas carols very, very loudly.

Daniel saw golden silvery flakes, like snow, but not snow, falling gently in the room. It lightly blanketed each of them.

*I think that is the Shekinah glory,* Daniel thought. *God's presence is in this room as we sing.*

He opened his mouth wide singing with the others, "Silent night, Holy night."

*

"Joy to the world, the Lord has come!" The little hospital room choir all sang loudly, except Zach, who pretended to hate singing.

*There is something healing about singing together,* Rebecca thought as she drank in the joy on her sons' faces. Daniel always said that singing together heals your body and your soul, and that it unites your heart with others.

They sang one carol after another. Soon a small crowd of nurses, aides, and the family members of patients in other rooms had gathered around the edge of the room and into the hallway. Some were just listening, but many sang along.

"Frosty the Snow Man" and "Rudolph the Red-Nosed Reindeer" were big hits.

Then between the first and second verse of "Silent Night" it happened.

"Look!" Titus yelled as he pointed to Daniel. "Daddy is singing!"

"Don't stop! Keep singing," Rebecca implored.

As they did, she studied Daniel's face. Sure enough, Daniel's lips were moving ever so slightly.

# CHAPTER 78
## 5:30 PM

Doris and the boys were at the door of the waiting room with their jackets on. Rebecca knelt down to be eye level with Titus and said, "Boys, you need to do exactly what Mrs. Garcia says at church tonight. It is Christmas Eve and there will be a lot of guests. People will bring family members who will be there for the first time."

Looking directly at Zach, she continued, "Do *not* do anything to distract."

"I wish that you and Daddy were going to be there," Titus said.

"I do too, honey. But Daddy needs to be here so he can keep getting better."

"Can we tell people about Daddy moving?" Caleb asked.

"Yes, please tell them. Also, tell them to keep praying that he will fully wake up and look at us and talk to us."

"Who's preaching tonight, Mom?" Elijah asked

"I think Pastor Carlos and Pastor Matthew are both going to say something."

"Will *we* get to light candles?" Titus asked.

"Yes," Rebecca said. "You all will. But be very careful and do exactly what Mr. and Mrs. Garcia say."

"Can we come back here after church?" Elijah asked.

Rebecca looked at Doris.

"Elijah and Travis will be coming back with Mr. Garcia," Doris said. "I'm taking the rest of you guys home with me. We need to wrap a few presents."

"We already got our present -- Dad moved," Caleb said.

"Wait till tomorrow. Tomorrow's Christmas. He is going to wake up all the way," Zach said.

## CHAPTER 79
### 5:43 PM

Rebecca had the room to herself. Everyone she knew was at church for the Christmas Eve candlelight service. After a noisy, eventful day in the crowded room, she was enjoying the relative quiet.

Her mind drifted back to the first few years of the new church. Back then, the little church was mostly made up of college students from UNLV and street people. The college students went home for Christmas. The street people primarily came to the service when there was a meal provided for them ahead of time. So, Rebecca and Daniel worked all day preparing a big meal to be served at 6:00 PM.

At 5:20, Daniel left Rebecca to finish the meal herself as he drove a bus around the neighborhood picking people up. At 5:40 he dropped off a load of people and went back out for more. When they got back at 6:00, everyone held hands and prayed. Then the meal began.

After the meal, Daniel, Rebecca, and several others, scrambled to clean it all up, to put away the folding tables, and to put the chairs in rows for the Christmas Eve service.

Rebecca played the piano and led the music and Daniel served as the emcee. Rebecca led Elijah and a few of the elementary children in singing a few little Christmas songs for their parents. Then she led the congregation in a few more Christmas carols. Daniel preached a short sermon. Following that, they all lit candles and sang "Silent Night." Then they wished each other a merry Christmas.

After that, Rebecca talked with the people and tried to keep track of her little boys. Daniel loaded up the bus and made two runs to get everyone home.

Then the family loaded up in the van, drove to Donut Hut and got the stickiest, most sugary donuts they could.

When they took the boys home and put them in bed, Rebecca and Daniel put the finishing touches on their meager Christmas gift wrapping, then got cleaned up and ready for bed. They cuddled briefly on the couch as they watched the fire and laughed about the events of the evening. Then they went to bed and quickly fell asleep, exhausted but happy.

*

That night, Grace City Church was full for the first of two Christmas Eve services. There was the expected excitement, but it was something different from previous years. There was a palpable absence. Just a few days earlier, Pastor Daniel had been gunned down right before the eyes of many of them. He was not here. He was in Paradise Hospital fighting for his life.

After a few songs, Pastor Matthew stepped to the center of the stage. "Let me address 'the Elephant in the room,'" he said. "Or better, 'the Lead Pastor not in the room.'"

"As most of you know, Pastor Daniel was shot right here on Sunday night. By the grace of God, his stubborn will, the work of a skilled doctor, and your prayers, added to the prayers of thousands from all over the world, he did not die."

Clapping and cheers filled the room from the multi-ethnic congregation. "Praise the Lords!" And a few "Amens!" were heard through-out the room.

"Tonight, he is alive and recovering at Paradise Hospital."

More clapping and cheers.

"He has been in a coma all week. But, what you don't know is that earlier today, he moved. He squeezed the hands of his family members, and just a short time ago, he even tried to sing a Christmas carol!"

At this, people exploded to their feet cheering, pumping their fists, high-fiving the people beside them, crying, laughing and clapping.

Many who had been there on Sunday night had thought they would never see Daniel alive again on this earth.

Many of these people had been laboring in prayer all week and were delighted to hear that God was answering.

The joyful ruckus lasted a full two minutes. Wiping tears off his cheeks and lifting his hands to shush the crowd, Pastor Matthew continued, "The job is still not done. We must continue to pray."

"Pastor's eight-year-old son, Zach, told me before the service that he believes that his dad will be fully awake tomorrow because it's Christmas. Let us all lift our voices in prayer and humbly ask the Lord to do that very thing: to wake Pastor Daniel up, healthy and whole tomorrow for Christmas."

The room was immediately filled in a beautiful symphony of prayers. About two minutes into the impromptu prayer meeting, the volume crescendoed upward, then began to slowly recede.

At just the right moment, the band broke into "Joy to the World" and the whole place burst into song.

*

Daniel was dreaming and saw himself rise up out of the hospital. There was music surrounding him and the next thing he knew, he was flying over the city. For a man cemented motionless in a bed all week, it was extra-exhilarating to be soaring through the cool night air above the ceaseless din of the city. He found himself flying over the Grace City campus on Flamingo Avenue. Amazingly, he could see right into the building. Every seat was taken and people stood around the walls.

Joy filled his heart as he thought back to the early days and how hard they worked just to have a handful of people. Tonight, the church would pack out two Christmas Eve services. On Sundays the morning service was usually packed out and the evening one was nicely full. If, or better, *when* he got out of this hospital, they would have to add a second service on Sunday mornings.

Quietly, he flew back to the hospital, passed through the wall into his room, and floated gently down into his bed. Next to him was Rebecca, holding his hand and resting in the chair beside him.

*She is still beautiful. Such a beautiful person.*

*How did I ever get her to say yes to me? Must have been a God-thing. With God all things are possible.*

*I wish she could hear me.*

*"Rebecca, I love you. Rebecca, I love you. Rebecca, I love you."*

\*

Rebecca jerked to attention, "Was that…?"

She looked at Daniel and then pressed her ear to his mouth.

"Rebecca, I love you. Rebecca, I love you," he croaked out in a tiny voice.

She squeezed his hand.

He squeezed back!

"I love you too!" she whispered. "I love you too!"

# CHAPTER 80
## 8:05 PM

"Hey, Mom!" Elijah said, as he entered Daniel's room.

"Merry Christmas, Mrs. Browning!" Travis said as he followed Elijah into the room.

"Merry Christmas, Rebecca!" Bobby Garcia, Doris' husband, said as he came in behind Travis.

"Merry Christmas!" Rebecca said. She had a huge smile.

"I know that this is Las Vegas and it is 56 degrees out, but also knowing that you are from the Midwest, I thought you'd like some hot chocolate," Bobby said, handing her a big Styrofoam cup.

"Thanks, Bobby," Rebecca said, taking the cup greedily. "You guys have been such a great huge blessing to us. Thanks for putting up with our boys all week."

"No problem. They have been *really* good. Except for this one," Bobby said giving Elijah a gentle shove. "You know what a pain he can be."

"Oh, don't I know!" Rebecca laughed. Then she smiled at Elijah warmly. "So, Elijah, how did church go tonight?"

"Well," Elijah said, "the first service was packed."

"Yes, but tell her the best part," Travis said.

"Pastor Matthew told everyone how Dad had squeezed our hands and that his lips were moving when we sang Christmas carols. When he said that everyone stood up and began cheering!"

"It was awesome, Mrs. B. They cheered for like five minutes."

"I didn't know that they loved Dad so much," Elijah said.

"Everyone loves your dad," Travis said.

Elijah looked at Rebecca. "How is Dad?"

"Well…" she started. "Well…" then she started to cry.

"Mom are you alright? What happened?"

She nodded and took a deep breathe. "Your dad -- spoke to me."

"He spoke to you? Really? What did he say?"

"He said that he loved me."

## CHAPTER 81
### 9:30 PM

"Mrs. B, I told you that my mom and her sister wanted me to come to lunch tomorrow," Big Tony said. He had been sitting in the lobby eyeing everyone who entered the unit.

"Yes, Tony. I understand. It is Christmas," Rebecca said.

"Well," he dropped his eyes and fingered the hat he held in his hands. "They just called and said my brother Billy had showed up. I don't know if I told you about Billy, but he was in prison for a while. When he got out he went to Chicago to be with some woman he met over the Internet and we have not seen him for years."

"So, your brother came to visit for Christmas. That's wonderful," Rebecca said.

"Yes, he's flying out Saturday night. So, I'd really like to spend some time with him," he said. "He got tickets for a MMA fight on the Strip for the two of us tomorrow night. So, I won't be in the lobby watching out for that shooter tomorrow during the day or tomorrow night."

"I see," Rebecca said slowly. "That's all right, Tony. I understand that you need to spend some time with your brother."

# CHAPTER 82
## 11:00 PM

Daniel was dreaming again. He saw the little Hispanic family gathered around the table. The chair that the father had occupied at the head of the table was noticeably empty. The mother was speaking in Spanish and Daniel could make out only a few words.

"No tenemos dinero para regalos de Navidad este año." the little mother said sadly. *We have no money for Christmas presents this year*. Sin dinero. *No money."*

The children nodded quietly. Their little faces were very sad, serious and subdued...all except the oldest. His eyes burned in rage.

\*

Maria and Ezekiel had banished their boys to their rooms for the night. Then Ezekiel went out to his vehicle and brought in several big bags of presents.

"What's this?" Maria asked. "We bought the boys their presents a few weeks ago. Plus, I thought I told you that I had gotten the other ones."

"They needed a few more," Ezekiel said quietly.

*If everything doesn't go well. These may be the last presents they get from me for a long time.*

## FRIDAY, DECEMBER 25 "CHRISTMAS"

## CHAPTER 83
### 1:30 AM

Maria had fallen asleep as soon as she had dropped into bed. But beside her, Ezekiel was deep in thought. He had the details of his plan worked out and memorized, all but one. Anxiously he went through every step. But he was indecisive regarding how he would actually kill the preacher and not get caught.

*Can't shoot him it; would attract too much attention.*

*Can't stab him, also too obvious.*

*Can't choke him; would leave DNA and possible finger prints on the* neck.

*No, it needs to look like he died naturally this time. I already made my point last time by shooting the guy in his church.*

*No, I need something that will not be noticed right away. Something that would definitely kill the preacher, but not attract attention or leave evidence traceable to me. I need something that would allow me to escape. Something where they would not even know he was dead until I was long gone.*

*Hum… Suffocate. That's it. I can use a pillow to suffocate him. They will think he just died in his sleep.*

# CHAPTER 84
## 6:15 AM

The clock in Maria's head went off at 6:15 AM every morning, whether she set her alarm or not, even on Christmas morning. She knew the boys would burst in the room any minute to wake Ezekiel and her up to open presents. But until then, she lay still and silently prayed.

*Father in heaven, thank you for this day when we celebrate the birth of your son. He truly is the gift of God. I do not know where I'd be without Jesus.*

*Pastor Daniel has said that if people choose not to forgive, they end up putting themselves in prison and are tormented by their bitterness. I hate seeing my husband so tormented with his bitterness. Other than his bitterness and anger, he is a good man. When he was a boy, he loved you. Please set him free.*

*Today, I have one big request. It is all I want for Christmas: Please touch my husband's heart and release him from his prison of bitterness, anger, guilt and shame. Please work mightily in any way you think is best to change his heart and change his life, before it is too late.*

*I do not know why I feel so urgent about asking you to do something this Christmas, but I do. Please work today.*

\*

Daniel was snoring in his hospital bed dreaming. He saw a Sunday evening service at Grace City Church. He was standing at the door, greeting people on their way in to the service. Maria Cruz was introducing him to her husband Ezekiel. As he was watching the scene play out, Daniel remembered facts about the Cruz family.

Maria had gotten saved not long after they started the church when the church prayed for her son, Miguel, who was miraculously healed. She had come faithfully with her four sons every week since.

Her husband, Ezekiel, had been sent to prison for dealing drugs and shooting a man in a drug deal gone badly. The church had all prayed for Ezekiel. He had gotten out of prison early on good behavior and had started a Limo Company that was doing quite well. But this was only the second time he had been to church.

In his dream, Daniel saw Ezekiel walking into the church service that night six months ago. He walked in; he looked anxious and refused to look Daniel in the eye. Like so many of these men, he acted very tough on the outside, but he was a scared, little boy on the inside.

Maria had told Daniel that Ezekiel's father had been a pastor in Las Vegas. But when his father died of a fast moving and extremely painful cancer, Ezekiel had gotten mad at God. As a teen, he had turned to selling drugs to support his widowed mother and his younger siblings.

The scene continued to play. Daniel noticed Ezekiel shifting back and forth uncomfortably during the worship part of the service. The man was sweating, and his eyes darted around like a scared animal. When Daniel got up to speak, he looked at Ezekiel. The look on the poor man's face changed. At one point, he looked at Daniel with burning rage. Then he jumped up and dashed out of the church.

Then everything went dark.

*

"Get a move on," Brian barked to Terri. "The police are probably looking for the van, so I'm going to steal a vehicle from that little ranch down at the foot of the hill."

"I didn't know that you knew how to steal vehicles," Terri said.

"My brother, Jessie, and I used to steal cars in Missouri. That's why I had to go to prison those three years."

"Oh, that's right. That was before I met you on that dating website."

"And you are glad you did, aren't you?" Brian laughed.

"Yes, I guess so." She paused and looked at Brian, "Hey, Brian, I was thinking, if you steal a vehicle, won't the police be looking for that too?"

*

"Knock, knock!" Karen said in a cheerful voice. "Merry Christmas!"

"Merry Christmas, Karen," Rebecca said sleepily.

"I am sorry to bother you so early, but Glenn will probably be discharged shortly!" Karen said. "I can't believe it. He'll be home on Christmas!"

"Wow!" Rebecca smiled. "That is so great!"

"Like I told you yesterday, he made such improvement on Wednesday night and yesterday, that the doctor said there was no sense keeping him in here. He is still on a very short leash, but at least he can be home and go back and forth to the doctor's office for appointments."

Karen was bubbly in her enthusiasm. "Here, these are for you," she said handing Rebecca a big box of chocolates.

"How did you know my weakness?" Rebecca laughed as she took the box.

Then Karen turned serious, "You know when you prayed the other day, it really touched me. More important, I think it really made a difference. You prayed that Glenn would turn around soon and he did."

"I don't usually pray that boldly," Rebecca said. "But I felt that I was supposed to."

"I am glad you did. When you told me that all things are possible with God, you were right," Karen continued. "I used to go to church when I was a girl. In fact, Glenn and I went to church even after we had kids. But we got away from it when we came out here."

Rebecca nodded as she listened to Karen.

"But now I *know* God is real," Karen said. "And I also believe that he is going to do a miracle for you and Daniel too. Like you said, with God all things are possible!"

Rebecca nodded, "I hope you are right."

"Where is your boldness?" Karen said. As she turned to leave she added, "You'll see. Oh, and I also wanted to tell you that Glenn and I will be at your church when Glenn's up to it. We want to hear your husband preach."

*

Doris was up early making pancakes. Quietly she prayed as she stirred the batter.

*Lord, I feel so sad that the Browning boys won't have the joy of waking up with their parents in their own home on Christmas. I am thankful that some of the ladies at the church have decorated Daniel's room and I know that Rebecca will do the best she can, but a hospital room is no place for anyone to spend Christmas, especially little boys. So, please use these pancakes to help remind these boys that you love them and that a lot of other people love them this Christmas.*

*And, Lord, I do thank you that Pastor Daniel was able to squeeze the boys' hands yesterday.*

*Now, would you please wake him up all the way today? And when he wakes up, please let him be healthy and whole.*

## CHAPTER 85
### 8:30 AM

The Cruz family were all gathered around the living room opening presents. Later the house would be full. In the afternoon, Maria's mother, and oldest sister, would be joining them. Also coming would be Maria's younger sister, Isabella, and her boyfriend; Maria's niece, her boyfriend, their two- year-old daughter, and her teddy bear.

This time was supposed to be *their* time to enjoy Christmas together. But something wasn't right, Maria could tell. Ezekiel was distracted and irritable.

Ezekiel had seen the ravages of alcohol abuse and only had a few beers now and then. So, Maria was surprised that even though it was still early in the day, he had starting drinking already.

"What's wrong, honey?" she asked as she reached for his hand.

"Nothing," he said as he withdrew his hand.

*What's wrong? What's wrong? You got to be kidding.* He thought. He opened another beer as the voices continued their relentless torture.

*Remember Christmas after your dad died?* The voices taunted him. *There was no money for presents. There was not even money for food, all because God killed your dad.*

*Remember how sad your mother and your brothers and sisters were? It was God's fault.*

*While you were in prison, your wife got religion. That was all the preacher's fault.*

*The only way to get God out of your life and away from your family is to kill that preacher.*

*You got to kill the preacher. You had better get it right this time. You better not get caught. We will never leave you alone until he is dead.*

# CHAPTER 86
## 9:30 AM

"Mommy!" Titus shouted when he ran into the room. "It's Christmas!"

Rebecca scooped him up and laughed.

"Merry Christmas, Mom," Elijah said, as he gave her a side hug.

"Merry Christmas," Caleb said as he came in carrying his guitar.

"Merry Christmas, boys," she replied.

Zach however, said nothing and instead walked right up to Daniel. "Merry Christmas, Dad," he said. "It's Christmas. You need to wake up soon."

\*

"@#$%^&%#!" Jason cursed. "No, don't eat that!"

Trying to keep a lamb in the tiny stone-covered, backyard of his little ranch house was proving difficult. The beast had already eaten all the flowers and had started eating the leaves off the little palm tree he had planted last month.

Plus, the lamb had kept Jason up most of the night crying for its mother. He had given it a bowl of milk, but it wanted more.

Beyond that, the lamb had messed all over the back seat of his car when he drove it back to Vegas.

"I'll be a happy man when Victor sticks a knife in you tonight," he said to the innocent little fellow. "A *very* happy man."

\*

"Can we go to the park and fly the drone?" Miguel asked. Ezekiel had given him the drone as a special Christmas present.

"All right," he said.

*Anything to get out of this house,* he thought.

The voices were persistent in their torture. *Remember when you were thirteen? You did not have a dad. God killed him.*

*The only way to get back at God is to kill the preacher. You got to kill the preacher. You got to kill him tonight.*

*

"I don't see any cop cars anywhere," Terri said. "Not many people out on Christmas morning."

"Keep looking," Brian ordered. "They can't all have the day off. There are Revolutionaries on the loose!" he cackled.

*

"He looks good," the nurse said to Rebecca. "His vital signs are very good. His breathing is not labored."

"Yes, he is doing so much better than he was the other day," Rebecca said.

"Hkkkkkh-sssss-Hkkkkkh-sssss-Hkkkkh-sssss...," Daniel was gently snoring.

"Has he squeezed anybody's hand or said anything this morning?" the nurse asked.

"No, not yet," Rebecca said.

"But he will," Zach said. "Today is Christmas!"

# CHAPTER 87
## 1 PM

"Merry Christmas!" Martha called as she stuck her head in Daniel's room.

"Martha, it is *so* nice to see you," Rebecca said.

"I hope I am not bothering anything," Martha said. In her right hand, she carried a shopping bag. "I brought you some pieces of pie that were left over from the Homeless Brunch this morning."

"Thank you, "Rebecca said.

"Pie?" Zach asked with huge grin on his face. "We like pie."

"We sure do," Caleb agreed.

"What type of pie did you bring?"

"I brought a few pieces of apple, cherry, and pumpkin."

"Give me one of each," Elijah said with a smile.

"Me too!" Titus yelled merrily.

"I don't think so," Rebecca laughed.

"Martha, how did the Brunch go? The boys were going to help, but when Doris called Carlos, he said they had plenty of helpers."

"Yes, we had plenty of help. The lunch went great! The church provided turkey, ham, drinks and paper products. Fifty of our church people signed up to bring side dishes for themselves and for fifty of our guests. So, one hundred of us, fifty homeless and fifty of us who are better off, all sat around tables *together* and enjoyed Christmas Brunch as one big family."

"Sounds awesome, I know Carlos has been wanting to do that for a while."

"Yes. As you know from our Wednesday night meals, eating all mixed together dignifies the homeless," Martha said. "It takes away the *us* and *them* mentally. It makes us all just *family*, especially on Christmas."

Then Martha got a very serious look on her face. "Rebecca, when I was praying this morning, I had a very, very strong impression that I think had to be from the Lord."

"Oh?" Rebecca asked curiously.

"I believe that God is going to give you and your boys a very special Christmas present."

"He did, he brought us pie!" Caleb said.

"Oh, this will be much better than pie," Martha smiled. "Much better."

*

"I can't believe that we can't find any cops," Brian said disgustedly.

"I must not be our day," Terri said. "Yesterday we shot two cops. That's more than anybody else did. Why don't we just go back home now?"

"No. We need to add a Christmas Day massacre to our credentials as the heroes of this Revolution," he said. Then he got a crazy look in his eye. "Wait, I got an idea. Let's start purifying this nation of Jews. Look on your phone and see if there are any Jewish synagogues near here."

*

"Hkkkkkh-sssss-Hkkkkkh-sssss-Hkkkkh-sssss...."

Apart from Daniel's snoring, and the sound of Christmas music playing quietly in the background, the room had grown quiet.

"I think we need to pray again," Zach said. "Dad needs to wake up."

"Good idea," Elijah added. "It worked yesterday."

"It can't hurt," Caleb said.

"All right, let's pray," Rebecca said.

"Pray that he wakes all the way up. It is Christmas," Zach directed.

"I want to go first. I never get to go first." Titus said.

"All right, you can go first," Rebecca said. "Come here and hold Mommy's hand."

"Dear Jesus, thank you for Christmas and for pie and for Christmas presents. Please make Daddy all the way better," he prayed.

"Father in heaven, I thank you for a good Christmas in a hard place. Thank you for the people that have blessed us so much this week. Thank you that we get to be together as a family," Rebecca prayed. "Thank you that Daniel is getting better. Please wake him up all the way, very soon. Even today. In Jesus' name, amen."

*

Daniel had begun dreaming. He and Rebecca were in the prayer chapel of the campus church before service. After they had gotten engaged, they had begun meeting there to pray about their future together.

Daniel was holding Rebecca's hand and she was praying. When she finished, she said, "in Jesus name, amen" and squeezed his hand.

He squeezed back and began to pray.

*

"Father in heaven, I want to thank ...." Elijah had began to pray, when he was interrupted by Daniel.

"Lord, we give our lives to you," Daniel's eyes were closed, but his voice was clear. "We surrender all of us to all of you. Take us and use us for your glory. In life or death, be glorifed."

"Dad!" Elijah said.

"Daniel!" Rebecca pressed on Daniel's shoulder.

Daniel shook his head and opened his eyes for the first time since Sunday evening. He blinked and squinted in the low light of the room.

"Daniel, Honey, Merry Christmas!" Rebecca said delightfully hugging him.

"Merry Christmas, Dad," Caleb said.

"Daddy, you are awake!" Titus yelled as he jumped up onto the bed to hug his father.

"He's awake," Zach pointed out. "After all, it *is* Christmas."

*

"Did you find one yet?" Brian asked.

"Um...yes," Terri said as she looked at her phone. "There's a synagogue not too far from here -- Temple Beth Shalom. Says that it is on Maryland Avenue, next to the Paradise Hospital."

# CHAPTER 88
## 2:15 PM

"Mom, Dad, we got a very special Christmas present this year." Rebecca was looking into her phone as she Facetimed with her parents in Ohio. Then she turned the phone slightly so they could see Daniel sitting up in the bed, weakly smiling, and waving.

"Merry Christmas," Daniel said weakly.

"Praise the Lord!" Rebecca's mom said in an astonished whisper. "Praise the Lord!"

"With God all things *are* possible," her dad said.

*

"Nobody is here," Brian said sadly as he pulled into the parking lot of Temple Beth Shalom. "I thought someone would be here on Christmas."

"But Christmas is *Jesus'* birthday," Terri said. "Jews don't celebrate Jesus' birthday. They killed Jesus."

"Oh, shut up!" Brian growled. "I knew that."

"So, what are we going to do?"

"Shoot up a Jewish synagogue," Brian cackled. "That's what we are going to do."

# CHAPTER 89
## 2:30 PM

"BOOM, BOOM!"

Brian laughed wildly as the sign with the words Beth Shalom went crashing to the ground.

He reloaded his shot gun and handed it to Terri. "Here, you try it."

"Boom! Boom," the windows of the glass door shattered.

"This *is* fun!" she laughed.

"Let's go inside and have some more fun. Bring your guns," he said as he opened the door to the van.

\*

"Praise the Lord!" Roberta said in her big booming voice. "Praise the Lord!" She had stopped in to check on Rebecca and the boys. Now she was snapping pictures with her cell phone of Daniel and his family around the bed. "I can't wait to post this on Facebook. *#resurrected from the dead; #Christmas miracle.*"

"You and your Facebook," Rebecca laughed.

"Don't you make fun," Roberta said. "It got thousands of people praying for you. And it got you mentioned on Fox news when that reporter got the request for prayer shared on her FB page by her friend."

"God can use anything, I guess," Rebecca said.

"Even Facebook," Roberta said smugly.

"God used a donkey in the Bible," Zach said.

\*

"Dispatch to Mike Bravo 112. Mike Bravo 112 are you receiving?"

"Mike Bravo 112 receiving loud and clear dispatch. PC Hunt and PC Elwell on duty."

"We have a report of gunfire on the corner of Maryland and Paradise Avenue. Seems someone is shooting up the Jewish synagogue there."

"Roger that Dispatch. We are on our way."

\*

"CRACK, CRACK."

"The shots are coming from inside," Elwell said as they pulled into the parking lot. She tried to calm the flow of adrenaline that was beginning to shoot through her body.

"We better call for back-up." Office Hunt said to Officer Elwell.

"CRACK. PING," a bullet hit the side of the vehicle.

"Get your head down," Hunt yelled.

"CRACK, CRACK!"

"CRASH!"

Two bullets shattered the window where Elwell's head had been just a second earlier.

"CRACK, CRACK, CRACK, CRACK!" A spray of bullets hit the windshield.

"BOOM, BOOM!" Brian's shotgun took out the tires on the passenger's side where Elwell was ducked down.

Brian and Terri dashed out of the synagogue toward their truck.

Hunt pointed his gun thorough the space where the window had been. He aimed in the direction of Brian and fired.

"CRACK, CRACK,"

Brian hit the ground, cursing as he fell. He grabbed his leg and yelled, "The Revolution continues!" Frantically he crawled toward the truck.

"CRACK, CRACK, CRACK!"

Terri fired at the police car. "CRACK, CRACK, CRACK!"

"Down with tyranny!" she screamed.

"Hunt, are you all right?" Elwell yelled. Hunt had blood coming from his shoulder and neck.

"You drive!" Brian yelled as he pulled himself to the truck. "I got an idea."

Terri jumped in the driver's seat and started the engine. Brian pulled himself into the passenger seat and reached into his backpack and pulled out a grenade. "Don't Tread on Me!" Brian yelled as he pulled the pin and tossed it toward the police car.

Terri jerked the truck out of the parking lot heading north.

"HONK!" she just missed hitting a car.

"CRACK," she fired at it, but missed. "Get out of my way!"

"KABOOM!" the grenade exploded back at the parking lot.

"The Revolution continues!" Brian yelled. Then he grimaced and grabbed his bloody leg.

Terri laughed, stomped on the gas and sped off.

# CHAPTER 90
## 5:05 PM

"Let me take the boys down to the cafeteria to get them something healthy to eat. People have been bringing us goodies all day and they need something healthy. That will allow you pastors some time to talk," Rebecca said as she shooed the boys out the door.

"Thanks, Rebecca," Carlos said. "Don't worry, we will keep a good eye on him."

Daniel was sitting up and his eyes were open. He was wearing a weak smile.

"Daniel, I have three questions that I can't get out of my head," Matthew said when Rebecca and the boys were gone.

"First, do you remember anything from the last week?" Matthew asked.

"Yes. I had some crazy dreams," Daniel said. "They were so real. I don't think I will ever forget them."

"What type of dreams?"

"Before I woke up, I had some nice dreams of good times with Rebecca and the boys," Daniel said.

"But then, there were also some extremely vivid spiritual warfare dreams, especially at first. It was as if the forces of good and the forces of evil were literally fighting over my bed," he continued.

"They were," Carlos said thoughtfully. "Many of us could feel it too, but certainly to a lesser extent than you did."

"Yeah, Wednesday when we were praying for you during your operation, for a while it was very, very strange. We felt sick and distracted. It was hard to pray."

"Spiritual warfare," Daniel said soberly.

"Get this. It turns out that the exact time we felt the attack was the exact time that you died in the Operating Room," Matthew said,

"Wow," Daniel said quietly.

"And when your fever got so high, several Grace City prayer warriors all over the city felt the Lord calling them to special prayer for you at that very time," Carlos said.

"Really?" Daniel said. "At that time, I was dreaming that a demon had shot me with a burning arrow. I was on fire."

"Sounds intense," Carlos said.

"It was the most intense dream I ever had," Daniel said.

"I think the enemy has been trying to take you out," Matthew said.

"Fortunately, he has not been successful," Carlos added.

"Thank God!" Matthew said.

"I had some other weird dreams too," Daniel said seriously. He frowned in concentration. "You know Maria Cruz's husband?"

"Oh yes, the one she is always praying for?" Matthew said.

"Yes."

"Wasn't his dad a preacher?" Carlos asked. "I think she told us that his dad died when he was a kid and he ended up in a gang, selling drugs to support his family."

"Yes," Daniel said. "It is the strangest thing. I have had a whole set of dreams about him as a kid."

"Did you know him as a kid?" Matthew asked.

"No, that is what makes them so strange."

Matthew and Carlos looked at each other.

"My second question is this," Matthew said. "When you died in the operating room, did you see a light and Jesus and all of that?

"Yes and no. They tell me that I was only dead a very short time. I guess that it was not long enough to see heaven," Daniel said. "But I did see the resurrected Jesus as the victorious warrior of Revelation chapter one. He also was the Resurrection and the Life who brought me back to life."

"Wow, I want to hear more about that sometime," Matthew said.

"Me too," Carlos added.

"Ok, I have third question," Matthew said. "This summer you were preaching that series of messages on the cross and what it means to really follow Jesus. You were talking about denying yourself and taking up your cross. You talked about the grain of wheat falling into the ground and dying before it could bear fruit. You were talking about cashing in all our chips for the treasure which is the kingdom of heaven. You told about the first century martyrs and the 21 century martyrs."

"Yes. I remember."

"I loved that series. But at the same time, I hated it," Carlos said with a smile.

Matthew was persistent. "You asked us the same question over and over every week, 'Would you die for Jesus?' Then you would say, 'You probably would never die for Jesus if you aren't living for Jesus now.'"

"I remember," Daniel said.

"One week you even asked us several times, 'would you take a bullet for Jesus?'"

"Yes."

"So, this is my question," Matthew continued. "When you were preaching those messages, did you think you would literally take three bullets for Jesus?"

Daniel smiled as he slowly took in the weight of the question.

"Matthew, you know that when we first got here, we started reaching addicts and rescuing prostitutes. Of course, some people got mad about it and I got some serious death threats," Daniel said.

"Yes," Matthew nodded.

"I had always thought I would be scared if I was ever in the situation where I had to take a bullet for Jesus. But surprisingly, I wasn't. Instead, I was filled with joy. We are all going to die one day anyway. What is a better way to die than dying for Jesus?!"

"Amen," Carlos said. "Amen."

"I get it!" Matthew said excitedly. "You can say that you would face a bullet for Jesus with joy because you are living sold out to Jesus already. It's like when Paul said, 'for me to live is Christ and to die is gain.' Paul was ready to die for Jesus because he was fully living for Jesus."

"That's right," Daniel said slowly. His eyes drooped, and shoulders sunk as his energy was waning.

"You guys know I have my faults and weaknesses. I am definitely *not* perfect. But every morning I try to give Jesus my whole heart, mind, and body. I surrender my family and my ministry. I give him my past, present and future. I try to give it all to him every day anyway."

Daniel's eyes fluttered closed.

"We know that you are tired. You have had quite a week. Let us pray for you. Rebecca will be back any minute," Carlos said.

Daniel smiled and nodded wearily.

## CHAPTER 91
### 8:07 PM

"Hello, Madam Mayor," McKnight said into his phone.

"Yes, ma'am, another crazy day. This is what we know.:

"About 3 PM, we received a report of shots being fired at the Temple Beth Shalom synagogue at the corner of Maryland and Paradise," McKnight continued.

"We sent a car to check it out. When the officers got in the parking lot they were immediately fired upon. One of the officers was hit in the exchange of gunfire. One of the shooters was wounded. A white male in his mid-thirties. The other was a white female. When they drove off, they threw a grenade at the officer's vehicle," McKnight paused.

Then he nodded, "Yes ma'am, a real grenade.

"Fortunately, the grenade hit the car and bounced off before it exploded. Neither of the officers were killed, but they did both sustain minor injuries. They were both treated and released. The officers got a description of the vehicle, a red Ford F-150 pickup truck. It matches the description of one that was stolen in Coyote Springs out by the Valley of Fire this morning. It has been sighted driving north on Interstate 15 and law enforcement is in pursuit."

# CHAPTER 92
## 9:00 PM

"Good night, boys, Merry Christmas," Rebecca said with happy weariness as she hugged each of her sons.

"Hkkkkkh-sssss-Hkkkkkh-sssss-Hkkkkh-sssss..." Daniel was sound asleep and snoring, worn out by the excitement of the day.

"Good night, Mom," Caleb said as he hugged Rebecca. "Love you."

"Love you, too," she replied.

"Thanks for the presents," Elijah said as he hugged Rebecca.

"I got my Christmas present when Dad woke up," Zach said.

"We all did, honey. We all did," Rebecca said.

"With God all things are possible," Elijah said.

"Yes. With God all things *are* possible," she replied.

"See you guys in the morning," Rebecca said.

"What day is tomorrow?" Caleb asked. "I am confused."

"Me, too," Titus said

"Tomorrow is Saturday," Elijah said. "It has been a crazy week that's for sure."

"Boys, remember, Grandma and Grandpa will be here Monday," Rebecca said.

"Yay!" Titus said. "Grandma and Grandpa!"

*

When the boys left, Rebecca welcomed the quiet. Finally, she was there by herself in the room with Daniel. Roberta and Freda were home with their families. Big Tony, who had done security duty the night before, was celebrating Christmas weekend with his mother, aunt and brother. So, it was just Rebecca and Daniel.

Rebecca was drained from the most exhausting week of her life. It had been a physical marathon and an emotional roller coaster. She just wanted to tip back in her reclining hospital chair, put her feet up, snuggle up in the blanket, and fall asleep next to Daniel's bed.

"Thank you, Lord, for a good day," she prayed quietly. "It was *so* good to see Daniel awake and talking and mentally whole. You have brought him this far. Please bring him all the way to complete healing."

"Hkkkkkh-sssss-Hkkkkkh-sssss-Hkkkkh-sssss...," Daniel added.

*I don't even mind the sound of his snoring,* she thought. *It sounds like music to my ears.*

\*

Daniel was dreaming again. He was in church at Grace City Flamingo on Sunday evening. He could see that attendance was down because of the pre-Christmas busyness and the absence of the UNLV college kids. The band had just finished, and he walked out on the platform. He gave the introduction to his message.

As he did, out of the corner of his eye, he saw a man slowly standing and pointing his right hand at him.

*Who is that man?* Daniel thought.

*Maria's husband. That man is Maria's husband.*

*What is he doing? It looks like he has a gun.*

"CRACK! CRACK! CRACK!" Gunshots exploded and crashed into him.

Everything went black.

## CH 93

### 10:30 PM

The kids and Maria were finally asleep. *Fortunately, Maria is a very deep sleeper,* Ezekiel thought.

"Maria, Maria," Ezekiel whispered as he gently shook her shoulder.

"Huh?" Maria said squinting up at Ezekiel. "What is it?"

"I just got a call. I got a driver who got in an accident on the 15. I'm going to see if everything is okay. I'll be back later," he said. He hated lying to her.

"Okay," she said. "I love you, Ezekiel. Merry Christmas."

"I love you, Maria," he said quietly. He felt guilty and ashamed.

*That's why I must do what I am going to do. I must get you away from God,* he thought.

*That's right,* the voices agreed. *You must kill the preacher. Tonight, you will kill the preacher and you will be set free.*

*I hope so,* he muttered. *I hope so.*

\*

As Ezekiel slipped out of the bedroom, Maria tried to go back to sleep. But something inside her told her to pray. She got down on her knees beside her bed and began, "Father, I am not sure what is going on right now, but you do. Ezekiel has been very distracted the last two days. I am not sure what is really going on right now. But something is not right."

"Please be very active my husband's life right now," She continued, "I am afraid that he has gotten himself into some trouble. I am worried for him."

"Lord," she said as the tears welled up in her eyes. "I have been praying for a Christmas breakthrough in his life. Christmas is almost over. There has been no breakthough yet. Please bring him to you. Please free him from his bitterness and shame."

She took a deep breathe, "Please, Lord, Please."

*

Daniel began another vivid dream. He saw the Hispanic boy in a bedroom, with several beds jammed into it where his little brothers slept. The boy had tears on his cheeks. "Why did you take my father? Why did you take my father?" he whispered as he pounded his fists into his pillow. "Why? Why? Why?"

Then the boy looked up into the heavens and shook his fists. "I hate you, God. I hate you."

Then the scene shifted.

The bedroom turned into Grace City Flamingo. It was a Sunday evening from the summer.

Daniel saw Maria Cruz and her husband, Ezekiel, sitting in the service. It was the night Ezekiel ran out of church while Daniel was still speaking.

Daniel saw Ezekiel as he darted to his large, black SUV and sit there alone while the rest of the family was still in church.

Tears streaked Ezekiel's face. "Why did you take my father? Why did you take my father?" he yelled as he pounded his fists into the dash. "Why? Why? Why?"

Then he looked up into the heavens and shook his fists. "I hate you, God. I hate you."

# CH 95

## 11:00 PM

"DING, DONG...DING, DONG!" Nine times the sound of a bell rang off the walls of a desolate canyon in the Buck's Mountain wilderness. The moon was full and the air brisk for Vegas in December. Victor, Rose, and eleven black-caped witches and warlocks gathered under the moonlight in a circle marked by stones. The circle was thirteen feet in circumference around a small fire. Inside, small candles formed an upside-down star called a pentagram. There were also large, black candles marking out the points of the star.

Solemnly the high priest, Victor, wearing a shiny, black robe, entered the circle, crossing himself counterclockwise with his left hand. Confidently, he strode to a stone altar on the south side of the circle. Stoically he began to chant the words of the sinister and sacred Black Mass, first in Latin, then in English. "In nominee de nostre Satanas: Lucifere Excelsis! In the name of Satan: The Great Lucifer!"

Solemnly twelve voices repeated: "In nominee de nostre Satanas: Lucifere Excelsis! In the name of Satan: The Great Lucifer!"

Victor's voice rang out rich and clear, "Introido as alatare Satanas; I will go the altar of Satan."

The coven repeated his words. "Introido as alatare Satanas; I will go the altar of Satan."

"In the name of Satan, ruler of Earth," Victor intoned, "I command the forces of darkness to bestow their infernal power upon us. Open wide the gates of Hell and come forth from the abyss bringing death to the one we curse this night."

"Glory to Satan and the evil spirits. In the name of Satan, glorious Lucifer!" The coven replied.

"Satanas vobiscum; Satan be with you." Victor says.

"Et cum spiritu tou; And with you," the coven replied as one.

"Raise your left hand and repeat after me: Will you serve Lord Satan with your whole mind, body, and soul?"

"Yes!" the coven stated emphatically.

"As a symbol of purging your minds from false teaching and renouncing all connections with the heresy of Jesus, the Liar, break your crucifixes and throw the pieces into the fire."

Each of the witches and warlocks around the circle snapped their thin, wooden crucifixes and threw the pieces into the fire in the middle.

"Let me remind all of you, that if you ever break your vow to follow Satan, we will pronounce sentence upon you in the name of Lord Satan. You will perish by a terrifying death. An eternal flame from Satan's mouth shall consume your soul forever in hell."

"Yes, Lord High Priest," they said solemnly.

*

Suddenly Rebecca was awakened as a sharp pain shot through her head. She felt foggy and dizzy.

She looked over at Daniel and the muscles in his faced tightened and he jerked slightly.

*What is going on?*

*

Zeke reached into his backpack and pulled out the nice gray and brown wig to cover his short, black hair. He then put on some clear glasses with large, heavy frames.

Then he got quietly out of his SUV and slipped on a backpack. He pulled the hood of his jacket over his head and took a deep breath.

*Tonight is the night. No turning back.*

Looking around and seeing no one, he dashed through a yard, hopped a wall, and walked quickly down the sidewalk toward the back entrance to the hospital. He had parked two blocks behind the hospital on Las Cruces Street so that his vehicle would not show on the hospital security video feeds of the parking lot.

*Leave no traces*, he muttered to himself. *Leave no traces*.

\*

Stanley did not mind working on Christmas night. First, it was overtime pay. Second, he had no family in Vegas anymore and he did not feel like being alone. Third, and best of all, his partner tonight was Raphael. Raphael's wife was a great cook and Raphael was on a new diet. Raphael's wife had loaded up a big basket of Christmas goodies for Stanley and the other security officers. He spread them out before him like a pirate examining his treasure.

Tonight, would be extra-special because the other two guards were putting down a fight that had erupted in the ER waiting room. He had at least half-an-hour to get a head start on the goodies before he would be disturbed.

"What shall I eat first?" Stanley asked greedily.

"It doesn't matter," Raphael laughed. "In a few hours, it'll be gone anyway."

## CH 96
## 11:15 PM

Zeke turned his face away from the security cameras when he entered the door to the ER. The ER was surprisingly full on Christmas night as alcohol intake and domestic incidents under the stress of the holidays must have increased the number of emergencies.

The people in the waiting area were riveted to the TV in the lobby watching a car chase between the police and some people who had fired guns at police officers earlier in the day.

Quickly, Zeke he walked through the waiting room and into the hallway headed to the wide main lobby and elevators.

*Unnoticed,* he thought. *Good.*

At the lobby, he turned right and walked down the long hall heading toward the cafeteria and the old section of the hospital.

He saw two nurses coming his way, so, he buried his face in the clipboard. They were busy talking and didn't really look at him.

*Whew,* he thought as he felt the adrenaline shooting through his body.

After they passed, he ducked into the men's bathroom just outside the cafeteria and locked the door.

He stripped off his jacket and tossed it into the large waste basket in the corner. Moving quickly, he pulled off the sweat pants and the hooded sweat shirt he was wearing and threw them into the waste basket.

Next, he reached in the backpack and pulled out hospital scrubs and slipped them on. He withdrew a carefully folded lab coat and put it on. He pulled out a name badge that he had stolen from Ezra when touring, clipped it on the pocket of the coat, and slipped a stethoscope around his neck. Looking in the mirror he adjusted the wig and the glasses. *Good enough,* he thought.

He took a deep breath trying to calm his nerves.

*Follow the plan.*

Piece by piece he recounted the plan:

*First, get in place. Check.*

*Second, create distractions.*

*Third, get in the preacher's room.*

*Fourth, suffocate the preacher.*

*Fifth, get out undetected.*

*Sixth, get home and get back in bed.*

*Simple enough. Freedom is almost here.*

Zeke stood on the commode and leaned out, reached up, and removed the vent in the ceiling in the middle of the room.

He jumped down and pushed the waste basket up against the toilet as close to underneath the vent as he could get it. He reached in the backpack and pulled out several carefully rolled-up newspaper cylinders and dropped them in the basket. Generously, he doused it with the charcoal lighter fluid.

He stood back and lit a match.

He tossed the lighted match into the wastebasket.

"Poof!" The contents burst in flame.

*Excellent! A perfect distraction. Now keep moving.*

Zeke slipped out of the door, turned left and walked until he came to the next men's room near the end of the hall. Once inside, he did the same thing, lighting a fire under the vent.

He excited the bathroom and hurried down the hall to the old section of the hospital.

*Two down. Keep moving.*

Just outside a rarely used stairwell in the old section of the building, there was a small, red and white fire alarm switch. Quickly, Zeke pulled the switch down and slipped into the stairwell.

"BEEEEEEP! BEEEEEP! BEEEEEP!" It blared.

*Good*, he thought. *A third distraction.*

He quickly descended the stairs to the basement.

"The basement is like a ghost town at night," Ezra had told him the other day.

Zeke saw no one.

Quickly, Zeke went to the big room where the HVAC units were located. Using his security card, he opened the heavy metal door and went in. The HVAC units were on his right.

"The Step Down unit is right overhead," Ezra had told him. "The HVAC units for the rest of the hospital are on the roof, but the ones for the old building are right under the Step Down."

*Perfect*, Zeke thought. *The smoke is going to go right up to the preacher's floor – Room 247.*

*

"Fire Alarm pulled on the first Floor. Area #5," Stanley reported, looking at the screen in front of him.

"I'll go," Raphael said. "Merry Christmas. I promised Camilla that for Christmas I'd watch my diet and walk more. So, you enjoy your pie."

"Thanks," Stanley said as he shoveled in a huge mouthful. He was watching the television as the big police chase of the alleged cop-killers was unfolding before the nation on Christmas night.

Raphael was a big man. He had played line for Las Vegas high school back in the glory days when their football team was good. Married life was good for him and he had put on a hundred pounds since high school.

Steadily, he waddled the full length of the hospital down the long hall to Area #5, the old section of the hospital. The beeping sound grew more intense the farther he walked. Looking around the area, he saw no smoke and no fire.

"Nothing here," he said on his walkie-talkie to Stanley. "Must be a false alarm."

He adjusted the switch on the alarm box and headed back to the Security Office.

# CH 97
## 11:30 PM

With a screw driver that he had carried in his hand under the clipboard, Zeke quickly took off the grates protecting the fans of the HVAC units. Carefully, he arranged more of his newspaper logs around the unmoving fans of the open units.

"The smoke should go up the vents to the preacher's floor," he said to himself. Standing back, he sprayed the logs with lighter fluid, one after another. Then, with a wicked grin, he pulled out his matches and flicked a match into the first unit.

"Poof!" It burst into flames. Moving methodically, he quickly lit fire in the three other units.

"Now the party begins," he said. "Say good-bye, Mr. Preacher."

*

Raphael was dripping sweat and huffing and puffing by the time he got back.

Just as he put his hand on the knob the hallway lights began to strobe and a new sound pierced his ears.

"Honk! Honk! Honk!"

"What now?" he yelled in the door to Stanley.

"Heat sensors going off in the men's rooms in Area #3 and #5 on the first floor." Stanley said. "I told Tim when he checked them last month that they were too sensitive. Probably somebody smoking in the boys' room."

"I was *just* on the first floor." Raphael groaned. Then he grunted, pushed open the door and waddled out.

*

"Oh, Spirit of Death, do not wait any longer," Victor said with great dramatic flair. As he did, he removed his cape and tossed it aside. Then he unbuttoned his vest.

"We join our voices to cry out for the death of this hated preacher," he intoned.

"Death, Death, death," the coven began to chant.

Then, in a flourish Victor ripped open his silky, white shirt, popping two pearl buttons in the process. In his right-hand he held a shiny dagger.

"We want death today," he said.

"DEATH! DEATH! DEATH!" the coven shouted louder.

"Cut the hated preachers heart out. Cut him to death!" he yelled as he slashed an X across his chest.

"DEATH! DEATH! DEATH!" the frenzied coven shouted.

Rose rushed up to him, swept her finger across his bloody wound and gleefully rubbed the blood across her mouth and licked her lips.

"DEATH! DEATH! DEATH!" the delighted group of witches and warlocks howled.

*

In his sleep, Daniel saw that the dark cloud that had been lingering outside the hospital earlier in the week was back. Now it was rapidly approaching his room and increasing in size as it neared him.

Then they materialized. The black hoard was back, fighting his angel guardians more viciously than ever. Leading the way was the gigantic, evil warrior with the burning red eyes. In his massive, bony hand he clutched a huge, golden dagger.

Daniel watched in horror. As if in slow motion, with one smooth, mighty motion, the giant demon slashed the dagger across his chest.

"AWWW!" he gasped.

His chest was on fire again with piercing pain.

Then everything went black.

# CHAPTER 98

## 11:45 PM

Daniel's cry startled Rebecca. "Daniel, Daniel what is it?"

She grabbed his hand and it was limp. Out of habit, she glanced up at the screen that displayed his vital signs. They were all plummeting.

\*

Martha awoke with a jolt and sat straight up in bed. *Something is not right.* She rubbed her eyes.

*Daniel. It's Daniel. Must pray for Daniel.*

She rolled out of bed, dropped to her knees, and began to pray in earnest.

\*

"We got a fire in the wastebasket of the restroom!" Raphael reported to Stanley over his walkie-talkie.

"What the heck is going on?" Stanley asked. "The fire alarms on all the floors of the old section are all going off. Smoke detectors are going crazy."

\*

"Bring me the sacrifice," Victor said theatrically. Dutifully, Jason pulled the young, white lamb into the center of the circle.

"Yesss!" the coven hissed in anticipation of what was about to happen.

"Today Christians celebrated the birth of their lamb. Tonight, we celebrate the death of the lamb. Lord Satan killed their lamb. Tonight, we ask that the Spirit of Death would kill the preacher.

"As I sacrifice this lamb, may the Spirit of Death sacrifice the preacher!"

"Yes, Yes, Yes!" the blood-thirsty coven hissed loudly.

\*

Zeke bounded up the stairs two at a time. *Got to be ready to strike,* he thought.

*Keep going.*

At the landing of the second floor, he collected himself and pulled a surgeon's mask over his mouth and nose.

*Good disguise and it helps with breathing through the smoke,* he thought as he recounted his plan.

Smoke was pouring out the vent overhead. *Excellent!* He thought.

Quickly, he walked toward the Step Down unit.

BEEP! BEEP BEEP!" the fire alarm pierced the air.

*Someone pulled the alarm on this floor. Good, that will add to the chaos,* Zeke thought.

Almost there, *I got to keep moving.*

*Kill the Preacher. Kill the preacher. Kill the preacher,* the voices were screaming at him now.

*Kill the preacher!*

\*

"Code Red! Code Red!" The voice of Stanley said over the intercom. "Code Red, all floors in #5. Repeat, Code Red! All other floors and areas, please await further instructions. "

# SATURDAY DEC 26
## CHAPTER 99
### 12:05 AM

*This smoke is perfect. It is like a Halloween dream*, Zeke thought as he knifed through the smoke toward the Step-Down Unit.

*Chaos is reigning.*

People were coming out of their rooms coughing and running here and there in every direction not sure what to do.

Zeke pushed past a patient with an IV tree struggling to flee the smoke. Then he pushed opened the door of the Step-Down Unit.

"Room 247," he said to himself. "Looks like it's the third door on the right."

*

"That should get rid of the smoke," the fireman said as he and his partner shot their fire extinguishers into each of the burning HVAC Units in the basement of the old building.

*

Rebecca had been ringing the bell to alert Daniel's nurse since his vitals were dropping but to no avail. She started to cough as smoke was coming into his room.

*I got to get the nurse,* she thought.

She jumped up, dashed toward the door, and pulled it open.

"Thwack!" the heavy door flew back and smacked her in the forehead. She paused, stunned.

In the hall, Zeke felt the door hit something. "Ugh," he grunted and pushed it as hard as he could the second time.

On the other side, the door slammed into Rebecca's head again. She slumped to the ground, knocked out by the blow.

Zeke pushed past her into the room.

*There he is,* Zeke thought as he headed toward Daniel.

*Kill him!* the voices said. *Kill him!*

But seeing the man lying there with tubes going into him and monitor wires coming out of him something shifted in Zeke. *It seems unfair. He is so weak. Like a child sleeping peacefully.*

*DO IT!* the voices in his head yelled. *Smother him.*

Suddenly, Daniel shot up in the bed, blinked his eyes and looked at Zeke.

"Ezekiel, Stop!" Daniel commanded.

Zeke was stunned to see the man in the coma sit up and speak. He was amazed to have the man call his name.

"Ezekiel, I know that you are Maria's husband. She weeps and prays for you almost every week in church," Daniel said.

"I also know that you are the man who shot me."

Zeke was paralyzed, his feet stuck to the floor. The only thing moving were his bewildered eyes.

"I forgive you," Daniel said looking him in his eyes.

"Your father, Pastor Cruz of the Iglesias de Dios Pentecostal, loved you and he would forgive you in spite of the things you have done."

Hot tears burned Ezekiel's eyes. *I can't believe what is happening. How does this man know so much about me?*

"Most importantly," Daniel continued. "Your heavenly Father knows you and forgives you. He knows why you started selling drugs. He knows that you just wanted to take care of your family. He knows all the pain you have felt."

Ezekiel dropped his head and wiped tears from his eyes. Each of Daniel's words were cutting deep into his heart.

"You must let go of your bitterness and receive forgiveness," Daniel said.

It was too much. Ezekiel buried his face in Daniel's lap and began to sob loudly. Daniel reached out his hand and placed it firmly on Ezekiel's head.

"The torture will stop for good when you ask God to forgive you for hating Him."

Each of Daniel's words was like a scalpel knifing into Ezekiel's heart slicing at cancerous tissue.

"The agony will end when you receive forgiveness. It will stop when you let God replace your bitterness and anger with love. You must also replace your guilt and shame with forgiveness."

"For-.... forgive me!" Ezekiel whispered in a soft, scratchy voice. "Please, oh please forgive me." Twenty years of guilt and shame, bitterness and anger began to pour out of Ezekiel in tortured sobs.

Rebecca began to stir. She reached her hand to her pounding forehead and felt a knot rising. She opened her eyes to see that the smoke had cleared. Then she heard Daniel's voice and saw a man wearing a cock-eyed wig with his head in Daniel's lap.

"Father in heaven, open Ezekiel's eyes to see how much you love him.' Daniel prayed. "Open his heart to experience how deeply you care."

Ezekiel blinked his eyes wide open as if thick blinders were being lifted from his eyes.

Rebecca shifted her weight so, she could kneel next to the man and put her hand on his shoulders. She quietly interceded for a breakthrough as Daniel prayed for the man. It was a familiar position as she and Daniel had often served as the prayer partner for one another as they led an imprisoned soul into freedom.

"Father," Daniel continued. "Please extend your arms, reach out, and draw Ezekiel to yourself with power and tenderness right now in the name of Jesus."

Ezekiel felt a golden light and a wonderful warmth wash over him. The dark cloud he had lived under for so many years was breaking up.

"Silence the voice of the enemy in his head." Daniel continued. "Father in heaven, please, set him free right now in the name of Jesus."

For twenty years, Ezekiel had felt like he had a huge, rusty chain around his heart. As the preacher prayed, the chain was shaking.

"Ezekiel, do you want to be free?" Daniel asked. "If you want to be free, nod your head."

Rebecca saw the man in the wig, deliberately and determinedly nod his head up and down.

"The Bible says submit yourself to God, resist the devil and he will flee from you. Right now, say, 'Jesus is Lord.'" Daniel said.

A weak voice came from the weeping man, "Jesus is Lord."

"Say, 'I submit my life to God," Daniel directed.

"I submit my life to God," Ezekiel whimpered

"I resist the devil and he must flee from me," Daniel directed.

"I resist the devil and he must flee from me."

"Chains of bitterness and anger be gone."

"Chains be gone," Ezekiel said. "Chains be gone!"

At that, Ezekiel felt as though the chain around his chest cracked in two, dropped off, and melted like hot butter. He could not believe it.

He tilted his head back and smiled. For the first time in twenty years he felt free. It was as though he was under a waterfall of grace with hope, joy, and love pouring down over him. A dam of condemnation burst in his chest and his tears turned to tears of joy.

# CHAPTER 101

## 12:25 AM

Suddenly, the wilderness was ablaze in light as a dozen trucks converged on the satanic circle. Soon a dozen spotlights blared into Victor's eyes.

"You better stop right there, boy, or I'll blow your head off," a deep voice boomed out of the darkness. A dozen rifles clicked as they were cocked.

Victor squinted his eyes and stumbled back.

"What? What is going on here?" he asked meekly.

"'*What's going on*' is you took my lamb and I aim to get 'er back," The voice boomed. "Let'er go and let'er go, now."

A tall man in jeans, boots, checkered shirt and cowboy hat stepped into the light holding a rifle trained at Victor's head. He surveyed the twelve black-robed witches and warlocks and then looked over Victor with his torn, silky, white shirt and blood on his chest. "What in blazes are you fools doing?"

"We were conducting a scientific psychological exercise," Victor said throwing out the first thing that came to mind. He was a skilled liar. "I am Professor Victor Dubois of UNLV and these are some of my students."

"It looked like you were fixing to kill my lamb," the rifle toting man said, aiming the gun at Victor's head.

Victor raised his hands and said, "On no, of course not. I was just going to cut off a bit of wool and burn it in the fire."

"What sort of science is that?" the man asked.

"Psychologically, if we burn the wool, we rid ourselves of bad memories of past Christmases."

The man shook his head and spit.

"If I may ask," Victor said, "who are you, sir?"

"Mitt, Mitt Bradford. I'm the captain of the Buck's Mountain Militia, the owner of the land you are standing on, *and* the owner of that lamb you have your hands on."

"I see," Victor said meekly.

"And what's with the rocks?" Mitt pointed his gun barrel at the rocks piled up as an altar where they were going to sacrifice the lamb.

"They represent negative events from our past," Victor lied.

"What about those stupid robes. Are you all in the ugly robe club?" He laughed. The voices of others laughing could be heard coming from the trucks.

"Yes, that's it," Victor said meekly. "Well, so sorry to trouble you. We had better be going now. So, sorry to trouble you."

"Listen you bunch of idiots. If you *ever* come back on Buck's Mountain again, it will be your last time," Mitt growled.

"Now, you better start walking if you hope to be near civilization by daylight."

"Oh, we have a van and a small bus parked down at the foot of the hill," Victor said.

"Those vehicles are yours?" Bradford asked innocently. "Sorry, but they won't be going anywhere any time soon. We needed some gas for our trucks. We did not think you would mind if we took it from your vehicles." Laughter came from the trucks surrounding the coven.

Bradford smiled as he pointed the gun back at Victor's head.

"And there just did not seem to be enough air out here in the desert tonight. So, since you won't be driving anywhere anytime soon, we let the air out of your tires."

"I see," Victor frowned.

"Now, give me back my lamb and get outta here."

He poked Victor hard in the ribs with the barrel of the rifle. "Did you hear me? I said, 'Get!'"

## EPILOGUE

## <u>MONDAY, JANUARY 13</u>

### CHAPTER 102
### 11:18 AM

"I see no reason that you can't go home today." Dr. Kim said to Daniel. "You have healed up nicely and as long as you limit your activities for a while, you should be fine."

"You are sure he will be all right?" Rebecca asked.

"If you would have asked me that three weeks ago, I would have had to tell you, 'No. He is not going to make it.'" Dr. Kim said. "But today, I can say, everything is healing nicely, and I am very confident that he will be fine if he does not overdo it."

*

"Rebecca, why are you crying?" Daniel asked as she wheeled him to Carlos' mini-van.

"Why am I crying?" She sniffed, "I am crying because three weeks ago you were shot three times in the chest and I never thought I would see you again this side of eternity. You were just discharged and tonight our whole family will finally be around the dinner table again."

"Why am I crying?" She continued, "because losing you has always been my biggest fear and God took us through the valley of the shadow of death and used it to defeat my fear."

"I am crying because Maria's husband, Ezekiel is truly a new man."

"I am crying because our son Zach showed powerful faith telling everyone that you would wake on up Christmas. Our son Elijah handled this whole situation like a grown man. And you should be proud of your other sons as well."

"Why am I crying? Because our church rallied around us in a powerful way that blew everyone away."

"All right, alright," Daniel laughed "I get it."

Then he asked, "So, are we going to stop and get me a strawberry milkshake on the way home?"

## APRIL 23

## CHAPTER 102

## 2:10 PM

Judge Addison Stevens was a very, large, distinguished man. "Does the defendant have a statement?" the ebony-skinned, giant said as he glared at Ezekiel.

"Yes, your honor. My statement is this: I am guilty. I tried to kill this man." Ezekiel said as he pointed to Daniel, who smiled and nodded at him. Daniel was sitting next to Rebecca and Maria on one side with Pastor Carlos and Freda on the other.

"Thank God, I failed in my attempt. By God's grace this wonderful man is still alive," Ezekiel gestured to Daniel.

"Your honor," Ezekiel said, looking over at the judge, "I take full responsibility for my actions. Sir, I deserve to pay for my crimes."

"I want to thank those two men," he said pointing at Daniel and Pastor Carlos. "Pastor Carlos went with me when I turned myself into the police. He visited me almost every day in the jail for the months prior to this trial. He read the Bible and prayed with me." He nodded at Pastor Carlos. "He also brought his laptop and that man, Pastor Daniel, skyped in to pray and read Scripture with me."

"I especially want to thank that woman," he said pointing at Maria. "She prayed for me every day." He paused, his eyes moist.

"She stayed with me when I was angry and bitter and miserable. No man deserves such a good wife."

"And your honor," Ezekiel broke into a wide grin. "I want to thank God. I want to testify that I am no longer the man I was. I was running from God and running with the devil. But God has changed all that. He has forgiven me and given me a new heart."

Cheers burst out from the Grace City contingent in the courtroom.

"Order in the court," the judge said, hitting his gavel, with a hint of a smile.

Ezekiel continued, "When I get out of jail I will serve Jesus, my family, my church, and my community. Instead of being a burden on society, I will be a blessing."

The judge nodded, rubbed his big hand through his snow-white hair and looked at Daniel, "Does the victim want to make a statement?"

"Ezekiel, I am very proud of you,' Daniel said as he smiled at Ezekiel. "You have opened your heart to God and received his forgiveness and love. You have let him change you. In the last four months you have read the New Testament through three times. You truly are a new man. When you get out, we -- your wife, and your church – we will be here for you. We will help you fulfill your calling, finally after all these years." Daniel's voice faded and his eyes dropped slightly. He was still weak during his recovery.

"Ezekiel Miguel Cruz, I hereby sentence you to three years in the Nevada State Prison. Two years for attempted murder and one year for use of a deadly weapon with no parole."

"Now, son," Judge Stevens said staring directly at Ezekiel. "Nevada is the only state in the union with the possibility of such a light sentence for such a heinous crime. I personally have never before given out such an unusually light sentence for such a serious crime."

The judge paused, raised his chin, and rubbed his hand over his tightly cropped, white beard.

"But this is an unusual case. Young man, I believe that your heart change is real. I see that you have a strong support system. May God grant you grace to do all you have promised. I wish you the very best."

# A NOTE FROM THE AUTHOR

When I was a church planter in Las Vegas, I received the threat that I'd be shot during our Sunday evening service at our Flamingo Campus. (Thankfully, the shooter never showed up).

Not long after that, I watched my son, Andrew, fight for every breath in the ICU of Sunrise Hospital. Then he was moved to a Step Down Unit to make room for a celebrity.

As a result of those experiences, I got the idea for this story. I hope that reading it stretches your faith and increases your prayer life.

# ACKNOWLEDGEMENTS

Great thanks goes out to Donna Davenport and Luke Earley for serving as editors. Also, special thanks to Brenda Hellern for proof reading and to Kay Hardman and Cathy Earley for being content readers. Thanks to Dr. Ron Routh for expert medical critique and to Captain Rich and Kim Fletcher for expert police critique. Thanks to Alton Loveless as the publisher. And very special thanks to Grace City Church, Las Vegas, Nevada.

17159115R00181

Made in the USA
Lexington, KY
17 November 2018